PENGUIN BOOKS
A GRAIN OF SAND: CHOKHER BALI

Born in 1861, Rabindranath Tagore was one of the key figures of
the Bengal Renaissance. He started writing at an early age, and by
the turn of the century had become a household name in Bengal as
a poet, a songwriter, a playwright, an essayist, a short story writer
and a novelist. In 1913 he was awarded the Nobel Prize for
Literature for his verse collection *Gitanjali*. At about the same time
he founded Visva Bharati, a university located in Shantiniketan near
Kolkata. Called the 'Great Sentinel' of modern India by Mahatma
Gandhi, Tagore steered clear of active politics, but is famous for
returning the knighthood conferred on him as a gesture of protest
against the Jallianwala Bagh massacre in 1919.

Tagore was a pioneering literary figure, renowned for his ceaseless
innovations in poetry, prose, drama, music and painting, which he
took up late in life. His works include some sixty collections of verse,
novels like *Gora*, *Chokher Bali* and *Home and the World*, plays like
Red Oleanders and *The Post Office*, over a hundred short stories,
essays on religious, social and literary topics, and over 2000 songs,
including the national anthems of India and Bangladesh.

Rabindranath Tagore died in 1941. His eminence as India's greatest
modern poet remains unchallenged to this day.

*

Sreejata Guha has an MA in Comparative Literature from State
University of New York at Stony Brook. She has worked as a
translator and editor with Stree Publications, Seagull Books and
Jacaranda Press. She has previously translated *Picture Imperfect*, a
collection of Saradindu Bandyopadhyay's Byomkesh Bakshi stories,
Taslima Nasrin's novel *French Lover* and Saratchandra
Chattopadhyay's *Devdas* for Penguin. Her translation of Tagore's
Home and the World is forthcoming in Penguin.

*

Swagato Ganguly did his PhD in Comparative Literature and Literary
Theory from the University of Pennsylvania, Philadelphia. He is
currently Assistant Editor with *The Statesman* in Kolkata.

A Grain of Sand

Chokher Bali

RABINDRANATH TAGORE

Translated from the Bengali by
Sreejata Guha

Introduction by Swagato Ganguly

PENGUIN BOOKS

PENGUIN BOOKS
Published by the Penguin Group
Penguin Books India Pvt Ltd, 11 Community Centre, Panchsheel Park, New Delhi
110 017, India
Penguin Group (USA) Inc., 375 Hudson Street, New York, New York 10014, USA
Penguin Group (Canada), 90 Eglinton Avenue East, Suite 700, Toronto, Ontario,
M4P 2Y3, Canada (a division of Pearson Penguin Canada Inc.)
Penguin Books Ltd, 80 Strand, London WC2R 0RL, England
Penguin Ireland, 25 St Stephen's Green, Dublin 2, Ireland (a division of Penguin Books
Ltd)
Penguin Group (Australia), 250 Camberwell Road, Camberwell, Victoria 3124,
Australia (a division of Pearson Australia Group Pty Ltd)
Penguin Group (NZ), cnr Airborne and Rosedale Roads, Albany, Auckland 1310,
New Zealand (a division of Pearson New Zealand Ltd)
Penguin Group (South Africa) (Pty) Ltd, 24 Sturdee Avenue, Rosebank, Johannesburg
2196, South Africa

Penguin Books Ltd, Registered Offices: 80 Strand, London WC2R 0RL, England

First published by Penguin Books India 2003

Typeset in *Perpetua* by SÜRYA, New Delhi
Printed at Pauls Press, New Delhi

A Note on the Title

Although *A Grain of Sand* is not a literal translation of the original title, I chose it because it powerfully evokes the most significant nuances contained in the phrase Chokher Bali, which literally means a grain of sand that lodges in the eye, an irritant, a source of discomfort. In itself an innocuous speck of dust, a grain of sand can bring tears to the eye, and cause a pearl to form inside the oyster's shell. Due to the tensile nature of the source language, the two words together evoke layers of meaning that make the phrase virtually untranslatable in English. One of the metaphorical evocations is that of the grain of sand that lodges inside the shell of an oyster and helps in forming a pearl. In my reading of Tagore's *Chokher Bali*, Binodini performs the function of this grain of sand. She lodges herself within Mahendra and Asha's household, afflicts their romance and through tears and tribulations, helps their relationship mature into a pearl. When Binodini suggests playfully to Asha that they be Chokher Bali to one another, she infuses an added dimension of reciprocity into the function of the grain of sand—it is an insight into the fact that both women will rub each other the wrong way, irritate each other's feelings and sentiments, just like the discordant grain of sand that the wind blows into one's eye. My choice of the title arises out of an attempt to capture this complex imagery implicit in the original phrase. It is, of course, one of many possible options and hence deserves this elaboration, following which I hope readers will feel free to name the text differently, depending on the dominant notes it strikes in each individual mind.

Bangalore   Sreejata Guha
August 2003

Author's Note

A glance at my literary output will reveal that *Chokher Bali* was something of a novelty, not just for me but also for the contemporary literary scene. It is difficult to say what prompted me to write it. The immediate cause was the demand made by a monthly journal for a serialized novel. Shrisha Chandra had just restarted the magazine *Bangadarshan*. My name was added to the list of contributors—not something I was entirely happy about. Following in the footsteps of famous predecessors is always a daunting task, and I was not sure that I would be up to it. But whenever my protests have come into conflict with an editor's request, I have seldom been able to win the fight—and this time was no exception.

Not too long ago we had all enjoyed the novel *Bishabriksha (The Poison Tree)*, serialized in *Bangadarshan*. Its taste had been new at the time. Now, the same *Bangadarshan* could be revived, but the old content could not be reverted to. The times had changed and the new editor would need to start off in a new direction. The assistant editor, Shailesh, was convinced that I could readily provide a year's worth of stories for the magazine. So I had to set to work. It was much like paying my monthly dues to an expectant editor. What resulted were the serialized instalments of a novel.

Until then I had never ventured into the territory of the novel. I had only indulged in brief meteor showers of short stories. I decided that the new-age novel must be fashioned in the workshop of the present day. The devil made poison trees today just as he did in the past, but its expressions were different now, at least in the literary arena. Today the images had to be clear and distinct. Any attempt to blur them with ornamentation would ruin their 'modern' character. So when I wasn't able to dodge the demand for a story, I had to go down to the factory-shed of the mind where hammer and bellows beat the raw metal from the fire into the shape of an image. A description of this harsh process of creation, where man looks into himself and formulates his own self, had not appeared before in Bengali fiction. Later, *Gora, Ghare Baire* (*Home and the World*) and *Chaturanga* (*A Game of Dice*) would follow in the same vein. The short story did not fall outside the ambit of this cruel world either—*Nashtaneer* (*The Broken Nest*) or *Shasti* (*Punishment*) are evidence of the same inner violence. Thereafter, the same struggle with life was to be reflected in the poetry of *Palataka*. If on the one hand *Bangadarshan* enabled me to give free rein to my political and sociological ideas, on the other it brought me into close and uncompromising contact with human nature in my stories and in my poetry.

In *Chokher Bali* it is a mother's envy that provides the vital thrust to the story. It is the situation that results from this envy that brings out Mahendra's illicit and undesirable propensities in a way in which they would never have been exposed in normal circumstances. It is as if the door to a bestial cage was thrown open and the vicious events that were contained within tumbled out unrestrained. Modern literature is not merely about describing the sequence of events, but also about analysing them and drawing out their inner meaning. It is this method that is employed in *Chokher Bali*.

Kolkata, 1940

Rabindranath Tagore

Introduction

In what has been called the first modern novel written in India, *A Grain of Sand*, whose Bengali original *Chokher Bali* was first published in 1903, has subjectivity and the probing of emotional and psychological depths as its hallmarks. The breakthrough it achieved can best be appreciated if it is counterpointed to Bankimchandra Chattopadhyay's 1873 novel *Bishabriksha* (*The Poison Tree*), which it rewrote and explicit references to which are strewn through it.

Both novels centre on the problematic figure of the upper-caste Hindu widow, whose remarriage was traditionally forbidden and who was enjoined to mortify the flesh and lead a spartan existence. Groups of social reformers had emerged by the latter half of the nineteenth century who placed the spotlight on women's issues such as lack of education, confinement to the home's inner chambers, the condition of widows, and the marrying off of child brides to adult men. Although widow remarriage had been legalized by 1856, social taboos were strong enough to ensure there were few takers of the legal privilege among the Hindu elite. At the same time, the custom of child marriages coupled with low life expectancies ensured that many women would be widowed at an early age. It is the troubling question of the sexuality of the young widow, officially purged through a regime of ascetic denial but nonetheless still thought to be present, that lurks at the centre of both novels.

The titles give away the difference in their approaches. In *The Poison Tree* Nagendra's wife Suryamukhi leaves home when he marries Kundanandini, a young widow. When Suryamukhi comes back to the household Kundanandini consumes poison and dies. The novel has an atmosphere of Gothic foreboding and dread, and Bankimchandra (or 'Bankim' as he is referred to in *A Grain of Sand*) reminds the reader through overt authorial intrusions of the ill consequences that flow from widow remarriage. This structure of a cautionary tale is underlined by the title—the poison tree which yields its fatal fruit, is the attraction the young widow has for the rich and well-established Nagendra.

A Grain of Sand, on the other hand, refers to sand that gets in the eye and can cause one to blink reflexively. It is the name (Chokher Bali, shortened to Bali or 'sand') that Binodini, the beautiful widow who is one of the most interesting and complex women characters in all of Tagore's fiction, playfully proposes she and her rival Asha, teenaged bride to wealthy rentier and spoiled mama's boy Mahendra, call each other in preference to more flowery nicknames. It becomes a precise and naturalist image for the stormy relationship that develops between the two women. Authorial intrusions are limited and the plot unfolds through psychological interplay between the characters. Moral judgements, if any, are made exclusively through the shape given to the narrative.

Bankimchandra's forte was historical romance and *The Poison Tree* has an epic flavour—we are granted limited access to the interiority of the characters. Kundanandini in particular is a cipher, an enigma, a child of nature who doesn't quite fit into any social order, a pawn in games that other people play. The only point at which she becomes voluble is after she has swallowed poison, when she confesses her desire for Nagendra. Tagore, by contrast and radically for his time, grants us unhindered access to the subjectivity of Binodini, a passionate woman who overthrows the norms of widowhood to make direct appeals to the men she loves, and whose emotions become the central pole of the novel. When Binodini tells Behari, a do-gooder who is also Mahendra's friend and consort, 'I may be bad, or wrong, but do try to see things from my point of view just this once and understand me,' it might as well be an appeal that Tagore is making to the reader of his day.

Tagore's characters are chock-full of sensibility, which makes the novel a *sturm und drang* tract where desire and jealousy circulate in a complex quadrangular chain between Mahendra, Binodini, Behari and Asha. The chain is made yet more complex if one throws in Mahendra's possessive mother Rajlakshmi, who is yet to get over her obsessive attachment to her son. *A Grain of Sand* brooks comparison with Tagore's novella *Nashtaneer* (*The Broken Nest*) published the same year (1903) and the 1916 novel *Ghare Baire* (*Home and the World*). In *The Broken Nest* Charulata, the central character, grows intimate with her husband's younger cousin Amal; *Home and the World* features a quadrangular relationship between the wealthy landlord Nikhilesh, his widowed sister-in-law, his wife Bimala and his friend Sandip. *Home and the World* was written after Bengal had been racked by the agitation against partition of the province decreed by the colonial government in 1905; politics finds its way into the narrative as transgressive sexuality appears in conjunction with militant nationalism. Both the latter novels have been turned into exquisite films by Satyajit Ray.

Tagore excels in portraying the delicate nuances of the

relationship between the Thakurpo (husband's younger brother) and Bouthakurani (brother's wife, often abbreviated to Bouthan) living under the same roof in a joint family household. A leitmotif that runs through all these works is the suppressed passion between them, often the gateway to tragedy. Binodini addresses both Mahendra and Behari as Thakurpo, while Binodini and Asha are Bouthan to Behari.

Tagore depicts the joint family under the stresses of modernity—an analogy may be the way global satellite television is shaping metropolitan mores in India a century later. Kolkata in Tagore's time had been at the leading edge of Western education in India for at least half a century, and the publishing industry was one of the city's largest indigenous enterprises. The biggest cluster of printing presses were in an area known as Bat-tala, whose name became synonymous with mass-produced scurrilous literature that was felt to be threatening to morals. The late nineteenth century equivalent of satellite television would have been the widespread dissemination of printed books and periodicals and the emergence of a reading public. Bankimchandra had adapted the Western romantic novel for a Bengali audience, causing a shocked contemporary to remark: 'We would have liked to quote some of the sentences [from his first novel] but they contain such explicit descriptions that they would not be acceptable to our readers . . . it is to be regretted that he has not always kept in mind that Bengali books are being read by cultured women.'

Women's education had, in fact, taken off in a manner that widow remarriage hadn't. One of its goals was to equip women to be proper marital companions to their husbands; another was to make them good homemakers. Binodini excels in these areas and we see that her father had invested a great deal in educating her—she has even taken lessons from a British woman. All that, however, is rendered nought by her widowhood, and her rage boils over when she sees Asha, an illiterate and unfinished 'child-woman,' running away with what should have been hers. In the course of her sexual rivalry with Binodini Asha, too, must painfully learn how to read and pick up the homemaking arts.

The mastery of letters is of great moment in the scenes of passion between Binodini and Mahendra, when Binodini reads aloud from Bankim's novels as her way of flirting with Mahendra. When it comes to *The Poison Tree*, though, Binodini conceals the book as she lies on Mahendra's mattress, and he struggles mightily with her to snatch the book from within the folds of her sari. The scene parallels the moment in Samuel Richardson's sensational novel *Pamela* (1740) when Mr B, a sexual predator in whose household Pamela has taken up employment as a maid, sets upon her only to get at the letters she had concealed beneath her bodice. For Mahendra there is a similar transfer of erotic charge from Binodini's body to her book: 'He pulled out the pillow on which Binodini had lain, and laid his head upon it; he picked up the book and began to turn the pages.'

There is a mirroring effect here, as *A Grain of Sand* is a rewriting of *The Poison Tree*. This is a novel that is highly alive to textual mediations. When Binodini plans on luring Mahendra away from his household, the conservative Behari tells her: 'The words you speak now, are all derived from the literature you're so fond of reading. Three-fourths of it is the language of dramas and novels . . . mere echoes of the printing press.' But above all, Tagore's novel heralds the entry of a new type of heroine whose attraction lies not so much in her beauty or status, but in the quality of her mind.

The contradictory pushes and pulls of tradition and modernity, the conflict between oral custom and the irruption of the written word, were experienced by Tagore in his personal life as well. Tagore's grandfather built an enormous commercial empire and is reported to have supped with Queen Victoria in London. His father, Debendranath Tagore, was a prominent religious reformer and headed the quasi-Christian Brahmo sect. Rabindranath was the youngest of fourteen children, and most of them were talented in one or more spheres of literature, music, theatre and other arts, making the Tagores the lead family of the Bengal Renaissance and the sprawling ancestral mansion at Jorasanko in northern Kolkata its epicentre. English romantic poetry and Victorian novels were avidly read in the household. At the same time, men in this reformist family were given in marriage to child brides; Tagore himself was married to Mrinalini Devi when he was twenty-two, and she nine. Tagore's companion since childhood had been elder brother Jyotirindranath's wife Kadambari Devi, who committed suicide within six months of Tagore's marriage. Given the great degree of artistic and romantic stimulation within the Tagore household, where a wife was more likely to adopt as companion a younger brother of her husband's, the stage may have been set for confusion and tragedies like this one by, as it were, the telescoping of several centuries.

While echoes of Tagore's personal tragedy have been read into the troubled Bouthan–Thakurpo relationships in his novels, this may not be the only reason why love affairs in Tagore's fiction tend to have an illicit and abortive quality. There is the preponderant influence in his writing of the Vaishnava padabali or lyric verse, celebrating the dalliance of Krishna with Radha. In one version of the legend Radha, a married woman, is on her way to Mathura when Krishna seduces her on the banks of the river Yamuna. It is in a farmhouse on the banks of the Yamuna that Binodini too awaits her tryst with Behari. But the Krishna–Radha affair is 'parakiya prem' (love with someone who belongs to another). It takes place in a timeless moment outside social space, and is inevitably accompanied by heartbreak.

There is a surprising turn towards askesis at the end of *Chokher Bali* when Binodini, having waited for Behari by the banks of the Yamuna, turns down his offer of marriage. While she had 'enjoyed her luxuries' and been quite casual about performing the self-mortifying rituals prescribed to widows, she now leaves for Kashi, or Varanasi, the traditional abode for widows where she will have to subsist on the most meager of necessities. Through this conservative ending Tagore may have been catering to the audience of his day although, in certain respects, Bankimchandra had gone much further thirty years earlier. In *The Poison Tree* Kundanandini gets to marry Nagendra, and when she swallows poison it remains ambiguous whether it is because of her rejection by Nagendra, or remorse at the transgression she has committed.

From the point of view of a modern audience the novel's denouement does not hold as much interest as the intensity of the emotional turmoil that Tagore reveals within a small canvas, as new forces make themselves felt in a traditional society. This turmoil is unfolded from inside, in the manner of an impressionist miniature, a first in Indian fiction. It is also leavened by Tagore's splendidly delicate irony and humour, not a common characteristic of *sturm und drang*-ers. And above all there is the character of Binodini, unashamed charmer and seductress, who oscillates violently between renouncing and reclaiming her desire.

On the centenary of its publication the novel has been filmed for the first time by director Rituparno Ghosh. It is fitting that this modern, colloquial English translation should also become available at the same time.

Kolkata   Swagato Ganguly
August 2003

1

BINODINI'S MOTHER, HARIMATI, CAME TO MAHENDRA'S MOTHER, Rajlakshmi with an appeal. They were childhood friends from the same village.

That same day, Rajlakshmi broached the topic with her son, Mahendra. 'Mahin, we must do something for this poor girl. I've heard she is very beautiful and she's even had lessons from a British woman—I'm sure she'll appeal to your modern tastes.'

Mahendra said, 'Mother, there are plenty of other boys who have modern tastes.'

'Mahin, this is the problem with you: you always shy away from the subject of marriage.'

'Mother, we can talk about other things, can't we? This unwillingness is not really such a great flaw in my character.'

Mahendra had lost his father as a child. His relationship with his mother was therefore rather unique. He was twenty-two; after completing his MA, he was now studying medicine. Yet, not a day passed when he didn't have a playful tiff with his mother and then patched up ceremoniously. Figuratively speaking, just as a kangaroo cub is most comfortable in its mother's pouch it was second nature for Mahendra to stay in his mother's sheltering shadow. He could not dream of eating, sleeping, or even lifting a finger without his mother's constant ministering.

When his mother began to bring up Binodini as part of every conversation, he said, 'Fine, I will go and see this girl.'

On the appointed day he grumbled, 'What's the point of seeing her! I would only be marrying at your insistence; so it's a waste of time trying to figure out if I like her or not.'

There was a trace of resentment in the words, but his mother was sure that when he finally saw the girl at the time of the wedding, her son would approve of her choice and his ruffled feathers would be smoothed.

Rajlakshmi began to prepare for the wedding with great enthusiasm. But as the day drew nearer, Mahendra grew more and more restless. Eventually, a few days before the wedding he blurted out, 'No Mother, I cannot go through with this.'

From the day he was born, Mahendra had been indulged by the gods and men alike; hence his desires were uncontrolled. He was completely incapable of respecting the desires of others. So, the fact that he was bound by his mother's request and his own promise to her made him very hostile towards the whole proposition of marriage; he now refused point blank.

Behari was a very dear friend of Mahendra's. He addressed Mahendra as Dada and Rajlakshmi as Mother. The latter looked upon him as a mere towboat trawling behind the ship that was Mahendra, a necessary attachment for her son, and as such she felt quite kindly towards him. She said to him, 'Behari, *you* will have to marry her now; otherwise the unfortunate girl—'

Behari folded his hands and said, 'Mother, forgive me, but I cannot do that. When Mahin da wastes a sweet because he doesn't like the taste of it, I've finished it off at your request often enough. But that's not going to work where a bride is concerned.'

Rajlakshmi thought, 'Behari and marriage? He dotes on Mahin so much that the thought of marriage probably never crosses his mind!' This only served to increase her compassionate regard for Behari.

Binodini's father was not a wealthy man. But he had taken great pains to get his only daughter educated and trained in domestic work by a British missionary lady. It had not occurred to him that the girl was growing past the marriageable age. After his death, his widow began to look for a match desperately. They had no money and the girl was now in danger of remaining a spinster.

Finally Rajlakshmi came to their aid and fixed Binodini's marriage to the son of someone she knew from her native village near Barasat. Soon after her marriage, Binodini was widowed.

Mahendra laughed as he said, 'Thank heavens I didn't marry her. With a widowed wife where would I be?'

Three years later, mother and son were having the following conversation:

'Son, people are talking, and I am the one they're blaming.'

'Why Mother, what harm have you done them?'

'They say that I am not getting you married for fear that you'll forget me when your wife comes.'

Mahendra said, 'Well, that fear is justified. If I were a mother I would never dare get my son married. I would much rather take all the criticism that people dish out without a murmur of protest.'

Rajlakshmi laughed. 'Just listen to yourself.'

Mahendra said, 'But it is a fact that when a wife comes in, she gets all of the son's sympathies. The mother who loved and nurtured him for so many years suddenly grows distant. Even if *you* can take that, *I* cannot.'

Secretly thrilled, Rajlakshmi called out to her widowed sister-in-law, Annapurna, who was passing by. 'Just listen to my son, Mejo-bou. He doesn't want to marry for fear that his wife would oust me from his affections. Have you ever heard such nonsense in your life?'

Annapurna said, 'My son, that is going a little too far. There's a time for everything in life. This is the time for you to leave your mother's lap and build a life for yourself with your wife beside you. Such childish behaviour at this age is unbecoming.'

These words did not please Rajlakshmi at all. The words she spoke in response may have been forthright, but they certainly weren't pleasant. She said, 'Mejo-bou, why does it distress you if my son loves his mother more than most other sons? If you had a son you would know what it means to a mother.'

Rajlakshmi felt that the empty womb was envious of the proud provider of the male scion.

Annapurna said, 'I said that only because you broached the subject of Mahin's marriage. Otherwise, what right do I have to speak?'

Rajlakshmi said, 'Why should it trouble you if my son refuses to bring home a bride? Actually, if I have been able to bring up my son and care for him all these years, I can carry on doing so for the rest of my life—I don't need anyone else.'

Annapurna shed some silent tears as she walked away. Mahendra felt upset over this fallout; when he came back from his college he went straight to his aunt's room.

He knew that his aunt had only spoken out of affection for him. He was also aware that his aunt had an orphaned niece and that the childless widow would like to see her married to Mahendra so that she could have her close at hand. Although Mahendra was opposed to marriage, he thought this little wish of his aunt's was a very natural one and he empathized with it.

When Mahendra walked into the room, the light was already failing. Annapurna was resting her head on the bars of the window and staring out despondently. Her lunch lay covered and untouched on a table.

Mahendra was given to tears easily. This vision of his aunt made his eyes moist; he went closer and said, 'Aunty.'

Annapurna tried to smile. 'Mahin, come, sit.'

Mahendra said, 'I am very hungry and I'd love to have some leftovers from your lunch.'

Annapurna understood that he was trying to comfort her and checked her tears with great difficulty. She ate her lunch and fed him at the same time.

Mahendra's heart overflowed with pity and affection. At the end of his meal, just to cheer up his aunt, he spoke on impulse, 'Aunty, remember that niece of yours you'd mentioned—won't you show her to me?' The minute the words were out, he wished he hadn't said them.

Annapurna laughed and said, 'Are you thinking of marriage now?'

Mahendra spoke quickly, 'No, no, not for me. I think I might get Behari to agree. You must arrange for us to see her once.'

Annapurna said, 'The poor girl, will fate be so kind to her? If only she is lucky enough to have Behari for a husband.'

Mahendra turned to leave; at the door he bumped into his mother. 'What were you two discussing all this while?' she asked.

Mahendra said, 'No discussion, I just came for a paan.'

Rajlakshmi said, 'But your paan is ready in my room.'

Mahendra went away without speaking. Rajlakshmi entered the room, took one look at Annapurna's tear-stained face and her imagination ran wild. 'Well, well, Mejo-bou, carrying tales to my son, were we?' she hissed as she turned and left without waiting for an answer.

2

MAHENDRA HAD ALMOST FORGOTTEN HIS PROMISE TO SEE THE GIRL, but Annapurna hadn't. She wrote to the girl's relatives (on her father's side) in Shyambazar and arranged a date for her to be seen. When Mahendra heard that a date was fixed he said, 'Why did you rush things so much, Aunty? I haven't even spoken to Behari yet.'

Annapurna said, 'But Mahin, now if you don't go to see her, it won't look good.'

Mahendra sent for Behari and explained everything. He said, 'Let's go and see her at least; then if you don't like her, no one will force you.'

Behari said, 'I am not so sure of that. I won't be able to reject a girl who happens to be Aunty's niece.'

Mahendra said, 'Well, that settles it then.'

Behari said, 'But this was a very rash thing to do, Mahin da. You cannot go around putting loads on other people's shoulders when you have kept yours conveniently free. Now it will be very difficult for me to do anything that'll hurt Aunty.'

Mahendra looked a little shamefaced. Then he said somewhat irritatedly, 'So what do you want to do now?'

Behari said, 'Since you have raised her hopes in my name, I will marry the girl—but all this show of going to see her is not necessary.'

To Behari, Annapurna was nothing less than divine. She sent for Behari and said, 'This is not right, son—you cannot get married without seeing her. And promise me that you will say no if you do not like her.'

Behari had to agree.

On the appointed day Mahendra came back from college and said to Rajlakshmi, 'Mother, could I have that silk kurta and my Dhaka-cotton dhoti?'

Mother asked, 'Why? Where are you going?'

Mahendra said, 'Just give it now—I'll explain later.'

Mahendra couldn't resist dressing up a bit. Though he was going to see a girl for someone else, the very occasion was cause enough for a youth to pat his hair down and spray some essence.

The two friends set out for Shyambazar.

Anukulbabu was the girl's paternal uncle. His three-storeyed house surrounded by gardens, built with his own hard-earned money, towered over the neighbourhood. When his indigent brother died, he had brought his orphaned niece to stay with him. Her aunt, Annapurna, had offered to take her in but although that would have relieved him of additional expenses, he had refused for fear of compromising his reputation. In fact, he was so fastidious about his status that he seldom ever sent the girl to meet her aunt.

Soon, it was time to look for a match for the girl. But where preparations for the girl's wedding were concerned, Anukulbabu was unable to keep up his ostentatious ways. His intentions may have been grand, but the lack of money prevented them from being executed. Whenever the question of dowry came up, Anukulbabu said, 'I have daughters of my own; how can I pay for all this?' Thus the days passed. It was at such a time that Mahendra made his appearance with his friend, dressed to kill and reeking of essence.

It was early April; the sun was about to set. At one end of the first-floor veranda, decorated with painted ceramic tiles, arrangements were made for the two friends, with silver trays laden with fruits and sweets and icy liquids that condensed into a latticework of glistening dew upon the silver glasses. Mahendra and Behari sat down to partake of the offerings diffidently. Down in the garden the gardener watered the plants. As the scent of wet earth wafted on the cool April breeze, it also swayed and tugged at Mahendra's shawl.

Through the doors and windows around them they could hear slight murmurs, gentle sounds of laughter and the tinkling of bangles.

When they had finished eating, Anukulbabu glanced into the interior of the house and called, 'Chuni, please get us some paan here.'

A little later a door behind them opened hesitantly and a young girl, shrouded in an invisible cloak of shyness, came and stood beside Anukulbabu, holding a tray of paan in her hands.

Anukulbabu said, 'Don't be shy, my child. Keep the tray in front of them.'

The girl bent low and placed the tray on the floor beside them with shaking hands. The rays of the setting sun touched her blushing face. Mahendra caught a quick glimpse of her tremulous expression. She made as if to run away but Anukulbabu said, 'Wait a minute, Chuni. Beharibabu, this is my younger brother Apurva's daughter. He is no more and I am all she has in this world.' He heaved a sigh.

Mahendra felt a bolt of pity strike through his heart. He glanced at the orphan girl once more.

No one had mentioned her age clearly. Close relatives always said, 'She'd be around twelve or thirteen,' which meant that she was perhaps closer to fourteen or fifteen. But her blossoming youth seemed caught up in a faltering timidity, perhaps because she was aware of her obligations as a dependent.

Mahendra's heart overflowed with sympathy as he asked, 'What is your name?'

Anukulbabu gave her encouragement, 'Tell him, child,

tell him your name.'

The girl answered in her habitually obedient manner, 'My name is Ashalata.'

Asha! Mahendra felt the very name was poignant and the voice very mellow. Asha, the orphan! Asha, the hopeful!

The two friends came out on the streets, let the carriage go and started walking. Mahendra said, 'Behari, don't let go of this girl.'

Behari avoided a direct answer and said, 'The girl reminded me of her aunt; perhaps she'd be just as charming and good-natured.'

Mahendra said, 'So, perhaps now the load I placed on your shoulders doesn't seem quite so heavy?'

Behari said, 'No, it seems bearable.'

Mahendra said, 'But I don't want to put you to any trouble. Let me relieve you of your burden—what do you say?'

Behari cast a solemn glance at Mahendra and said, 'Mahin da, are you serious? There's still time. If you marry her, Aunty will be the happiest. She would then have the girl close to her all the time.'

Mahendra said, 'Are you mad? If that were possible, it would have happened long ago.'

Behari didn't raise any further objections and went his way. Mahendra took a long-winded route home and walked back slowly. Rajlakshmi was busy frying puris and Annapurna had not yet returned from her niece's.

Mahendra went up to the terrace all by himself and lay down on a mat. The half moon was casting its own silent, unique spells upon the concrete skyscape of Kolkata. When

Rajlakshmi came to call him for dinner, Mahendra replied lazily, 'I don't feel like getting up.'

Rajlakshmi said, 'Let me send it up here then?'

Mahendra said, 'I don't want dinner tonight. I have already eaten.'

Rajlakshmi asked, 'Where did you eat?'

Mahendra said, 'That's a long story. I'll tell you later.'

Rajlakshmi was miffed at her son's inexplicable behaviour and made as if to leave. But Mahendra composed himself in a minute and spoke out repentantly, 'Mother, please send my meal up here.'

Mother answered, 'What's the point if you are not hungry?'

A small emotional scene ensued between mother and son following which Mahendra had to sit down to eat again.

3

THAT NIGHT MAHENDRA DIDN'T SLEEP WELL. EARLY THE NEXT morning he landed up at Behari's house and said, 'Behari, I gave it a lot of thought and finally came to the conclusion that Aunty wishes *me* to marry her niece.'

Behari said, 'She has made that wish known to you many times in many ways—there was no need to give it fresh thought.'

Mahendra said, 'Yes, well, that's why I feel that if I don't marry Asha she will be a little hurt.'

Behari said, 'It's possible.'

Mahendra said, 'I feel that would be very wrong of me.'

Behari spoke up with a trace of unnatural enthusiasm, 'Great news, that is wonderful—if you say yes, there's nothing more to be said. It would have been even better if you had woken up to your duty yesterday.'

Mahendra said, 'Well, better late than never.'

The moment Mahendra let the thought of marriage take hold of his mind it was difficult for him to show even the slightest patience. He felt that the deed should be done without any further ado.

He went to Rajlakshmi and said, 'Mother, I am agreeable to your wish—I'm ready for marriage.'

Rajlakshmi said to herself, 'Now I know why Mejo-bou rushed off to see her niece the other day and why Mahendra dressed up and left too.'

She felt angry at the entire universe; in spite of her repeated requests, it was Annapurna's plan that had succeded! She said, 'Let me look for a good match for you.'

Mahendra said, 'Oh, that has been arranged.' He told Rajlakshmi about Asha.

Rajlakshmi said, 'Let me tell you, child, that girl will not do.'

Mahendra controlled his feelings and spoke mildly, 'Why Mother, isn't she a nice girl?'

Rajlakshmi said, 'She has no one to call her own. If I bring her in, I will have no relatives and family to look to from her side.'

Mahendra said, 'I wouldn't mind that, but Mother, I rather liked the girl.'

Rajlakshmi's heart grew harder at the sight of her son's persistence. She went to Annapurna and said, 'You want to get that orphaned, unlucky girl married to my only son so that you can control him, don't you? What audacity, what treachery!'

Annapurna wailed, 'There's no talk of Mahin marrying her; I do not know what he has felt prompted to tell you.'

Rajlakshmi didn't believe her one bit. Annapurna sent for Behari and implored him with tears in her eyes, 'Wasn't everything arranged with you? Why did you turn it all around? You will have to give your consent once again. If you don't help me, I will be greatly embarrassed. The girl is very nice, she won't be unworthy of you.'

Behari said, 'Aunty, you don't have to tell me that. Since she is your niece, there is no question of my disapproval. But Mahin da . . .'

Annapurna said, 'No, my child, there is no way she can marry Mahin. Let me be very honest with you—I'll be happiest if she marries you. I wouldn't consent to a match between her and Mahin.'

Behari said, 'Aunty, if you don't give your consent, the matter is settled.' He went to Rajlakshmi and said, 'Mother, Aunty's niece's wedding is fixed with me. There are no women in my family and so I had to be shameless enough to come and give you the news myself.'

Rajlakshmi said, 'Really, Behari? This makes me very happy. She is a very good girl. Don't let her go.'

Behari said, 'Why would I? Mahin da himself went and fixed this match for me.'

All this got Mahendra well and truly worked up. He was

so upset with his mother and aunt that he left home and took up a room in a students' hostel. Rajlakshmi went to Annapurna in tears. 'Mejo-bou, it looks like my son is about to leave the house in misery. Please do something.'

Annapurna said, 'Didi, please be patient; his anger will evaporate in a few days.'

Rajlakshmi said, 'You don't know him. He can go to any extent if he doesn't get what he wants. You must do whatever you can and get him married to your niece.'

Annapurna said, 'Didi, how can I do that? I have given my word to Behari.'

Rajlakshmi said, 'That word can be taken back.' She sent for Behari and said, 'Son, I will find you a better match— you'll have to let this girl go. She isn't worthy of you.'

Behari said, 'No, Mother, that's not possible. It is all fixed.'

So Rajlakshmi went to Annapurna again and said, 'I beg of you, Mejo-bou, please help me. If you tell Behari, he'll do it.'

Annapurna said to Behari, 'Son, I hate to say this to you and I don't know how to say it. I would have been happiest if Asha were to marry you. But you know all that is happening—'

Behari said, 'I understand, Aunty. I will do as you say. But never, ever again will you request me to marry anyone.'

Behari left. Annapurna's eyes filled with tears. But she brushed them away for fear of bringing ill luck on Mahendra. She told herself again and again that whatever happened was for the best.

Thus the day of the wedding drew close, even as a silent,

cruel battle of emotions raged between Rajlakshmi, Annapurna and Mahendra. The lights came on, the music played loudly and there was feasting and merry-making all around.

Asha stepped into her new home, decked in bridal finery, swathed in fetching shyness. Her gentle, trembling heart did not envision even a single thorn lining the fabric of her cosy haven. On the contrary, she was filled with joy that she was coming home to her aunt Annapurna, the closest thing to a mother that she had ever known.

After the wedding, Rajlakshmi called Mahendra and said, 'I think Bou-ma should go and stay with her uncle for a while now.'

Mahendra asked, 'Why, Mother?'

Rajlakshmi said, 'Your exams are coming up and you may not be able to concentrate.'

Mahendra said, 'I am not a child. I know how to look after myself.'

Rajlakshmi said, 'May be. But it's only a matter of another year.'

Mahendra said, 'If she had her parents, I wouldn't mind sending her to them. But I refuse to send her away to her uncle's house.'

Rajlakshmi muttered to herself, 'My, my, we are devoted, aren't we? Mother-in-law has no say in the matter! Married for a day and already tied to her apron strings. In our days when our husbands married us, such shameless fawning was unheard of.'

Mahendra said confidently, 'Don't worry, Mother! My exams will be fine.'

4

RAJLAKSHMI BEGAN TO TEACH HER NEW DAUGHTER-IN-LAW THE household duties with untold enthusiasm. Asha's days were spent in the store-room, kitchen and puja room. At night Rajlakshmi took her in to sleep in her own room, so that the young girl wouldn't miss her relatives too much.

After much deliberation Annapurna decided to keep her distance from her niece.

Mahendra's state was like that of the greedy child who watches the adult chewing the sugarcane stick dry, unable to do a thing about it. He could barely tolerate the vision of his newly wedded young wife being crushed under the wheels of household duties.

He went to Annapurna and said, 'Aunty, I cannot stand the way mother is working the new bride half to death.'

Annapurna knew that Rajlakshmi was overdoing things. But she said, 'Why Mahin, it's a good thing to teach the bride some household chores. It's better than her reading novels, sewing or sitting around doing nothing like these modern girls.'

Mahendra got worked up and said, 'A modern girl *will* be a modern girl, be it good or bad. If my wife can read a novel and appreciate it like me, I don't see what's wrong with it.'

Rajlakshmi heard her son in Annapurna's room, dropped whatever she was doing and rushed in. She asked sharply, 'What are you two discussing?'

Excited beyond words, Mahendra replied, 'Nothing, Mother, I just can't stand by and watch my wife working like a slave.'

Rajlakshmi controlled the burning spikes that jabbed within and answered in her most acerbic voice, 'And what, pray, should her ladyship do?'

Mahendra said, 'I will teach her to read.'

Rajlakshmi left the room without a word and a moment later she returned, pulling Asha by the hand. 'Here, take your bride and teach her to read.'

She then turned to Annapurna and bowed in mock obeisance, 'Forgive me, Mejo-bou, I didn't realize the true worth of your niece. I have stained her soft hands with turmeric in the kitchen; now you can wash them out carefully and hand her over to Mahin—she can put her feet up and study. I am always there to do the slave-work.' Rajlakshmi stomped into her room, slammed the door shut and bolted it noisily. Annapurna sank to the floor under the weight of her misery. Asha failed to get the full implications of this unexpected family spat; but she turned pale with shame, fear and wretchedness. Mahendra felt very angry as he thought to himself, 'Enough is enough. I must take my wife's life in my own hands, or it won't be right.'

These newly emerged feelings of duty fanned the flames of desire like a friendly breeze which bore away his college-work, exams, friends, social sense and all else. Mahendra was fired by the enthusiasm to teach his wife and he went into his room and shut the door, paying no heed to work or people.

A piqued Rajlakshmi thought, 'If Mahendra and his bride come and bang on my door, I will not answer. Let me see how he manages without his mother.'

Days passed and no repentant footfall sounded by the door.

Rajlakshmi decided that if he came to beg forgiveness, she'd forgive him, or he would be too hurt. But there were no entreaties for mercy.

Then Rajlakshmi decided to go to Mahendra's room and say that she had forgiven him. Just because the son was upset, the mother didn't have to be the same way.

Mahendra had a small room all to himself on the second-floor terrace, where he studied and slept. All these days Rajlakshmi had totally neglected cleaning his room, making the bed, putting his clothes away. Her heart was in turmoil since she had not performed her usual motherly duties. One afternoon she decided to go upstairs and tidy up his room while he was away in college; the minute he walked in, he'd know his mother had been there.

Rajlakshmi mounted the stairs. The door to Mahendra's room lay open and when she stood before it, she felt shock ripple through her. Mahendra was lying on the mattress on the floor, sleeping, and Asha sat with her back to the door, caressing his feet. Rajlakshmi was revolted at this blatant display of conjugal affections in broad daylight, with the door ajar. She went downstairs silently.

5

WHEN LONG-FAMISHED MUSTARD CROPS RECEIVE A SUDDEN BURST OF rain, they make up for lost time and flourish in leaps and bounds, laying spontaneous claims to the earth around them.

That is how it was with Asha. She had never truly felt that she belonged in the household to which she was related by blood. But after she came into this unfamiliar house, suddenly an intimate relationship, involving total trust, was hers for the asking; when her husband crowned the hitherto neglected orphan with his own hands, she didn't hesitate to rise to the occasion and take what was offered. She brushed aside the hesitant shyness of the new bride and took her rightful place at her husband's feet with artless pride and joy.

That afternoon, when Rajlakshmi spotted this newly arrived stranger-girl occupying her pride of place with such unconscious, easy grace, she came downstairs fuming and fretting indignantly. Since she was burning up with wrath, she went to singe Annapurna too. She said, 'Mejo-bou, just go and have a look at the royal heritage, the kind of thing your ladyship has learnt in her family. If only the elder men of this house were alive—'

Annapurna moaned in agonized distress, 'Didi, she is your daughter-in-law and you must scold her and teach her as you please. Why drag me into it?'

Like a strung bow, Rajlakshmi shrilled, 'My daughter-in-law? As long as you are ministering to her, would she even heed me?'

Annapurna went up to the couple's room, making a lot of noise, startling the pair of them. She looked at Asha. 'Is this how you are going to humiliate me, you stupid girl? Have you no shame, no sense of time or day, that you are resting here while your mother-in-law works herself to the bone? Serves me right for bringing you into this house!' The tears fell from her eyes as she spoke. Asha stood shocked in a corner, picking at her sari, tears streaming down her face.

Mahendra said, 'Aunty, why do you scold her? *I* am the one who holds her back.'

Annapurna said, 'And is that a good thing you're doing? She is young, an orphan, she has never been trained by her mother in the ways of this world. What are you teaching her?'

Mahendra said, 'Look, I have bought a slate, books and pen-and-paper for her. I am going to teach her to read, even if the world points fingers at me or all of you get angry.'

Annapurna said, 'But do you have to teach her all day long? An hour or so in the evenings would be quite enough.'

Mahendra said, 'It's not so simple, Aunty. Education is time consuming.'

Irked, Annapurna left the room. Asha took slow and hesitant footsteps to follow her. But Mahendra blocked her way, not heeding the pleading in her sad, lustrous eyes. He said, 'Wait, we have to make up for the time I lost sleeping.'

There may be earnest fools who might presume that Mahendra had indeed slept and wasted precious study-time; it is solely for their information that one needs to mention that Mahendra's educational methods would not be endorsed by any school inspector.

Asha trusted her husband. She truly believed that learning did not come easily to her and yet she must pursue it as a duty to her husband. For this precise reason, she did her best to collect her thoughts which ran helter-skelter.

She sat on a corner of the mattress on the floor, pored over her books fervently and began to learn them by rote, swaying to the rhythm. At the other end of the bedroom, her teacher sat at a small table with his medical books open. Every once in a while he cast an oblique glance at his student, apparently to measure her concentration. Suddenly, at some point, he would slam his books shut and call Asha by her pet name, 'Chuni!' Startled, Asha would look up. Mahendra would say, 'Bring the book to me—let me see what you are reading.'

Asha was scared she'd be tested. There was little chance of her passing the test. Her unruly mind was seldom equal to the task of acquiring knowledge from the book of alphabets. The more she tried to learn about the bumblebee, the more the letters swam before her eyes like a pile of mustard seeds. At her teacher's command Asha would guiltily bring the book and stand beside Mahendra's desk. One of his arms would snake round her waist and imprison her to his side firmly; he would hold the book in the other hand and ask, 'How much have you read today?'

Asha would point to the lines she had read.

Mahendra would sound forlorn. 'Ooh, that much? Want to see how much I have read?' He would point to the chapter heading in his medical text. Asha would widen her eyes. 'So what were you doing all this while?' Mahendra would caress her chin and say, 'I was lost in somebody's thoughts—a heartless person who was in turn lost in the life and times of the bumblebee.' Asha could have responded to this unfair accusation. But alas, modesty compelled her to accept this iniquitous defeat in the battle of love.

This will be proof enough that Mahendra's little school did not follow any private or public schooling methods.

If on a certain day Asha tried to concentrate on her books

while Mahendra was away, he'd sneak up from behind her and cover her eyes. Then he'd snatch away her books and say, 'You are so cruel, you don't think of me when I am gone?'

Asha would say, 'Do you want me to remain illiterate?'

Mahendra would reply, 'Well, thanks to you I am not very literate myself these days.'

The words sounded harsh to Asha. She would make as if to leave and say, 'How have I stopped you from studying?'

Mahendra would grab her hand and say, 'How would you know that? I can't pore over books when you are gone as easily as you can in my absence.'

A serious accusation! This would naturally be followed by a sudden burst of tears, like an autumnal shower, and soon enough it would disappear to reveal the sunshine of love, leaving behind a golden glow.

If the teacher is the greatest barrier in the path of knowledge, the helpless student can scarcely make her way through the wilderness. Sometimes Asha recollected her aunt's scornful rebuke and felt ashamed. She was aware that her studies were only an excuse for togetherness. Every time she met her mother-in-law she felt mortified. But Rajlakshmi never asked her to do any chores, never had a word of advice for her. If Asha volunteered to lend a hand in the kitchen, she immediately restrained her saying, 'Oh no, no, you go to the bedroom—or your studies will suffer.'

Eventually, Annapurna said to Asha one day, 'Your education, or the lack thereof, is quite apparent to me. But are you going to let Mahin fail *his* exams too?'

Asha hardened her mind with great resolve and said to Mahendra, 'Your exam preparations are suffering. From now on I shall stay in Aunty's room downstairs.'

Such severe penance at this tender age! Exiled from the bedroom all the way to Aunty's room! Even as she uttered these harsh words Asha's eyes grew heavy with tears, her truant lips trembled and her voice held a tremor.

Mahendra said, 'Fine, let's go to Aunty's room. But then she'd have to come upstairs and take our room.'

Asha felt angry when her solemn, magnanimous gesture was laughed at. Mahendra said, 'Better still, why don't you guard me day and night and see for yourself if I am studying for my exams or not?'

The matter was settled very easily that day. Details of the intimate guarding that took place are needless. Suffice it to say that Mahendra failed his exams that year and despite the elaborate descriptions in her book, Asha's knowledge of the habits of the bumblebee remained meagre.

But it would be wrong to say that such fascinating educational exchanges were conducted uninterrupted. Sometimes Behari dropped in and caused a major disturbance. He'd herald his arrival shouting, 'Mahin da, Mahin da.' He wouldn't rest till he'd dragged Mahendra from his hibernating nest of the bedroom. He chided Mahendra severely for neglecting his studies. To Asha he'd say, 'Bouthan, you can't gulp your food and digest it; you have to chew it. Now you are gulping down the rice greedily—later you'll be hunting for digestive tablets!'

Mahendra would reply, 'Chuni, don't listen to him. He's jealous of our happiness.'

Behari would say, 'Since you hold your happiness in your own hands, consume it in a way that doesn't make others jealous.'

Mahendra would say, 'But it's fun to make others jealous. Chuni, you know, the ass that I am, I had nearly handed you over to Behari.'

Behari would blush and mutter, 'Enough, Mahin da.'

Such exchanges did not endear Behari to Asha. She felt quite hostile towards him, perhaps because at one time her marriage had been fixed with him. Behari knew this, and Mahendra liked to make fun at his expense.

Rajlakshmi often complained to Behari. He said, 'Mother, the silkworm weaving the thread isn't as scary as the moth that cuts the bonds and flies away. Who could tell he'd break away from you thus?'

When Rajlakshmi heard that Mahendra had failed his exams she went up in flames like a forest fire in summer. But it was Annapurna who bore the true consequences of his failure. She gave up food and sleep.

6

ONE CLOUDY EVENING, WHEN THE LAND WAS FLOODED WITH THE first shower of the season, Mahendra entered his bedroom cheerfully, with a perfume-sprayed shawl on his shoulder and a fragrant garland around his neck. He tiptoed in, meaning to surprise Asha. But as he peeped in he found the window on the eastern corner open wide, the rain lashing in through it; the strong wind had snuffed out the lamp. Asha lay on the mattress, weeping her heart out.

Mahendra took quick steps into the room and asked, 'What's the matter?'

The young girl wept afresh. Many minutes passed before Mahendra finally got an answer: Annapurna couldn't take it any more and had gone away to her cousin's house.

Mahendra thought irately, 'If she had to go, why did she have to go today and spoil this nice, rainy evening for me!' But eventually all his wrath turned towards his mother. *She* was at the root of this. Mahendra said, 'Let us go and stay with Aunty—I'll see with whom Mother bickers.'

He kicked up a great fuss, began to pack his things and sent for bearers. Rajlakshmi understood what was afoot. She came up to Mahendra slowly and spoke to him calmly, 'Where are you going?'

At first he didn't answer. When she asked a few more times, he said, 'I am going to stay with Aunty.'

Rajlakshmi said, 'You don't have to go anywhere. *I* will go and fetch your aunt.'

She got into a palki and left for Annapurna's new home. Once there, she bowed low and said, 'Please don't be angry, Mejo-bou, and forgive me.'

Utterly embarrassed, Annapurna rushed to touch her feet as she wailed, 'Didi, why do you put me in the wrong thus? I'll do whatever you say.'

Rajlakshmi said, 'My son and daughter-in-law are leaving the house because you went away.' As she spoke, she burst into tears, tears of anger and humiliation.

The two sisters-in-law came back home. It was still raining. Asha had almost stopped weeping and Mahendra was doing his best to get her to smile. It appeared as if the rainy evening could be salvaged still.

Annapurna said, 'Chuni, you don't let me stay in this house, and you won't let go if I go away! Don't I deserve some peace?'

Asha looked up, startled like the wounded gazelle.

Mahendra was immensely irked as he said, 'Why Aunty, what has Chuni done to you?'

Annapurna said, 'I went away because I couldn't stand a new bride going about so brazenly. Why, you wretched girl, did you have to make your mother-in-law cry and fetch me back?'

Mahendra had not known that mothers and aunts were such a great hindrance to the poetry of one's life.

The next day Rajlakshmi sent for Behari. 'Son, please tell Mahin that I want to go to our ancestral home in Barasat— I haven't gone there in ages.'

Behari said, 'If you haven't gone there in ages, you need not go now. Anyway, I'll tell Mahin da, but I don't think he will agree to it.'

Mahendra said, 'Well, one does wish to see one's birthplace. But Mother shouldn't stay there for too long—the place gets uncomfortable when the rains come.'

Behari was annoyed to see Mahendra agreeing so easily. But he smiled and said, 'If Mother goes alone, there'll be no one to look after her. Why don't you send Bouthan with her?'

Mahendra sensed the covert criticism in Behari's words and disconcerted, he said, 'Of course I could do that.' But the matter didn't go any further than that. Behari only succeeded in alienating Asha's sympathies once again; the knowledge of that fact seemed to give him a wry pleasure.

Needless to say, Rajlakshmi wasn't all that keen to see her birthplace in Barasat. When the river runs dry in summer, the boatman drops the oar every now and then to check how deep the water runs. At such times of emotional rift between mother and son, Rajlakshmi too was plunging the oar here and there from time to time, checking on the depth of the emotions. She had not expected that her proposal of going away to Barasat would be accepted so easily. She said to herself, 'There's a difference between Annapurna leaving the house and my going away. She is a spell-casting witch and I am just a mother. It's better that I leave.'

Annapurna understood the workings of her mind and she said to Mahendra, 'If Didi leaves, I will go with her.'

Mahendra said, 'Did you hear that, Mother? If you go, Aunty will go with you and then how will our household run?'

Consumed with hatred, Rajlakshmi said, '*You* will come, Mejo-bou? That's impossible—without you the household cannot run. You *have* to stay.'

Rajlakshmi couldn't wait any longer. The following afternoon she was ready to leave. Everyone including Behari had assumed that Mahendra would escort her. But when the time came it turned out that Mahendra had arranged for a bearer and a guard to accompany his mother.

Behari said, 'Mahin da, you are not dressed yet?'

A little shamefaced, Mahendra said, 'I have college—'

Behari said, 'Fine, you stay. I'll go with Mother.'

Mahendra was offended. When they were alone, he said to Asha, 'Really, Behari is going too far. He wants to prove that he is more concerned about Mother than I am.'

Annapurna was forced to stay back. But she shrank into her shell from shame, grief and exasperation. Mahendra was angry at this distant behaviour from his aunt; Asha too, felt hurt.

7

RAJLAKSHMI ARRIVED AT THE BARASAT HOUSE. BEHARI WAS SUPPOSED to drop her off there and return at once. But when he saw how things were, he stayed back.

There were only a few very old widows living in Rajlakshmi's ancestral home. Thick forests of bamboo and foliage ran wild all around, the water in the pond was a deep, mossy green and jackals howled nearby all day long. Rajlakshmi was quite distressed.

Behari said, 'Mother, it may be your motherland, but "more glorious than all else" it is not. Let's go back to Kolkata. It'd be a sin to leave you alone here.'

Rajlakshmi was close to giving up and returning. But at this point Binodini arrived, seeking shelter with Rajlakshmi and at the same time providing her with loving care. Binodini needs no fresh introduction. At one time her marriage had been fixed first to Mahendra and later to Behari. But the husband that fate had ordained for her, had a spleen disorder that proved fatal very soon. Ever since his death, Binodini had spent her days alone in the cheerless household, like a lone flowering plant in the barren wilderness. Today the orphaned girl came and bowed respectfully, touched her aunt-in-law Rajlakshmi's feet and placed herself at her service. And it was service worthy of its name. There was not a moment's rest for her. Every chore was executed perfectly, meals were cooked to perfection and there was such lovely, gracious conversation.

Rajlakshmi would say, 'It's late my child, why don't you go and have some lunch?'

Binodini wouldn't hear of it. She didn't leave before she fanned her aunt to sleep.

Rajlakshmi said, 'But you'll fall ill, my child.'

But Binodini showed the least concern for her own health and said, 'Unfortunate souls like us don't fall ill, Aunty. You have come to your home after so many years—I have nothing here with which to care for you properly.'

Behari, meanwhile, became the local expert in a couple of days. Some came to consult him for their illnesses while others came to seek his advice on legal matters. If someone sought him out to find a good job for his son, someone else brought an application for him to fill out. He mingled with everyone with his intuitive curiosity and concern, be it the geriatric band of card players or the drinking group of the lower castes. No one resented him and he was welcome everywhere.

Binodini did her best to lighten the burden on this city-bred youth who was unfortunate enough to have landed in this godforsaken place. Every time Behari came back from his rounds, he found his room cleaned up, a bunch of flowers placed by his bed in a brass tumbler and Bankim and Dinabandhu's works neatly placed on his bedside table. On the inside covers of the books Binodini's name was inscribed in a feminine but firm hand.

There was a distinction between this kind of solicitude and the kind one normally encountered in a village. When Behari mentioned this to Rajlakshmi she said, 'And this is the girl both of you turned down.'

Behari laughed and said, 'It wasn't wise, Mother, we have been fools. But it's better to be fooled by *not* marrying than to be fooled by marrying.'

The thought churning in Rajlakshmi's mind was, 'This girl could have been my daughter-in-law. Why didn't it happen?'

If Rajlakshmi so much as mentioned going back to Kolkata, Binodini's eyes brimmed with tears and she said, 'Aunty, why did you have to come for a couple of days? When I didn't know you, my days passed somehow or other. Now, how will I live without you?'

Overwhelmed with emotion, Rajlakshmi blurted out, 'Child, why didn't you come into my house as a bride—I would have kept you so close to my heart!' These words made Binodini blush and run away.

Rajlakshmi was waiting for a letter from Kolkata, begging her to return. Her Mahin had never been away from his mother for so long in his entire life. He must be missing her terribly by now. Rajlakshmi was waiting eagerly for that letter from her son, bearing all his hurt feelings, tantrums and yearning for her.

Instead, Behari got a letter from Mahendra: 'Perhaps Mother is very happy to be back in her birthplace after so many years.'

Rajlakshmi thought, 'Dear me, Mahin must be very hurt. Happy! How could his wretched mother be happy anywhere without her Mahin!'

'O Behari, do read what more Mahin has written,' she said.

Behari said, 'There's nothing after that, Mother.' He crumpled up the letter, stuffed it into a book and dumped it in a corner of the room.

Rajlakshmi could scarcely contain herself. Mahin must have written such angry words that Behari couldn't read them out to his mother! Sometimes the calf butts against the cow's udder and procures both milk and maternal love. Rajlakshmi felt a similar surge of love for her son at the thought of his wrath. She forgave Mahendra readily and said to herself, 'If Mahin is happy with his bride, let him be. At any cost, he must be happy. I'll not trouble him any more. Poor thing, how angry he must be when his mother, who has never been away from him, has left him and come away.' Her tears overflowed at the very thought.

That day Rajlakshmi went again and again to Behari and hustled him, 'Go and have your bath, son; it's getting late.'

But Behari seemed to have lost interest in bathing or eating. He said, 'Mother, a little indiscipline is good for a hopeless wretch like me.'

Rajlakshmi coaxed him firmly, 'No, son, go and have your bath.'

After such continual badgering Behari went into the bathroom. The minute he left the room, Rajlakshmi rescued the crumpled letter from within the book, gave it to Binodini and said, 'Child, read out to me what Mahin has written to Behari.'

Binodini began to read. At first he had written about his mother, but that was very little. Not much more than what Behari had read out to her earlier. Then he had spoken of Asha. It was as if Mahendra was delirious with joy, mirth and a strange intoxication. Binodini read a little bit, blushed and stopped short, 'Aunty, what do you want to hear all this for?'

Rajlakshmi's yearning, loving face turned to stone in a moment. She was silent for a while and then she said, 'Stop.' She walked away without taking the letter back.

Binodini went into her room holding the letter. She bolted the door from within, sat on her bed and began to read again. Only she could say what she gleaned from that letter. But it certainly wasn't amusement. As she read it over and over again, her eyes began to burn like the desert sands at noon and her breath became as fiery as the desert winds. Her mind was awhirl with thoughts of Mahendra, Asha and their passionate romance. She held the letter on her lap, leant against the wall, stretched her legs out in front and sat still for a long time.

Behari couldn't find Mahendra's letter ever again.

That same afternoon, all of a sudden, Annapurna arrived in Barasat. Rajlakshmi paled at the thought of some bad news. She didn't dare ask anything and just looked at Annapurna with an ashen face.

Annapurna said at once, 'Didi, everything's fine in Kolkata.'

Rajlakshmi said, 'Then why are you here?'

Annapurna said, 'Didi, please take over your household. I have lost interest in these chores. I have set off to go to Kashi. I came here to take your blessings before I go. I may have wronged you, with or without intention, many a times. Please forgive me. And your daughter-in-law,' her eyes filled with tears, 'she is a child, she is motherless. Whether she is guilty or innocent, she is still yours.' She could speak no further.

Rajlakshmi got busy arranging for her bath and meal. Behari came running from Gadai Ghosh's gathering when he heard the news. He touched Annapurna's feet and said, 'Aunty, this is not possible; you cannot be so heartless as to leave us.'

Annapurna checked her tears and said, 'Don't try to hold me back, Behari—all of you be happy; nothing will stop on my account.'

Behari was silent. Then he said, 'Mahin da is very heartless to have bade you goodbye.'

Annapurna looked shaken. 'Don't say that—I am not angry with Mahin. But no good will come to the family unless I leave.'

Behari looked into the distance and sat there in silence. Annapurna undid the knot in her sari and took out a pair of gold bracelets. 'Son, keep these bracelets—give them to your wife with my blessings, when she comes.'

Behari touched them to his forehead and went into the next room to hide his tears.

As she left, Annapurna said, 'Behari, look after my Mahin and my Asha.'

She handed a piece of paper to Rajlakshmi and said, 'This is a deed whereby I give to Mahin my share in the ancestral property. Just send me fifteen rupees every month.'

She bent to the ground and took Rajlakshmi's blessings before she set off on her pilgrimage.

8

ASHA WAS VERY SCARED. WHAT ON EARTH WAS GOING ON! RAJLAKSHMI had gone away, and Annapurna followed suit. Mahendra's and her pleasure seemed to drive everyone away. It would end up driving *her* away. Their newly-wed love games struck her as a little incongruous amidst the vacant, deserted household.

If the flower of romance is plucked from the tree of life, it cannot sustain itself. Asha could also gradually see that there was a weariness, an ennui in their never-ending romance. It seemed to wilt every now and then—it was difficult sustaining it without the firm and liberal support of household life surrounding it. If romance has no link with other activities, play alone cannot bring out its true colours.

Mahendra tried to rebel against his family, lit all the lamps of his love-life all at once and tried to play out his grand romance amidst the gloom of his deserted household. He tried a dig at Asha, 'Chuni, what's the matter with you these days? Why are you so upset over your aunt's departure? Isn't our love enough to make up for all the loves in the world?'

Asha was miserable as she thought, 'Then there must be a lack in my love. I think of my aunt so often; I am so upset that Mother has left us.' She then tried her best to compensate for this lack in the extent of her love.

The household chores remained half done these days. The servants made hay and work was neglected. One day the maid claimed to be sick and was absent, the next day the cook was too drunk to come in to work. Mahendra said to Asha, 'That's great. Today we shall cook our own meals.'

Mahendra drove down to New Market to shop. He had no idea of what to buy and how much—he just picked up a lot of things and came home happy. Asha didn't have a clue either about what was to be done with the horde that he had brought home. Trial and error drove the clock hands past three o'clock and Mahendra was amused by the end result—a variety of inedible dishes. Asha failed to join him in his mirth—her own ignorance and incompetence shamed her.

Everything was scattered about so untidily in all the rooms that it was difficult to find anything when it was needed. One day, Mahendra's scalpel was used to cut vegetables and it took permanent refuge in the pile of debris. His notes were used to stoke the kitchen fire, whereupon they gave up the ghost on the ashen bed of the stove.

These and many other disasters gave Mahendra much cause for mirth while Asha continued to feel more and more upset. To the young girl such abandoned drifting of the household on the waves of confusion and waste was nothing less than a nightmare.

One evening the two were sitting on a bed they'd made on the covered veranda. Before them stretched the open terrace. After a spurt of rain the skyline of Kolkata was awash with moonlight on the horizon. Asha had gathered rain-drenched bakul flowers from the garden; she now sat with her head bent, weaving them into a garland. Mahendra was pulling at it, hindering her, criticizing and generally trying to pick a mock squabble. If Asha opened her mouth to chide him for such misdeeds, he immediately silenced her by a contrived move and nipped the reproach in the bud.

At this point the neighbour's koel called out from its cage. Immediately, Asha and Mahendra looked up at the cage that hung over their heads. Their koel never let the neighbour's koel go unanswered. Why was it silent today?

Asha was worried. 'What's wrong with the bird?'

Mahendra said, 'It's heard your voice and is too shy to open its beak.'

Asha pleaded, 'No, seriously, please have a look.'

Mahendra brought the cage off the hook. He opened its doors and found the bird had died. After Annapurna left, the bearer had gone on leave. No one had looked after the bird.

Asha's face turned ashen. Her fingers stilled over the flowers piled on her lap. Mahendra was saddened too; but he was more afraid of the mood being spoilt and so he tried to laugh it off, 'Actually it's all for the best. When I go to college the damned bird cried its heart out and disturbed you.' Mahendra reached for Asha and tried to hold her close.

Asha disentangled herself slowly and emptied her sari of the bakul flowers. 'No more,' she said. 'Shame on us! Please go quickly and bring Mother back.'

9

AT THAT VERY MOMENT THERE WAS A SHOUT OF 'MAHIN DA, Mahin da' from below. Mahendra replied, 'Hello there, come on up.' Behari's voice actually lifted Mahendra's spirits. Since their marriage Behari had often come between them as a barrier—but today that very barrier seemed welcome and imperative. Asha too felt relieved at Behari's arrival. When she drew the sari over her head and made as if to rise, Mahendra said, 'Where are you off to? It's only Behari.'

Asha said, 'Let me arrange for Thakurpo's tea.'

Asha's dejection lifted a little at this opportunity to do something. She wanted to hear about her mother-in-law and so she stood there awhile. She still never addressed Behari directly.

As he walked in Behari said, 'Oh no, I seem to have run headlong into intense poesy. Don't worry, Bouthan, you sit down and I'll be on my way.'

Asha glanced at Mahendra, who asked, 'Behari, how is Mother?'

Behari said, 'Don't bring up Mother and Aunty today, my friend, there's time yet for all that. Such a night was not made for sleep, nor for mothers and aunts.'

Behari was about to turn back when Mahendra dragged him back by force and made him sit down. Behari said, 'Look Bouthan, it's not my fault—he held me back by force—it's Mahin da's sin and the curse shouldn't come upon me!' Such bantering always irked Asha because she could never respond. Behari did this on purpose.

Behari said, 'Well, the house is a sight. Isn't it time yet for you to fetch Mother?'

Mahendra said, 'Certainly! In fact we are waiting for her.'

Behari said, 'It won't cost much of your time to write that to her and it'll give her immense joy. Bouthan, I appeal to you: please spare Mahin da for a few minutes so that he can write the note.'

Asha stomped away in anger—she had tears in her eyes.

Mahendra said, 'What a moment it was when you two set eyes upon one another—your squabbles never seem to end.'

Behari said, 'You have been spoilt by your mother and now your wife is doing the same. I find it so appalling that I protest ever so often.'

Mahendra asked, 'And what's the upshot of all this?'

Behari replied, 'None where you are concerned, but there is some for me.'

10

BEHARI MADE MAHENDRA WRITE THE LETTER TO RAJLAKSHMI AND took it with him the next day, meaning to bring her back. Rajlakshmi could tell the letter was written as a result of Behari's coercion, but she couldn't stay away any longer. She brought Binodini along with her.

When she returned and found the house in utter disarray and chaos, Rajlakshmi felt even more hostile towards Asha. But what a change there was in Asha! She followed Rajlakshmi around like a shadow now, trying to lend a hand everywhere even without being told. Rajlakshmi exclaimed anxiously, 'Let it be, you'll ruin it! Why do you try to do what you don't know anything about?'

She reached the conclusion that this change in Asha was

brought about by Annapurna's departure. But she felt Mahendra should not think that when Annapurna was around he could spend his days freely with Asha and now under his mother's regimen he had lost his wife. He would perceive his aunt as his well-wisher and his mother as an enemy. What was the point?

These days, if Mahendra called her in the day, Asha hesitated to go up. But Rajlakshmi reprimanded her, 'Can't you hear, Mahin is calling you? Can't you answer him? Too much love has gone to your head. Go on, you don't have to do the vegetables now.'

It was back to the mockery of the slate, pencil and the alphabets, blaming each other for the alleged paucity of love, pointless squabbles over who loved whom the most, turning gloomy days into nights and moonlit nights into sunny days, staving off ennui and boredom by sheer force. It was a kind of deadly grip on each other, where even when togetherness yielded no great joy, there was morbid fear in letting go of one another for even a single second—the pleasure of mating turned to ashes and yet, one couldn't move away from it, fearing a vacuum elsewhere. Such was the terrible curse of over-indulgence that although the pleasure wasn't long-standing, the bonds were lethally binding.

Then one day, Binodini came and twined her arms about Asha's neck and said, 'My friend, may your happiness last forever, but don't you think you could spare this hapless soul a mere glance sometimes?'

Asha had a natural reserve in front of strangers, having grown up in another's home. She feared rejection. When Binodini had arrived with her arched brows and sharp glance, her flawless face and her pristine, youthful beauty, Asha hadn't dared approach her to make her acquaintance. She noticed that Binodini was perfectly natural in Rajlakshmi's presence. Rajlakshmi also took pleasure in praising Binodini in Asha's presence, giving her more than her due share of importance. Asha perceived that Binodini was adept at all the household chores and supervision came naturally to her. She never hesitated to set the maids to work, scolding them and ordering them about. All this made Asha feel very small beside Binodini. But when that epitome of perfection, Binodini herself came to seek Asha's friendship, her pleasure drowned her hesitation and flooded her heart with joy. As if a magician had waved his wand somewhere, their friendship grew, blossomed and flourished in the space of a single day.

Asha said, 'Come, let's give our friendship a name—let's be something to each other.'

Binodini laughed. 'Like what?'

Asha suggested many pretty names like flower and bee, Ganga and Yamuna. But Binodini said, 'All those are outdated; an affectionate name is no longer worthy of love.'

Asha said, 'What would you like us to be?'

Binodini laughed and said, 'A grain of sand in the eye. Chokher Bali.'

Asha was more inclined towards the sweeter names, but she took Binodini's advice and settled for the affectionate invective of Chokher Bali—a grain of sand in the eye that drew pearly tears. She hugged Binodini and said, 'Chokher Bali,' and rolled to the floor, giggling.

11

ASHA WAS BADLY IN NEED OF A COMPANION. EVEN A ROMANCE IS incomplete if there are just two players—extra ears are needed to spread the words of love around. A famished Binodini drank up the details of the new bride's new-found romance like a drunkard swigging at a bottle. Her ears reddened as she listened and her blood fairly simmered in her veins.

In the muted afternoons, when Rajlakshmi was asleep, the servants disappeared into the rooms downstairs to rest and Mahendra went to college after much cajoling from Behari, when the faint cries of the kite could be heard from the far end of the blistering horizon, Asha lay flat on the bed with her hair spread out on the pillow and Binodini pulled up another pillow under her breast as she lay on her stomach; the two of them were lost in whispered tales—Binodini's face became flushed and her breath quickened. She always asked eager questions and got the tiniest details, heard the same stories over and over again and once they were told, she took recourse to her imagination and asked, 'What if things happened like this or like that?' Asha too enjoyed dragging the discussions onto those uncharted paths of what-if.

Binodini asked, 'Tell me, Chokher Bali, what would you do if you'd been married to Beharibabu instead?'

Asha said, 'Oh no, don't ever say that—oh God, I feel so embarrassed. But *you* would have suited him well; there *was* some talk once, wasn't there?'

Binodini said, 'Oh, there were talks about so many men for me. It's good it didn't happen—I am fine the way I am.'

Asha protested. How could she accept Binodini was happier than she was? 'Just think for a moment, Bali, if you'd got married to *my* husband! It nearly happened, too!'

Of course it had nearly happened. Why didn't it? Once this bed of Asha's was waiting for her. Binodini glanced around at this well-decorated room and simply couldn't push the thought out of her mind. Today she was a mere guest in this room, here today and gone tomorrow.

In the evening Binodini often took it upon herself to tie Asha's hair in a fancy hairdo and send her to greet her husband. Her imagination, veiled and hidden, crept behind this bedecked bride and entered the isolated room for a tryst with the spellbound young man. On some other days she refused to let Asha go. 'Oh come on, sit a little longer. Your husband won't run away. He's not the fleet-footed buck of the woods, he's the tame deer tethered at your threshold.' She would try to hold Asha back with such comments.

Mahendra got impatient and said, 'Your friend never seems to want to leave—when will she go back home?'

Asha rose to Binodini's defence zealously. 'No, you shan't be angry at my Chokher Bali. You'll be surprised to know that she loves hearing about you—she dresses me up so tenderly with her own hands and sends me to meet you.'

Rajlakshmi didn't let Asha do any household work. Binodini took Asha's side and let her in on some of the chores. Binodini was busy all day long with a variety of housework and now she wanted Asha at her side as well. She had woven a chain of household tasks so skilfully that it was impossible for Asha to find even a few minutes to steal away to Mahendra. Binodini laughed a cruel, jagged smile to herself when she thought of Asha's husband sitting in a corner of that lonely room on the terrace, bursting with impatience and thwarted passion. Concerned and anxious, Asha would remark, 'I'll be off now, Bali dear, or he'll be very angry.'

Quickly Binodini would say, 'Oh wait, just finish this bit and go—it won't take long.'

A little later Asha would grow restless again. 'No my friend, he'll be really angry now—let me go.'

Binodini would say, 'Oh dear, and I suppose that would be so terrible? There's no fun in romance if there isn't a bit of provocation sprinkled on the love—it's like the spice in the curry, it brings the flavour out.'

Actually, only Binodini knew the taste of this spice, but in her life the vegetables were missing from the curry. The blood flamed in her veins; wherever she glanced, her eyes showered sparks of burning embers: 'Such a happy household, such a loving husband—I could have made it a home fit for royalty and turned him into my devoted slave. This home then wouldn't be in this sorry state, and this man would have turned heads. But in my place rules this child of a girl, this infantile doll!' She hugged Asha and said, 'Dear Bali, please tell me what happened last night, won't you? Did you say all that I taught you to say? When I hear of your love, I lose both sleep and hunger.'

12

ONE DAY MAHENDRA GREW ANNOYED AND SAID TO RAJLAKSHMI, 'DO you think this is a good idea? Why do we have to take on the responsibility of a young widow from another family? I am not for this at all—you never know what troubles may lurk around the corner.'

Rajlakshmi said, 'But she is my Bipin's wife—I think of her as family.'

Mahendra said, 'No, Mother, this is not right. I would advice you to send her back.'

Rajlakshmi was well aware that Mahendra's wish couldn't be ignored easily. She sent for Behari and said, 'Behari, why don't you speak to Mahin? I am able to get a bit of rest in this old age simply because Bipin's wife is here. Call her whatever you like, but I have never got such loyal service from any of my own.'

Behari didn't answer Rajlakshmi, but he did go to Mahendra and say, 'Mahin da, have you thought about Binodini?'

Mahendra laughed and said, 'I am losing sleep over her. Why don't you ask your bouthan—Binodini is all I think about these days.'

Asha chided him silently from behind her anchal raised over her head.

Behari said, 'Well, well, we have a situation rivalling Bankim's *The Poison Tree* on our hands!'

Mahendra said, 'Exactly. Now Chuni is hell-bent on sending her away.'

From behind the veil, Asha's eyes seethed with silent rebuke.

Behari said, 'But it won't take long for her to come right back. I suggest you marry off this widow—that'll take care of her for good.'

Mahendra laughed. 'Kunda in *The Poison Tree* was married off too.'

Behari said, 'Fine, let that analogy be for now. I think of Binodini sometimes. She cannot possibly stay here forever. But sending her back to that godforsaken place is also a severe punishment.'

Binodini had not come face to face with Mahendra yet. But Behari had seen her and realized that she was worthy of more than the wilderness that passed for a home in Barasat. However, he was also wary of the fact that the flame that burned beautifully in an oil-lamp could as well set a house on fire.

Mahendra teased Behari about Binodini in various ways and Behari stood up to the test valiantly. But he stood firm in his belief that this woman shouldn't be toyed with and neither should she be ignored.

Rajlakshmi threw a word of caution at Binodini. 'Be careful my child, don't cling to Asha like that. You are used to the usual customs of a village household and know nothing of the modern ways. You are intelligent, you will know what I mean; just watch what you do.'

Following this, Binodini began to keep Asha at arm's length with great ceremony. She said, 'Oh, who am I? People like me should know their place and stay there or you never know what may happen.'

Asha wept and pleaded, but Binodini stood firm. Asha was fairly bursting with confidences unuttered, but Binodini paid no heed.

Meanwhile, the fervour of Mahendra's embraces slackened somewhat and his fascinated gaze on Asha grew rather weary. The foibles and oddities in Asha that had seemed amusing to him at first now irked him no end. He was piqued every moment by Asha's incompetence around the house, but he never spoke his mind. Even so, Asha could sense that familiarity had taken the sparkle out of the romance. Mahendra's lovemaking struck the wrong chords—some of it seemed excessive and some self-deceptive. At such times, escape was the only route, separation the only remedy. In the naturally intuitive fashion of women, Asha tried to leave Mahendra alone more often these days. But she had nowhere to go, except to Binodini.

Coming back to earth from the dizzy clouds of romance, Mahendra opened his eyes slowly and cast them at last on his studies, and other household chores. He began to retrieve his medical textbooks from all kinds of impossible places, wiped the dust off them and attempted to air out his college clothes.

13

WHEN BINODINI REFUSED TO ACQUIESCE, ASHA TRIED ANOTHER PLOY. She said to Binodini, 'Dear Bali, why don't you ever come before my husband? Why do you always run and hide?'

Binodini's answer was brief and snappy, 'Shame!'

Asha said, 'Why? I have heard from Mother that you are related to us.'

Solemnly, Binodini replied, 'In this world, there are no fixed rules for telling who is a relative and who a stranger. Whoever you feel close to is your relative; and whoever perceives you as an intruder, may well be a relative, but is still a stranger.'

Asha felt this remark could not be countered. It was a fact that her husband had wronged Binodini; he had thought of her as an intruder and often felt quite irked by her presence.

That same evening Asha pleaded with Mahendra, 'You must have a meeting with my Chokher Bali.'

Mahendra laughed. 'That's a grave risk you're taking.'

Asha said, 'Why, what's there to fear?'

Mahendra said, 'The kind of beauty you have described your friend to be, it's no safe haven for a man to venture into.'

Asha said, 'Oh, I can handle that. Please be serious—say you will meet her?'

It wasn't as though Mahendra wasn't curious to see Binodini; in fact, lately he'd even felt an urge to see her. But he felt this unwarranted impatience was somehow unethical. In matters of the heart, Mahendra's beliefs on what was ethical and what wasn't were a little more stringent than most people's. In the past he had not heeded the idea of marriage for fear that after marriage his mother's place wouldn't stay the same. These days he wanted to hold his relationship with Asha so sacred that he wouldn't let even the slightest curiosity about another woman tarry in his heart. He prided himself on the fact that his love was fastidious and pure. Similarly, he never wanted to acknowledge anyone else as his friend since that position was already given to Behari. If anyone ever felt attached to him and tried to further their acquaintance, Mahendra would go out of his way to be rude to them; he took pleasure in deriding them to Behari, and declaring himself absolutely indifferent to the average men around him. If Behari protested, Mahendra said, '*You* can do that Behari—wherever you go, you make plenty of friends. But I'm afraid I don't feel like making friends with every Tom, Dick and Harry.'

Thus, when Mahendra's heart lurched with inevitable eagerness and curiosity at the thought of meeting this unfamiliar woman, he felt he was letting down his own ideals. Eventually, he had lost his patience and gone to Rajlakshmi, requesting her to send Binodini away from their home.

He now said to Asha, 'No, Chuni, I don't have the time to meet your friend. I have my studies to attend to and you are there: where is the space for another friend?'

Asha said, 'It's all right, I won't take up your study time; I'll give my share of the time to Bali.'

Mahendra said, 'You may well want to give it, but why would I let you do that?'

Mahendra claimed that Asha's love for Binodini was eating into her love for her husband. With great pride he would say, 'Your love is not as constant and steadfast as mine.' This often caused the pair to squabble. Asha wouldn't accept it—she'd cry and fight but never was she able to win the argument.

Mahendra grew to take pride in the fact that he was

unwilling to let Binodini have even a hair's space between the two of them. Asha hated this pride, but one day she bowed before it humbly and said, 'All right then, will you please meet my Bali for *my* sake? Just once?'

Mahendra, after establishing the supremacy of his love over Asha's, finally agreed to meet Binodini as a favour to his wife. But he made it clear, 'That doesn't mean she'll be free to disturb me every now and then!'

The following morning Asha went into Binodini's room and woke her up with a hug. Binodini said, 'Wonder of wonders, the sunflower has left the sun and turned to the clouds today!'

Asha said, 'I'm no good at all that poetic stuff, my dear, so don't waste your breath. Why don't you go and say all this to the one who'd appreciate it most?'

Binodini said, 'And who is this poetic genius?'

Asha said, 'Your brother-in-law, my husband! No really, I'm not joking—he's very keen to meet you.'

Binodini said to herself, 'Your wife has begged you to and so you've sent for me—if you think I'll come running, you couldn't be more wrong.'

Binodini refused doggedly. Asha lost face before her husband.

Mahendra was also very angry. How dare she refuse to come before him! Did she think he was like any other man? Others may have tried to find some excuse in all these days to talk to Binodini, to see her face. The fact that Mahendra never tried any such tricks should be enough for Binodini to realize that he was different. If she ever came to know him well, she'd surely see how extraordinary he was.

A couple of days ago Binodini had also felt quite upset. 'I've been in this house for so long and Mahendra has never once tried to catch a glimpse of me. When I am in his mother's room he never ever cooks up an excuse to come and speak to his mother. Why all the indifference? I am not a piece of furniture, I am a person, I'm a woman! If he ever got to know me well, he'd know the difference between me and his cherished Chuni!'

Asha came to her husband with an idea. 'I'll go and fetch my Chokher Bali to our room saying you have gone to college. And then you'll come in suddenly and confound her totally.'

Mahendra asked, 'What has she done to merit such a harsh sentence?'

Asha said, 'No, really, I am very angry indeed. She has refused to meet you! I'll break her tenacity or my name is not Asha.'

Mahendra said, 'I am not exactly dying to meet your bosom friend. I refuse to meet her like that, by stealth.'

Asha held his hand and begged, 'Please do this for me, just this once? I want to shatter her pride somehow, on this one occasion; thereafter you two are free to do what you like.'

Mahendra did not reply. Asha pleaded, 'Please dear, for my sake?'

Mahendra was actually getting more and more fired up— and so, with a great show of indifference, he conceded.

It was a sheer, silent autumn afternoon. Binodini was seated in Mahendra's room, teaching Asha how to knit a woollen shoe. Asha was restive, looking at the door every now and then, dropping stitches frequently and revealing her own incompetence to Binodini.

Finally, Binodini lost her temper, snatched the knitting from her hands and said, 'Oh, you are no good at this; I have work to do—I'm going.'

Asha said, 'Sit for a little longer; let me try again—I won't go wrong this time.' She went back to the knitting diligently.

Meanwhile, Mahendra came up soundlessly and stood at the door behind Binodini; Asha smiled without looking up from her knitting.

Binodini asked, 'Now what is making you smile?'

Asha couldn't check her laughter; she burst into giggles and flung the knitting over Binodini's head, saying, 'You're right my dear, this is not for me.' She threw her arms around her friend and went on giggling.

Binodini had understood everything right at the start. Asha's restlessness and gestures had revealed all. She was well aware that Mahendra had come and stood at the door. But she let herself fall into Asha's transparent trap, like a simple, naïve fool.

Mahendra stepped into the room saying, 'Pray share the joke with this hapless soul?'

Startled, Binodini tried to raise her anchal over her head. Asha caught her wrist.

Mahendra laughed. 'Either you sit and I leave, or we both have a seat.'

Binodini didn't go in for a great show of embarrassment, tugging her hands away from Asha's grip and clamouring to leave, like most women would have. She spoke naturally and easily, 'I shall sit because you've asked me to. But please don't curse me and speak ill of me when I am gone.'

Mahendra said, 'I'll curse you so that you lose the power to move for a long time.'

Binodini said, 'Oh, I am not afraid of *that* curse because your "long time" won't be too long—it's already over probably.'

She tried to get up again and Asha pressed her, 'Please, please do sit a little longer.'

14

ASHA ASKED, 'TELL ME HONESTLY, WHAT DID YOU THINK OF MY Chokher Bali?'

Mahendra said, 'Not bad.'

Asha was a little hurt. 'You never *really* like anyone.'

Mahendra said, 'Except for one person.'

Asha said, 'All right, I'll know if you've liked her or not once the two of you get to know each other a little better.'

Mahendra said, 'Better than this! So this will happen frequently from now on?'

Asha said, 'Even courtesy demands that you further your acquaintance with some people. If you stop meeting her after just one conversation, what would she think? You are so strange. Anyone else would have been dying to meet such a girl as often as possible—but for you it seems like a great burden.'

Mahendra was happy to have this difference with other people reiterated. He said, 'All right, don't get upset. I have nowhere to run away and your friend shows no signs of leaving—so we'll certainly meet every now and then. And never fear, when we do, your husband has the social graces to be polite and cordial.'

Mahendra was under the impression that Binodini would find excuses and keep running into him from now on. He was wrong. Binodini never came anywhere near him and he never bumped into her accidentally, ever.

Mahendra couldn't bring up the subject with Asha for fear of even a hint of eagerness showing through. His efforts at suppressing the occasional wish to meet and talk to Binodini only served to stoke his desire. And Binodini's seeming indifference turned it into a blazing fire.

The day after he met Binodini, Mahendra asked Asha with carefully arranged airiness and laughter, 'How did your Chokher Bali like this unworthy husband of yours?'

Mahendra had hoped he'd get a gurgling, detailed report from Asha on this subject without his having to ask. But when he waited for it and it didn't come, he playfully brought up the question himself.

Asha felt very awkward. Binodini hadn't said a word on the subject and Asha was quite miffed with her because of this. She said to her husband, 'Be patient, let her get to know you better; how can she say anything on the basis of yesterday's short conversation?'

Mahendra felt crestfallen at this response and it grew even more difficult for him to feign indifference towards Binodini. But before he could ask any more questions, Behari walked in and asked, 'Mahin da, what are you two arguing about today?'

Mahendra said, 'Just listen to this: your bouthan has gone and become a hair-band or fish-bone or something to a Kumudini or Promodini or someone; good for her, I suppose. But now if I too have to be cigar's ash or match-stick to that lady, it's really going too far!'

Behind her veil Asha showed signs of a storm gathering perilously. Behari glanced at Mahendra and laughed silently; then he said, 'Bouthan, this is not a good sign. These are mere smokescreens. I have seen your Chokher Bali and I can swear that if I see her more often I wouldn't call it my bad luck. But if Mahin da protests too much, I do see a cause for concern.'

This was fresh proof to Asha that Mahendra was very different from Behari.

All of a sudden Mahendra developed a desire for photography. Once long ago he had started learning photography and then given it up. Now he got his camera fixed, bought some film and began to take pictures of everything and everybody. He didn't even spare the servants and bearers of the house.

Asha was very keen that he take a picture of her friend.

Mahendra said brusquely, 'Fine.'

But Binodini's answer was even more brusque. 'No.'

Asha had to resort to another ruse and once again, it was obvious to Binodini from the very start. The plan was that Asha would somehow get Binodini to come up to her room in the afternoon and put her to sleep. Mahendra would take her picture as she slept and that would serve her adamant friend right indeed! The strange thing was that Binodini never took a nap in the afternoon. But that day when she came into Asha's room, for some reason her eyes drooped at once. Draped in a red shawl and facing the window, she rested her head on her arm and fell asleep in such a lovely posture that Mahendra said, 'She seems to have posed for a picture even in her sleep.'

Mahendra tiptoed around and fetched his camera. In order to decide on the best angle, he had to look at her from all sides. For art's sake he even had to brush away a few strands of hair from her forehead—and when he didn't like the effect, he had to correct it again. He whispered to Asha, 'Just move the shawl a little to the left near her feet.'

The inept Asha whispered back, 'I can't do it, she'll surely wake up. You do it.'

Mahendra did the needful.

Eventually, just when he had loaded the plate into the camera, Binodini seemed to sense the sound, sighed, turned her head and woke up with a start. Asha chortled in delight.

Binodini was extremely angry. Her sparkling eyes showered wrath upon Mahendra as she exclaimed, 'This isn't right!'

Mahendra said, 'I agree with you. But how can I bear it if after all my stealth I'm not even able to bring home the loot? Pray let me finish my crime and then punish me as you please.'

Asha begged and pleaded with Binodini. The picture was taken. But this first picture was spoilt. So the photographer insisted on taking another one the following day. Finally, Binodini couldn't say no to the proposal of taking one picture with both girls in it as a symbol of their everlasting friendship.

But she said, 'This will be the last one.'

So Mahendra deliberately spoilt that one. And then, over pictures and more pictures the acquaintance and camaraderie between them progressed in leaps and bounds.

15

DYING EMBERS GET A FRESH LEASE OF LIFE IF THE FIRE IS STOKED FROM without. The slight breach that had come about in the newly-weds' romance soon healed itself and their passion burned afresh after the introduction of a third party in their midst. Asha lacked the capacity to laugh and make witty conversation. But Binodini could provide that in abundance; and so Asha found a safe haven behind Binodini's strong persona. She no longer had to try so hard at keeping Mahendra entertained and amused all the time.

Within the short span of a few months, Asha and Mahendra had almost poured themselves out to each other—their song of love had started on the highest possible note—it was as if they were intent on eating up the principal instead of living off the interest. How were they to translate this deluge of recklessness into the mundane simplicity of daily life? How could Asha provide the fresh stimulation that Mahendra looked for every time tedium gripped him after traversing the heights of intoxication? It was then that Binodini brought in a colourful goblet filled with the fresh and the new—and Asha was relieved to see her husband in good humour again.

Now she no longer tried so hard herself. When Mahendra and Binodini laughed and joked, she simply laughed along joyfully. When Mahendra tried to cheat her at card games, she appealed to Binodini for justice. If Mahendra teased her or spoke out of turn, she expected Binodini to take her side and protest. In this fashion the threesome got accustomed to one another.

But this didn't stop Binodini from tending to her household chores. She only joined in the fun after she had finished cooking, cleaning, supervising the servants and taken proper care of Rajlakshmi. Mahendra would get impatient. 'You're going to spoil the servants by doing everything yourself.' Binodini would answer, 'That's better than spoiling yourself by not doing a thing. Go on, you had better go to college.'

Mahendra would say, 'It's a nice cloudy day—'

Binodini would reply, 'Oh no, you don't get away with that—the carriage is ready—you must go to college.'

Mahendra would argue, 'But I cancelled the carriage.'

Binodini would retort, 'I called it back.'

She would bring his clothes for college and stand before him.

Mahendra would say, 'You should have been born in a Rajput household—you'd have had fun placing the armour on your loved one when he went to war.'

Binodini did not like the idea of dropping out of classes or skipping studies for fun. Under her strict regulation the practice of lounging about and having fun at any time of the day became a thing of the past in the household. And hence the evening sessions turned into an oasis of pleasure for Mahendra. His days yearned for themselves to end.

Earlier, when his meals weren't ready on time, Mahendra gladly used this as a pretext to stay back home. These days Binodini took care to see that his meal was ready first thing in the morning and the minute he finished it, he was told that the carriage was waiting for him. Earlier, he seldom found his clothes neatly folded and laid out for him: on the contrary, they usually languished in a forgotten corner of some cupboard instead of going to the laundry and turned up many days later when one was searching for something quite different.

At first Binodini often chided Asha playfully in front of Mahendra, for these and other muddles. Mahendra too smiled indulgently at Asha's helpless ineptitude. But soon, out of affection for her friend, Binodini relieved Asha of her duties. Everything in the household had a changed look since then. If a shirt button broke and Asha stood gazing at it helplessly, Binodini snatched the garment from her nerveless fingers and stitched it up in no time. One day a cat got to Mahendra's plate of rice first and had a few mouthfuls. Asha was worried sick; Binodini went into the kitchen immediately, looked into various pots and pans and deftly rustled up another plate of food. Asha was dumbfounded at her proficiency.

Mahendra felt Binodini's caring touch in his clothing and food, at work and leisure. The woollen shoes on his feet and the woollen scarf around his neck—made by Binodini—felt like a tangible emotional contact. These days Asha came to Mahendra, neat, tidy and all decked up by her friend: she felt like she was partly herself and partly someone else; she and Binodini seemed to have united like the Ganga and the Yamuna.

Behari was no longer as welcome as he was before—he

was rarely sent for. Once Behari wrote to Mahendra to say that he'd like to come the next day at noon, a Sunday, and taste his mother's cooking. Mahendra felt the Sunday would go waste. So he quickly wrote back that the next day he had some work and would have to go out. But Behari dropped by in any case to look them up after lunch. The bearer informed him that Mahendra had not left the house. Behari yelled out 'Mahin da,' as he bounded up the stairs and went straight into Mahendra's room. Caught unawares, Mahendra said he had a headache and lay down facing the wall. Asha grew nervous when she saw the complexion of Mahendra's mood. She glanced at Binodini hopefully. Binodini was well aware that it wasn't a serious matter; but she said anxiously, 'You've been sitting up for too long, why don't you lie down. I'll get some eau-de-cologne.'

Mahendra said, 'It's all right, don't bother.'

Binodini paid no heed and quickly fetched some eau-de-cologne mixed with cool water. She handed the wet towel to Asha and said, 'Put this on Mahendrababu's temple.'

Mahendra went on saying, 'It's all right.'

Behari checked his laughter as he watched this performance. Mahendra felt smug that Behari could witness how precious he was to the two women.

Shyness in Behari's presence caused Asha's fingers to tremble and she wasn't very deft with the towel; a few drops of eau-de-cologne sloshed into Mahendra's eyes. Binodini took the towel from her hands and applied it skilfully; she then wet another piece of cloth with the liquid and wrung it out over the towel. Asha veiled her head and fanned her husband quietly.

Binodini asked in soothing tones, 'Mahendrababu, do you feel better?'

Having spoken such honeyed words, Binodini shot an oblique glance at Behari's face. She found his eyes twinkling in merriment. The whole thing was a farce to him. Binodini realized this man couldn't be fooled easily—nothing escaped him.

Behari laughed. 'Binod-bouthan, with therapy like this the ailment is likely to intensify rather than subside.'

Binodini said, 'How would I know that, we are only ignorant women. Is that what they say in your medical textbooks?'

Behari said, 'Of course. This kind of treatment is making my own head throb. But my head had better get all right on its own. Mahin da's head carries a far greater weight.'

Binodini dropped the wet cloth and said, 'Forget it then; let the friend treat his comrade.'

Behari was growing quite impatient with what he saw. He had been busy with his books and wasn't aware of just how complicated a relationship this trio had cooked up in the meantime. Today he observed Binodini carefully and she too took her measure of him.

Behari spoke a trifle harshly this time, 'Fair enough. A friend *must* indeed care for his friend. I brought on the headache and now I shall leave with it. Don't waste the eau-de-cologne.' He glanced at Asha. 'Bouthan, prevention is better than cure.'

16

BEHARI THOUGHT, 'I CAN'T STAY AWAY ANY LONGER. SOMEHOW, I must make my place among these people. None of them will want it, but it must be done.'

So he began to infiltrate Mahendra's circle without waiting to be invited. He said to Binodini, 'Binod-bouthan, this man has been spoilt by his mother, by his friend and then by his wife; I beg of you, don't spoil him further; show him a different path instead.'

Mahendra said, 'Meaning—'

Behari said, 'Meaning that a man like me, whom nobody spares a second glance—'

'Should be spoilt instead?' Mahendra quipped. 'It's not that easy; simply putting in an application is not enough.'

Binodini laughed. 'One has to have the capacity to be spoilt, Beharibabu.'

Behari said, 'That depends on who is doing the spoiling. Why don't you give it a try?'

Binodini said, 'It doesn't work if you are forewarned and forearmed; unawares is how it has to catch you, isn't it, dear Chokher Bali? Why don't *you* take on this brother-in-law of yours?'

Asha lifted two fingers and pushed her away. Behari also refrained from joining in the joke. It had not escaped Binodini that Behari wouldn't stand any nonsense where Asha was concerned. It hurt her that Behari idolized Asha but wanted to pull her down a peg or two. She looked at Asha again and said, 'This poor brother of yours is actually begging your love, though he addresses me—so give him some, dear friend.'

Asha was very cross. Behari blushed for an instant and in the next he laughed and said, 'So when it's my turn you pass the plea on to others but when it's Mahin da you take the matter in your own hands, do you, and deal in cash?'

It was obvious to Binodini that Behari was intent on upsetting her applecart; she'd have to be careful where he was concerned. Mahendra was annoyed—all this straight talk rang a false note in the melody. He addressed Behari a trifle harshly, 'Behari, your Mahin da doesn't need to go into any deals; he's happy with what he has.'

Behari said, 'He may not need to go into it, but if fate ordains it, a succession of such deals will come and crash on his doorstep like as many waves.'

Binodini said, 'You have nothing in hand at the moment; but where are your waves crashing right now?' She laughed at Asha and poked her in jest. Incensed, Asha got up and walked away. Behari held his tongue in thwarted rage; as he made to rise, Binodini said, 'Don't go away unhappy, Beharibabu. I'll go and send my Chokher Bali to you right away.'

When Binodini left, Mahendra was displeased that the gathering had broken up. His disgruntled face set Behari's nerves on edge and he burst forth, 'Mahin da, you are free to court disaster for yourself—it's something you have always done. But please don't ruin the simple, pious woman who has sought refuge with you. I beg of you, don't ruin her life.' Behari choked on the last words.

Mahendra shouted in righteous anger, 'Behari, I don't understand what you are saying. Don't speak in riddles; clearly say what you want to.'

Behari said, 'I'll do that then. Binodini is leading you astray on purpose and you are stepping on to the forbidden path like a fool.'

Mahendra roared, 'Lies! If you dare to make such false accusations about a lady from a respected family, you should be barred from the inner chambers.'

At this point Binodini walked in with a plate of sweets and smiling, placed it before Behari. He said, 'What's all this? I am not hungry.'

Binodini said, 'Well, that's how it is. You cannot go without eating some of this.'

Behari laughed, 'Does this mean that my application has been accepted and my "spoiling" has begun?'

Binodini smiled coyly and said, 'Since you are a younger brother-in-law, you have a right; why beg where you can demand? You may choose to seize affection if you wish, isn't that so, Mahendrababu?'

Mahendra was lost for words.

Binodini said, 'Beharibabu, is it modesty or anger that makes you refrain from touching the sweets? Must I call someone else here?'

Behari said, 'There's no need for that; what I have here is more than enough.'

Binodini said, 'Mockery? You are incorrigible. Even sweets cannot silence you.'

That night Asha condemned Behari to Mahendra and he supported her unconditionally, unlike other days when he would laugh and brush aside her complaints against his friend.

The next morning Mahendra visited Behari and said, 'Behari, all said and done, Binodini is not really a member of the family and in your presence she seems to feel a bit uncomfortable.'

Behari said, 'Is that so? That's a pity. Well, if it bothers her I guess I should stay away.'

Mahendra was relieved. He hadn't expected this unpleasant task to be accomplished so easily. He was a little scared of Behari.

The same day Behari strolled into Mahendra's inner chambers and said, 'Binod-bouthan, I beg your pardon.'

Binodini asked, 'But why?'

Behari said, 'I heard from Mahin da that my presence in the inner chambers offends you. So I shall beg your pardon and take my leave.'

Binodini said, 'Oh, that's not right, Beharibabu; I am here today and gone tomorrow. Why should you leave on my account? Had I known there would be such trouble I would never have come here.' Binodini's face fell and she looked as though she was holding back her tears as she walked away.

In that instant Behari felt, 'My suspicions were wrong— I have wrongly accused Binodini.'

That evening Rajlakshmi came to Mahendra in despair and said, 'Mahin, Bipin's wife is determined to leave us.'

Mahendra asked, 'Why Mother, what's troubling her here?'

Rajlakshmi said, 'Nothing. But she says if a young widow like her stays on in another's house for too long, tongues will wag.'

Mahendra was angry. 'This is not exactly "another's house", is it!'

Behari was sitting there and Mahendra threw him an incensed look.

Repentant, Behari mused silently, 'Yesterday I was perhaps too critical of Binodini and she's upset about it.'

Both husband and wife felt offended with Binodini.

One said, 'So you think we are "others"?' and the other said, 'After so long you still don't think of us as your own.'

Binodini said, 'But really, did you think you could keep me here forever?'

Mahendra said, 'Oh no, we wouldn't dare to presume any such thing!'

Asha said, 'Why did you steal our hearts like this if you meant to go away?'

That day nothing was decided. Binodini said to Asha, 'No, my friend, let me go. It's best to leave before the tie grows stronger.' She threw a poignant look at Mahendra as she said this.

The next day Behari came and said, 'Binod-bouthan, why do you speak of going? Have we offended you—is this a penalty we have to pay?'

Binodini turned her face slightly and said, 'Why would you offend me—my own fate is at fault.'

Behari said, 'But if you leave I can't help feeling it would be my fault.'

Binodini raised her eyes full of pleading and asked of Behari, '*You* tell me, is it right for me to stay?'

Behari was put in a spot. How could he answer in the affirmative? He said, 'Of course, you must leave at some point; but why don't you stay a while longer?'

Binodini lowered her eyes and said, 'All of you are

begging me to stay—it *is* rather difficult for me to override the requests—but this is really very wrong of you.' As she spoke, the tears fell thick and fast through the dense curtain of her long lashes.

Behari was unnerved by this silent, severe deluge of tears and exclaimed, 'In the short while that you've been here, you have won the hearts of everyone around you. And that is why no one wants to let you go. Please don't take it to heart Binod-bouthan, but who would want to be separated from such grace and charm?'

Asha sat in a corner with her sari pulled over her head, and wiped her eyes repeatedly. After this incident, Binodini never spoke of leaving again.

17

IN AN EFFORT TO WIPE OUT THE MEMORY OF THIS UNPLEASANTNESS, Mahendra proposed a picnic in the farmhouse at Dumdum the following Sunday. Asha welcomed the idea but Binodini refused. Both Mahendra and Asha were crestfallen at her refusal. They thought, 'Binodini is trying to distance herself from us these days.'

That evening, the minute Behari arrived, Binodini said, 'Beharibabu, listen to this, Mahinbabu wants to go to the farmhouse at Dumdum for a picnic and because I refused to go, the two of them have been sulking all day.'

Behari said, 'I can't blame them. If you don't go, the

bedlam that'll pass for a picnic can't be wished upon one's worst enemies, let alone on these two.'

Binodini said, 'Why don't you come along, Beharibabu? If you come, I'm willing to go.'

Behari said, 'Brilliant suggestion. But it awaits the master's approval—what does the master say?'

Both the master and her ladyship were miffed at this predilection on Binodini's part towards Behari. Hearing the proposal, Mahendra's eagerness for the outing dwindled. He was keen on persuading Behari that the latter's presence was distasteful to Binodini at all times. But now it would be difficult to hold him back.

Mahendra said, 'That's fine, sounds good. But Behari, you always kick up a ruckus wherever you go—perhaps you'll invite a whole bunch of local children there or stir up a fight with a whiteskin, one never knows what to expect with you.'

Behari understood why Mahendra was dragging his feet and he smiled quietly to himself as he said, 'But that's the fun of life—one never knows what's to come, what will happen next. Binod-bouthan, we'll have to leave at the crack of dawn. I'll be here on time.'

At the appointed time two carriages pulled up in front of the house: an ordinary one for luggage and bearers and a deluxe carriage for the gentlemen and ladies. Behari arrived early with a huge box. Mahendra said, 'What is that? There's no room in the servants' carriage.'

Behari said, 'Don't worry, Mahin da, I'll take care of everything.'

Binodini and Asha got into the carriage. Mahendra

hesitated, wondering what he should do about Behari. But Behari hauled the box on top of the carriage and jumped into the coachbox beside the coachman.

Mahendra heaved a sigh of relief. He was afraid Behari would want to sit inside the carriage and then there was no telling what he would do. Binodini was concerned. 'Beharibabu, isn't that rather unsafe?'

Behari answered her, 'Don't worry, my role in the performance doesn't include "falls to the ground and bites the dust".'

As soon as the carriage rolled away, Mahendra said, 'Why don't I go and sit out there and send Behari inside?'

Asha didn't like this. 'No, you won't sit there.'

Binodini said, 'Please don't. You are not used to it; you may fall.'

Mahendra got worked up. 'Fall indeed! Not on your life!' He made to open the door and get off.

Binodini said, 'You may well blame Beharibabu, but you take the cake in kicking up a fuss.'

Mahendra was in a huff. 'Fine then,' he said, 'let me hire a second carriage and go in that and let Behari come in and sit here.'

Asha said, 'If you do that, I'll come with you.'

Binodini said, 'And I suppose I should jump off the carriage?' The conversation ended amidst this hullabaloo. But all the way to Dumdum, Mahendra sulked and frowned.

The carriage finally reached the farmhouse. The servants' carriage had left long before theirs, but there was still no sign of it.

Autumn mornings could be very pleasant. The sun had

risen high by now and dried up the dew; the trees glistened in the fresh morning light. The compound walls were lined with shefali trees, the earth below them was strewn with fallen flowers and the air redolent with fragrance.

Freed from the concrete jungle of Kolkata and let loose in a garden, Asha ran about excitedly like a wild fawn. She dragged Binodini along, picked up heaps of flowers, plucked ripe custard apples off the trees and ate them raw, and then the two friends had a long and leisurely bath in the pond. Between the two of them, they filled the shade of the trees, the light off the branches, the water in the pond and the flowers in the garden with a sense of sheer delight.

After their bath, the two friends came back to find that the servants' carriage had still not turned up. Mahendra was sitting on a stool on the veranda, looking quite forlorn and reading an advertisement of a foreign store.

Binodini asked, 'Where is Beharibabu?'

Mahendra answered curtly, 'I don't know.'

Binodini said, 'Come on, let's look for him.'

Mahendra said, 'I don't think anyone will steal him away. He'll turn up even without our looking.'

Binodini said, 'But he may be worried sick about you, for fear that he might lose his precious jewel. Let's go and comfort him.'

Near the pond there was a mammoth banyan tree with a cemented bench around its girth. At that spot Behari had opened up his box, taken out a kerosene stove, lit it and started heating some water. The minute everyone arrived, he welcomed them, made them sit on the bench and served them cups of steaming tea and little plates laden with sweets and snacks. Binodini repeated again and again, 'Thank goodness Beharibabu came so well prepared; or else I shudder to think what would have happened to Mahendrababu without his cup of tea.'

Mahendra was greatly relieved to have his tea, but he still protested, 'Behari takes things too far. It's a picnic and it takes the fun out of it if one comes so well prepared.'

Behari said, 'Very well my friend, please hand back that cup of tea. You are most welcome to stay unfed and enjoy the true spirit of the picnic.'

The day wore on and there was still no sign of the servants. Behari's box now began to yield all the necessary food items: rice, dal, vegetables and even tiny jars of ground spices. Binodini was stunned and said, 'Beharibabu, you amaze me. Considering you do not have a wife at home, how did you learn to be so methodical?'

Behari said, 'Necessity has forced me to this—I have to look after myself, you see.'

Behari spoke in jest but Binodini was solemn as she looked at him with eyes full of sympathy.

Behari and Binodini went about setting things up for cooking lunch. Asha offered to help, albeit very hesitantly, but Behari stopped her. Mahendra, inept as he was, did not even proffer his services. He leaned against the tree trunk, hoisted one leg over the other and immersed himself in watching the play of light on the trembling leaves of the banyan tree.

When lunch was nearly ready, Binodini said, 'Mahinbabu, you won't ever finish counting those leaves. Go and have your bath.'

By now the bunch of servants had arrived with their cargo. Their carriage had broken down on the way.

After lunch a game of cards under the tree was proposed. Mahendra refused to join in and by and by he drifted off to sleep in the shade. Asha went indoors, shut the door and planned to have a lie-in.

Binodini raised her sari a little over her head and said, 'In that case let me go inside too.'

Behari said, 'Where are you off to? Sit for a while and chat. Tell me about your home.'

Every now and then the warm afternoon breeze shivered through the leaves and branches, a koel twittered through the thick foliage of the berry tree beside the pond. Binodini spoke of her childhood, her parents, her playmates. As she spoke, the sari slipped off her head. The brightness of her sharply etched beauty was softened by the shadows of childhood memories. The mocking, knife-edge flash of her eyes, that had made Behari feel much concern heretofore, settled into a calm and serene look as she spoke, and Behari glimpsed a different person altogether. The tender heart that was at the centre of her flashing radiance was still full of gentle affection and the burning embers of unquenched desires and all her sharp banter had not yet succeeded in withering the woman in her. Never before had Behari been able to visualize Binodini tending to her husband as a shy, homely wife or holding her child in her arms like a loving mother—but today, all of a sudden, the performing stage that he always seemed to see her on, vanished before his eyes, and he could envisage her in a happy home. He said to himself, 'Binodini may appear to be a teasing, coy temptress, but deep in her heart a chaste woman rests in silent prayer.' He heaved a sigh as he thought, 'One doesn't know one's own true self completely; that is only known to God. The self that emerges circumstantially is the one that the world takes for real.' Behari didn't let the conversation drift. He badgered Binodini with questions and kept her talking; she had never before found a listener like this and never had she so forgotten herself, spoken so much about herself to a strange man. Today, the endless torrent of words spoken so simply and from the heart made her entire self feel drenched, as though cleansed by the first rain shower, tranquil and at peace.

Mahendra woke up at five, still tired from having woken up early that morning. Quite irritated, he said, 'Let's start getting back now.'

Binodini said, 'What's the harm in staying a little while longer?'

Mahendra said, 'Oh no, then we'd run into drunken white men on the way back.'

By the time they finished packing and were ready to leave it was nearly dark. At this point a servant came and informed them that the rented carriage was nowhere to be seen. It had been left waiting outside the gates. Two white men had bullied the coachman and taken it off to the station. The servant was despatched to go and fetch another carriage. Mahendra was thoroughly put out as he thought, 'The day has been an utter waste.' He could scarcely conceal his impatience.

Gradually, the full moon disentangled itself from the web of boughs and branches, and rose high in the sky. The silent, still grounds were etched with shadows. This evening, in this charming, magical world Binodini felt her own identity defined as never before. Today, when she went and put her arms around Asha in the forested grove, her affection was entirely genuine. Asha saw that Binodini's cheeks were wet with tears. Concerned, she asked, 'What's this, Chokher Bali, why are you crying?'

Binodini said, 'Oh it's nothing, my dear; I am fine. It's just that I had a wonderful day.'

Asha asked, 'What was so great about it?'

Binodini replied, 'I feel as if I have died and come to heaven, as if I can get everything here.'

A dumbstruck Asha could make neither head nor tail of this. But she didn't like all this talk of dying and said, 'Shame, my darling Bali, don't talk that way.'

Another carriage was found. Behari took the seat in the coachbox once again. Binodini gazed out of the window in utter silence. The rows of trees, petrified in moonlight, rushed past like a dense shadow-fall in motion. Asha slept in one corner of the carriage. Mahendra sat in forlorn silence all the way back.

18

EVER SINCE THE DEBACLE OF THE PICNIC, MAHENDRA WAS EAGER TO re-establish his hold over Binodini. But the very next day Rajlakshmi contracted the flu. It wasn't serious, but she was weak enough to be confined to bed. Binodini took it upon herself to look after her and was at Rajlakshmi's side all day and night.

Mahendra said, 'If you work yourself so hard, *you* will fall sick very soon. Let me hire a servant to look after Mother.'

Behari said, 'Mahin da, don't get so worked up. If Binod-bouthan wants to nurse her, let her do it. This is not something a servant can do.'

Mahendra began to frequent the sickroom. The diligent Binodini found it intolerable that a person who wasn't doing anything, was always underfoot when there was work to be done. Irritated, she did mention a few times, 'Mahinbabu, you are not doing anyone any good by sitting here—don't absent yourself from your classes needlessly.'

Secretly, of course, Binodini was proud and thrilled that Mahendra was following her around. But at the same time she was impatient with this supplication, this 'waiting with a starving heart' even at his sick mother's bedside—she found it somewhat revolting. When Binodini took on a responsibility, she lost sight of everything else. No one could ever find her inattentive as long as there were household chores to be done, a patient to be fed, washed and helped—she was also intolerant of frivolity at moments of greater need.

Behari came sometimes to ask after Rajlakshmi. These were short visits. The moment he entered the room, he'd sense what needed to be done, what was missing—within minutes he'd set things right and then take his leave. Binodini was well aware that Behari approved of the way she was taking care of the patient. And hence Behari's visits were like a special reward for her efforts.

A feeling of indignity forced Mahendra to leave for college every day on time. His temper was already frayed and to add to that—what a change had come over his daily routine! Food was never ready on time, the driver would disappear, the ladders in his socks kept inching higher and higher. Such aberrations no longer charmed him. In the last few weeks he had grown accustomed to having his every need anticipated and looked after. Now, the absence of that attentiveness and Asha's bungling incompetence failed to amuse him.

'Chuni, how many times have I told you to keep my clothes pressed and ready before I go for my bath? It never happens that way. After my bath I have to spend two hours hunting for my clothes and sewing on buttons,' he exploded one day.

This was like a crack of thunder for Asha. She had never received such a dressing down. She could not summon up a suitable reply such as, 'It was you who stopped me from learning anything useful.' She was entirely unaware of the fact that competence in housework was all about practice and experience. She believed, 'I am unable to do a single thing properly because I am inept and stupid.' When Mahendra forgot himself and slighted her with an unfair comparison to Binodini, Asha accepted it humbly and without resentment.

Asha often hovered around her mother-in-law's room— sometimes she even stepped in tentatively. She would have liked very much to make herself indispensable to the household, she wanted to show everyone her willingness to work, but no one seemed to want it. She did not know how to take control of the household, how to run it in her own way. Her diffidence about her own incompetence kept her always outside the circle. A sense of deep misery festered in her heart, growing every day, but she was unable to articulate it, to give this formless agony a name. She perceived that she was not being able to do anything about the household falling apart all around her; but she didn't know how it had all taken shape, why it was eroding away and what would bring it back to life. She wanted to bawl her heart out every now and then, crying, 'I am really quite hopeless and incompetent; my stupidity is unparalleled.'

Earlier, Asha and Mahendra had often spent hours in a corner of the house, sometimes talking and sometimes not, but perfectly happy in each other's company. These days, in Binodini's absence, when Mahendra was alone with Asha he seemed lost for words. And he wasn't comfortable not saying anything either.

One day Mahendra saw a bearer carrying a letter and asked, 'Who is that letter for?'

'It's for Beharibabu.'

'Who gave it?'

'Bou-thakurani.'

'Let me see,' Mahendra took the letter. He was tempted to tear it open and read what Binodini might have written to Behari. He turned the letter over and over in his hands a few times and then hurled it back at the bearer.

If he'd opened it, he'd have found this: 'Aunty is refusing to eat gruel and barley water, may I give her a lentil soup today?' Binodini never consulted Mahendra on any medical matters. On such issues she trusted Behari implicitly.

Mahendra paced the veranda for some time, then entered his room and noticed that a picture hung crookedly on the wall—the string holding it was threadbare. He scolded Asha roundly, 'You never seem to notice anything; this is how everything gets spoiled.' The bunch of flowers that Binodini had brought back from the farmhouse in Dumdum and placed in a vase, was still in the same place, withered and dry. Mahendra usually didn't notice these things. But today his glance fell on it and he said, 'These will never be thrown away unless Binodini comes and does it.' He hurled the vase, flowers and all, out of the room and it bumped down the stairs with a metallic thud. 'Why can't Asha be what I want, why can't she work the way I like, why is her innate lassitude and feebleness making me so restless instead of binding me to the path of domesticity?' The words roared through Mahendra's head as he turned and realized that Asha was standing by the bed, holding one of the four-poster pillars, ashen-faced and lips trembling—then she turned away and dashed out of the room.

Mahendra took measured steps and picked up the discarded vase. His desk stood in a corner of the room. He sat at the desk with his head in his arms as the minutes ticked away.

After dark someone brought in the lamps, but there was no sign of Asha. Mahendra paced the terrace with impatient steps. The clock struck nine and the lonely house grew silent as the depths of the night—but Asha still did not come. Mahendra sent for her. Asha came up diffidently and stood by the terrace doorway. Mahendra approached her and drew her in to his heart. In an instant Asha's tears flooded her husband's bosom; she couldn't stop, her tears were ceaseless, her sobs threatened to tear away from her throat. Mahendra held her tight and kissed her hair—from the mute sky the stars looked down at them in mute silence.

Mahendra sat on the bed that night and said, 'I have too many night shifts to work in college. So I guess I should stay at a place near my college for some time now.'

Asha thought, 'Is he still angry? Is he moving away because he's upset with me? Am I so useless that I am pushing my husband out of his home? Death would have been a better fate.'

But Mahendra didn't show any signs of anger. He was silent as he held Asha's head on his chest and played with her hair, running his fingers through it repeatedly so that her hairdo came undone. In the early days of their romance he often did something like this and Asha protested vehemently. But today, far from protesting, she lay there in quiet contentment. Suddenly, she felt a teardrop on her temple, Mahendra raised her face to him and called in a voice choked with emotion, 'Chuni.' Asha did not respond in words. She merely held him closer with her gentle hands. Mahendra said, 'I was wrong, please forgive me.'

Asha pressed her petal-smooth palm to his mouth and said, 'Oh no, don't say that. You haven't done any wrong, it's all my fault. Please take me to task like a truant servant and make me worthy of a place at your feet.'

On the morning of his departure, before he left the bed Mahendra said, 'Chuni, my precious, I shall hold you the highest in my heart, no one can take away that place.'

Reassured thus, Asha steeled herself for all kinds of sacrifices and placed before him her only and slight demand: 'Will you write to me every day?'

Mahendra said, 'I will, if you promise to reply.'

Asha said, 'I wish I could write well.'

Mahendra pulled a few strands of hair tucked behind her ears and said, 'You write better than Akshaykumar Dutta—you could write the *Charu-path!*'

Asha said, 'Go on, stop teasing me.'

Before he left, Asha took it upon herself to pack his portmanteau. Folding and packing Mahendra's winter clothes were difficult. Between the two of them, they pushed and stuffed all the things into two suitcases where perhaps one would have sufficed. The things that got left out went on to form an array of discrete bundles. Although Asha was shamed by this, yet the squabbling, tugging at things, jesting and hurling reproofs at one another brought back memories of happier days. For a while Asha forgot that all this was in aid of imminent parting. The coachman sent word to Mahendra at least ten times saying that the carriage was ready. Irritated, he finally said, 'Tell him to unharness it.'

Gradually, the morning wore into afternoon and then dusk. Finally, the two of them cautioned one another once again to take care of themselves, promised to write frequently and with a heavy heart, parted company.

Rajlakshmi's fever had abated and she had been sitting up the last couple of days. At dusk she wrapped herself in a thick shawl and sat playing cards with Binodini. She was feeling quite fresh and fit today. Mahendra stepped in and without glancing at Binodini said to Rajlakshmi, 'Mother, I have to work nights in the college and it's difficult living here. I have rented a place near the college. I am going there today.'

Rajlakshmi felt deeply wounded but only said, 'Go ahead. Naturally, you must do what's good for your studies.'

Although she was now in good health, the minute she

heard Mahendra's plan to leave, she felt very ill indeed. She said to Binodini, 'Child, could you please hand me that pillow?' She lowered her head on the pillow as Binodini massaged her head and arms gently.

Mahendra felt his mother's temple, took her pulse. Rajlakshmi pulled her wrist away and said, 'As if the pulse tells you everything. Don't you worry, I'll be fine.' She turned away feebly.

Mahendra touched her feet and walked away, without so much as a word to Binodini.

19

BINODINI WAS WONDERING, 'WHAT IS THE REAL REASON——WOUNDED ego, wrath or fear? Does he want to prove to me that I don't matter to him? So he'll go and stay in a rented house, will he? Let me see how long this lasts.'

But Binodini herself was affected by Mahendra's departure and felt quite restive.

She had been keen on teaching Mahendra a lesson, throwing barbs at him; now that this didn't occupy her day, she felt time hanging heavy on her hands. All her interest in the household vanished. Asha, without Mahendra at her side, was bland fare indeed. Mahendra's affection, caresses and love towards Asha had always kept Binodini's heart astir. The intense awareness of pain their togetherness roused in Binodini's grief-stricken imagination, was cause for a compelling excitement. She could not figure out whether she loved the man or despised him, whether she should penalize him or give her heart to him; it was the same Mahendra who had deprived her of all fulfilment in life that was due to her, the same Mahendra who had rejected a gem of a woman like her and instead embraced a weak, feeble-minded child like Asha. He had succeeded in lighting a fire within her and she couldn't figure out if it was love, hate or a mixture of both. She would smile bleakly to herself and say, 'Is there another woman with a fate like mine? I cannot even understand if I wish to slay or to be slain.' But either way, whether to be burned by or to set fire to, Mahendra was indispensable to her. Where else would she shoot her poisoned arrows?

Binodini's breath came thick and fast as she muttered, 'Where can he go? He will be back. He is mine.'

Asha was in Mahendra's room, fiddling with his books, pictures, papers on the desk, his chair, on the pretext of tidying up. Her evening of separation was being spent in touching his belongings, picking them up, dusting one, putting another away. Binodini approached her slowly; Asha felt a trifle sheepish to be caught in the act—she stopped what she was doing and pretended to be hunting for something. Solemnly, Binodini asked, 'So, what are you doing, my friend?'

Asha drew up a small smile and said, 'Nothing much.'

Binodini wound her arms around Asha's neck and asked, 'Bali dear, why did Thakurpo take off like that?'

Binodini's question threw Asha into deep quandary and anxiety as she replied, 'As you probably know——he had some college work and so he had to leave.'

Binodini raised Asha's chin with her right hand, silently staring at her with a mixture of pity and concern as she heaved a great sigh.

Asha's heart sank. She considered herself to be stupid and Binodini to be clever. This expression on her friend's face turned her world upside down. She didn't dare to ask Binodini the question. Instead, she sat down on a sofa by the wall. Binodini sat beside her and drew her into her arms tightly. Held in the embrace of her friend, Asha couldn't check her tears as they flowed from her eyes unrestrained. Outside the house the blind beggar twanged his fiddle and sang, 'Give me the shelter of your feet, O mother Tara.'

Behari came looking for Mahendra and from the door he saw Asha weeping and Binodini holding her to her heart as she wiped away the tears. He stepped aside, went into the adjoining room which was dark and sat down. He gripped his head in his hands and began to wonder why Asha should be weeping. Who could be heartless enough to bring tears to the eyes of the girl who was innately incapable of doing wrong to anyone? He recalled the image of Binodini consoling Asha and said to himself, 'I really misjudged Binodini. In her nursing, comforting, and unselfish love for her friend, she is nothing less than a goddess on earth.'

Behari sat there in the dark for a long time. Once the blind beggar had stopped singing, Behari made a lot of noise, shuffled his feet, coughed and walked towards Mahendra's room. Before he reached the doorway, Asha veiled her head and scuttled towards the inner chambers.

The moment he stepped into the room Binodini exclaimed, 'Beharibabu, are you unwell?'

He said, 'Not at all.'

Binodini asked, 'Why are your eyes red?'

Behari avoided answering that as he asked, 'Binod-bouthan, where is Mahendra?'

Binodini grew sombre. 'I've heard that he has work at the college and so he has taken up a room near there. Beharibabu, please step aside and let me pass.'

Behari had been barring her way to the door absentmindedly. He stepped aside quickly as he realized this. Suddenly he remembered that if he were found talking to Binodini alone in a darkened room at dusk, people could take it amiss. As she left, Behari quickly spoke up, 'Binod-bouthan, please look after Asha. She is naïve, she doesn't know how to wound others or to defend herself from hurt.'

In the dark, Behari could not see Binodini's face—or he would have seen the resentment sparked in it. She had realized the minute she set her eyes on Behari today that he was overwhelmed with concern for Asha. Binodini herself didn't matter in the least! She seemed to be born to protect Asha, to free Asha's path of thorns, to fulfil every wish she ever had! Since Mahendrababu wished to wed Asha, Binodini had to be exiled to the wilderness of Barasat and married off to an uncouth ape. Since His Highness Beharibabu couldn't bear to see tears in dear Asha's eyes, Binodini must keep her shoulders ready at all times for her to weep on. Just once, Binodini wanted to smite this Mahendra, this Behari down to the dust at her feet and make them understand the difference between Asha and Binodini! Her helplessness at the injustice of fate, that had prevented her from planting a victory-flag in any man's heart, burned like wildfire inside Binodini and her very soul became combative.

As she left, she spoke to Behari in honeyed tones, 'You can rest assured Beharibabu, and don't worry yourself to death on account of my Chokher Bali.'

20

SOON AFTER, MAHENDRA RECEIVED A LETTER IN A FAMILIAR HAND, written to his new address. He didn't open it in the bustle of the day's work—but kept it safe in his pocket, near his heart. As he sat through his classes in college, or did the rounds at the hospital, he felt the bird of romance nestling in its nest next to his heart. If he woke it, his heart would be filled at once with its twittering and chattering.

In the evening he switched on the lamp in his room and leaned back comfortably in a chair. He fished out the letter from his pocket, warmed now by his body-heat. He scrutinized the address on the envelope for a long time, without opening it. He knew that the letter itself wouldn't have much to say. There was scant possibility that Asha would be able to articulate her feelings lucidly. He would have to read between the crooked lines of childlike scrawls to be able to reach her heartfelt thoughts. His own name spelt out in Asha's inept hand struck up a melodious note in Mahendra's mind—it was a pure love song from the concealed depths of a chaste woman's heart.

In the few days of absence from home, all vestiges of the

ire of familiarity had vanished from Mahendra's heart and was replaced by his old love for his new bride. In his last few days at home, the mundane, quotidian details had upset and irritated him. All traces of that disappeared now, only to be replaced by an abstract, unadulterated romantic light, which illuminated Asha's image in his mind.

Mahendra opened the envelope very slowly and brushed it across his forehead and cheeks. The scent of the perfume he had gifted to Asha once wafted from the notepaper and pierced his heart like a wayward sigh.

Mahendra unfolded the letter and read it. But what a surprise! The lines were crooked all right, but the language was by no means youthful. The letters were formed in a raw hand, but the words were scarcely so. It said:

Dearest,

Why should I bring to your mind the one you went away to forget? When you have ripped away the creeper and tossed it to the ground, she should be ashamed to try and creep up on you again. She should ideally sink through the earth.

But just this little bit should do you no harm, my heart. Let the memories come for just a few seconds. Will it hurt you terribly? Your dismissal has lodged itself in my heart like a thorn. All day, all night, in whatever I do or think, wherever I turn, I feel the knife twist cruelly. Please tell me how to empty my mind of your thoughts, the way you seem to have done with mine.

Dearest, was it my fault that you loved me? Did I, ever in my dreams, think I would hold such happiness in my hands? I am a nobody from nowhere in particular. If you never looked at me twice, if I had to be a serf without wages in your household, I would still not grudge my fate. I do not know what you saw in me, my heart, and why you raised me to the pinnacle of joy. And today, if lightning had to strike, why did it have to leave me charred, why couldn't it strike me dead instead?

In the past two days, I have been very patient and thought things over at great length—but I couldn't make sense of one thing: couldn't you have pushed me away without leaving home? Did you have to go away to distance yourself from me—do I take up so much room in your life? If you had cast me away to a corner of the room or even out of the door, would I ever have drawn your eyes to myself? Why did you leave? Isn't there someplace I could have gone instead? I came from nowhere and I could have gone the same way.

What a letter! It was very obvious to Mahendra whose language this was. He sat there, stupefied, like someone who has been wounded without warning. He felt as if his mind had been running along a rail track as its own pace when it had been hit from the opposite direction so suddenly, that all his thoughts had skidded off track and lay crumpled in a heap by the wayside.

He was deep in thought for a long time and then he read the letter again, twice, thrice. What had been, for quite some time, a vague notion began to take shape before his eyes. The comet that had hovered like a mere shadow on his horizon now rushed to occupy the whole sky, its massive tail blazing with a glowing light.

This letter had to be from Binodini. The naïve Asha had

presumed it to be hers and written it all down. As she wrote down the words dictated by Binodini, thoughts that had never crossed her mind began to take root in her head. Notions that were not her own took her fancy and became part of her thoughts; Asha could never have expressed in so eloquent a language the new pathos that surfaced. She wondered, 'How on earth did Bali know my mind so well? How did she say the exact words that were on my mind?' Asha clung to her bosom friend more ardently now, because the language of expression for the pain that was in her heart was in Binodini's hands— she was completely helpless.

Mahendra stood up, frowned and tried his best to be angry on Binodini. But instead, his anger fell on Asha. 'Just look at this girl's foolishness, how could she subject her husband to such nonsense?' he thought. As if to vindicate himself, he flopped onto the chair and read the letter yet again. As he read it, he felt a secret thrill course through his body. He tried and tried to read the letter as if Asha had written it. But these expressions could never come from the unpretentious Asha. A couple of lines into the letter, a stimulating suspicion bubbled through his mind, like fizzy, overflowing wine. This mark of romance, covert yet uttered, forbidden yet intimate, poisonous yet honeyed, proffered yet retracted, made him feel quite inebriated. He wanted to slash his hands or legs or do some harm to himself to take his mind off this matter. He brought his fist down on the desk with a bang, jumped off his chair and exclaimed, 'Off with you, let me burn this letter.' He held it close to the lamp. But instead of burning it, he read it all over again. The next morning the servant did clear the table of a pile of ashes, but those weren't from Asha's letter. Mahendra had set fire to the many replies that he had tried to write.

21

MEANWHILE ANOTHER LETTER ARRIVED:

You haven't answered my letter. It's a good thing actually. The truth can hardly be penned down on paper; I have perceived your answers deep in my heart. When the devotee prays to her lord, He seldom gives an answer to her face. But I suppose this poor soul's devout offering has found a place at your feet.

But if the devotee's prayers wrack your concentration, please don't take it amiss, lord of my heart! Whether you grant her wish or not, whether you turn your eyes to her or not, whether you come to know of her or not, this devotee has no option but to offer you her heart. Hence I write these lines today—O my stone-hearted god, stay steadfast on your course.

Once again, Mahendra tried to write a reply. But in the attempt to write to Asha it was a response to Binodini that flew swiftly to his pen. He could not write covertly like Binodini had, naming one but meaning the other. Many attempts and many torn sheets later he did manage to write something, but when he put it into the envelope and was about to address it to Asha he felt a whiplash on his back. A voice whispered, 'You brute, is this how you betray the trust of a credulous girl?' Mahendra tore up the letter into tiny bits and spent the rest of the night sitting at his desk, hiding his face in his hands as if to shield it from his own gaze.

The third letter arrived:

> Can someone who is incapable of indignation ever be a true lover? How will I give you my love if it is received with slights and rebuffs?
>
> Perhaps I have not read your mind right, and hence this impudence. When you left me behind, I felt prompted to write the first letter; when you didn't answer, I still poured my heart out to you. If I have misread you, is it entirely my fault? Just try to look back on the past and tell me if I haven't understood what you wanted me to understand?
>
> Anyway, whether it was truth or illusion, what I have written cannot be erased and what I have given cannot be withdrawn—that is my only regret. Oh, that my fate had to bring me such shame! But let this not assure you that the one who gives her love is also willing to drag it through the mud at all times. If you do not want my letters, then I must stop. If you do not reply, then this must be the end . . .

Mahendra couldn't stay still after this. He thought, 'I will have to go back home, however angry it makes me. Binodini is under the impression that I have left home in order to forget her!' Mahendra decided to return to his home simply to disprove this defiant misreading on Binodini's part.

Even as he reached the decision, Behari walked into the room. Mahendra was very pleased to see him. Earlier, his doubts and suspicions had made him feel jealous of Behari and the friendship had worn a little thin. But after reading the letters, Mahendra's jealousy had disappeared and he welcomed Behari with open arms and extravagant cheer. He got up and slapped Behari on the back, pulled him by the hand and offered him a seat.

But Behari looked crestfallen. Mahendra thought the poor wretch must have gone to meet Binodini and she must have snubbed him. He asked, 'Behari, have you gone to the house in the last few days?'

With a grave face Behari replied, 'I am coming from there right now.'

Mahendra speculated on Behari's anguish and felt quite amused. He thought, 'Poor, unfortunate Behari! He is really unlucky in love.' And he stroked his pocket once, where the three letters rustled noisily.

He asked, 'And how is everyone there?'

Behari didn't answer him and asked instead, 'What are you doing here away from home?'

Mahendra said, 'I often have to work nights these days—it's inconvenient from home.'

Behari said, 'You have had night-shifts in the past as well, I have never seen you leaving home.'

Mahendra laughed. 'Are you doubting me?'

Behari said, 'I'm serious. Come home with me right now.'

Mahendra was mentally prepared to go back home. But Behari's request made him dig in his heels. He said, 'How can I do that, Behari? My entire year's work will be ruined.'

Behari said, 'Look here Mahin da, I have known you since you were this high. Don't try to fool me. What you are doing is not right.'

Mahendra said, 'And who, my lord, am I subjecting to this injustice?'

Upset, Behari said, 'You have always bragged about your big-heartedness. Where is your heart right now?'

'These days, at the college hospital,' Mahendra answered.

Behari said, 'Stop, Mahin da, stop. Here you are laughing and joking at our expense and over there Bouthan is weeping her heart out, sometimes in the living room and sometimes in the inner rooms.'

This news of Asha's tears was a bolt from the blue for Mahendra. His new obsession had driven all thoughts of anyone else from his mind. Startled out of his reverie, he asked, 'Why is Asha weeping?'

Behari was impatient. 'Am I supposed to know that or are you?'

Mahendra said, 'If you must be angry because your Mahin da is not omniscient, I think you must direct the wrath at his maker, not at him.'

Behari then told Mahendra all that he had seen. As he spoke, he remembered Asha's tearful face burrowed into Binodini's bosom and his voice nearly choked with emotion. Mahendra was astounded by this display of intense affection. As far as he knew, Behari didn't have a heart to call his own—this was a new development! Did it start the day they had first gone to see Asha? Oh, poor, poor Behari! Mahendra did think him a poor soul, but the thought tickled him rather than making him feel sorry. He was very sure where Asha's loyalties lay. His heart swelled a little with pride as he thought, 'Those who for others are unattainable stars to be wished on, have actually come within my reach of their own accord.'

He said to Behari, 'All right then, let's go. But do send for a carriage first.'

22

THE MOMENT MAHENDRA CAME INTO THE HOUSE, ASHA TOOK ONE look at his face and all her complaints were forgotten, like the lifting of a fleeting mist. Thoughts of the letters she had sent made her cringe coyly and she could scarcely look him in the eye. Mahendra rebuked her, 'How could you accuse me of such things?'

He fished out the three oft-perused letters from his pocket. Asha wailed vigorously, 'Please, I beg of you, destroy those letters.' She made to snatch them from his hands. But he held them away from her and put them back in his pocket saying, 'I left on the call of duty and you thought I was running away? You actually doubted me?'

Asha's eyes filled with tears. 'Please forgive me, just this once? This will never happen again.'

Mahendra said, 'Never?'

Asha said, 'Never.'

Mahendra drew her to him and kissed her. Asha said, 'Give me those letters—I'll tear them up.'

Mahendra said, 'No, let them be.'

Asha humbly thought, 'He has kept them to punish me.'

On the issue of these letters, Asha felt a trifle displeased with Binodini. She didn't go to her friend with the good news of her husband's return home—instead she avoided her. Binodini noticed this and on the pretext of work, she too didn't stray that way.

Mahendra thought, 'That's strange! I had imagined Binodini would be far more visible now. But this is quite the reverse! So what was the meaning of those letters?'

Mahendra had hardened his heart and decided to abstain from all attempts at penetrating the mysteries of the female heart. He had decided that even if Binodini tried to come closer, he'd stay away from her. But now he changed his mind. 'This is not right. It's as if there is really something between us. I must laugh, talk and joke with Binodini naturally and brush away these niggling doubts.'

Mahendra said to Asha, 'It looks like *I* have now become the grain of sand in your friend's eye. She is nowhere to be seen these days.'

Asha was indifferent. 'I don't know what's wrong with her.'

Meanwhile, Rajlakshmi came to Mahendra in tears. 'Bipin's wife is really determined to leave us.'

Mahendra concealed his surprise and asked, 'What's the matter, Mother?'

Rajlakshmi said, 'I don't know, son, she is quite determined to go home now. You really don't know how to make someone feel welcome. She's a genteel woman, living in a strange home—how can she stay unless you treat her as one of your own and make her feel at home?'

Binodini was darning a bedcover in her bedroom.

Mahendra stepped into the room and said, 'Bali.'

Binodini looked up and asked, 'What is it, Mahendrababu?'

Mahendra said, 'Oh dear, since when did Mahendra become babu again?'

Binodini lowered her eyes and fixed them on her darning. 'What should I call you then?'

Mahendra said, 'What you call your friend, Chokher Bali.'

Binodini didn't give a mocking reply as she usually did— she continued silently with her sewing.

Mahendra said, 'Has that become our true relationship now, and so it cannot be played at any more?'

Binodini paused, bit off some extra thread from her sewing and said, 'I don't know, you would know better.'

She turned very grave and stopped whatever Mahendra would have said, by asking, 'Why did you suddenly decide to come back home from college?'

Mahendra said, 'How long can you keep dissecting cadavers?'

Binodini bit off some more thread with her teeth and without looking up, she asked, 'Do you need live people to cut up now?'

Mahendra had decided he would really liven up the evening by chatting and laughing with Binodini in the most friendly fashion. But he was taken aback by her acute seriousness and the light and friendly responses did not come readily to him. Whenever Mahendra found Binodini maintaining a harsh distance, his entire being just rushed towards her blindly—he was sorely tempted to shake the wall raised by her between them and to raze it to the ground. He didn't reply to the last of Binodini's taunts. Instead, he went up to her, sat beside her and asked, 'Why do you want to leave us and go away? What have we done?'

Binodini moved away a little, looked up from her sewing and fixed her large, bright eyes on Mahendra's face. 'Everyone has duties to perform. When you went away to college, leaving everything, was it because of someone doing something wrong? Don't I have to go? Don't I have duties to perform there?'

Mahendra thought hard but failed to come up with a good response. After a pause he said, 'What are the duties that are forcing you to leave?'

Threading the needle with great concentration Binodini said, 'My heart knows what my duties are. I can hardly give you a list of them.'

Mahendra sat in silence, looking grave and concerned, and gazed at a coconut palm outside the window. Binodini continued with her sewing wordlessly. There was complete silence in the room for a while. Then suddenly Mahendra spoke up. At the abrupt shattering of the silence, Binodini pricked her finger with the needle.

Mahendra said, 'Can we say nothing to hold you back?'

Binodini sucked the drop of blood from her finger and said, 'Why would you say anything? How does it matter whether I stay or go? Does it matter to you at all?' Her voice seemed to choke as she spoke. She bent low over her work and it felt as if her lowered eyelashes were checking a trace of tears that threatened to spill over. It was that time of the day when the winter afternoon was poised to surrender itself to the darkness of dusk.

In a flash Mahendra gripped Binodini's hands and said, 'And if it does indeed matter to me, would you stay?'

Binodini drew back her hands swiftly and moved aside. The spell broke for Mahendra. His own words of a minute ago kept ringing in his ears like a huge travesty. He bit down on his culpable tongue and spoke no more.

At this point Asha stepped into the room echoing with silences. Immediately, Binodini laughed and spoke as if in response to something Mahendra had said earlier, 'Since you all have placed me in such high regard, it's my duty to heed your request at least once. I'll stay until you send me away.'

Asha was thrilled at her husband's success and threw her arms about her friend. She said, 'Then that is the last word. Promise me that you will never leave as long as we don't send you away!'

Binodini promised. Asha said, 'Dear Bali, when you were going to stay back, why did you make us beg and plead so? Finally you had to bow your head before my husband, didn't you?'

Binodini laughed. 'Thakurpo, who was it that had to bow down, you or me?'

Mahendra was speechless all this time. He was feeling that the room resounded with his culpability, and shame was lashing away at him. How would he speak to Asha normally? How could he turn his uncouth rashness into a smiling jest at a moment's notice? This web of deceit was beyond his reach. He answered quietly, 'Of course, it was I who had to bow down,' and walked out of the room.

He came back in there immediately and said to Binodini, 'Please forgive me.'

Binodini asked, 'And what are you guilty of, Thakurpo?'

Mahendra said, 'We don't have the right to keep you here under compulsion.'

Binodini laughed and said, 'But where is the compulsion— I don't see it anywhere. You spoke out of kindness and concern and asked me to stay. Is that called coercion? You tell me, dear Bali, can love and coercion ever be the same?'

Asha agreed with her entirely. 'Never.'

Binodini said, 'Thakurpo, that you would like me to stay, that you'll be sorry to see me leave, is an honour in itself. Isn't that so, dear Bali? After all, how often does one find such a well-wisher? If fate is so kind as to hand me such a friend in need, a comrade in sorrows and joys, why would I be so keen to brush aside the friendly hand and leave?'

Asha was distressed to see her husband defeated and silenced and she said, 'Oh, you can never be beaten at words. My husband has laid down his arms, now you should stop.'

Mahendra rushed out of the room once again. At the same time Behari came looking for him, after having spent a few minutes talking to Rajlakshmi. Mahendra ran into him at the door and exclaimed, 'Oh Behari, I am the biggest scoundrel on this earth.' The force of his words carried them into the room.

Immediately, the summons came from within, 'Behari-thakurpo!'

Behari said, 'Just a minute, Binod-bouthan.'

Binodini said, 'Please come and listen to this.'

As he stepped into the room Behari shot a quick glance at Asha's face. The little that could be seen behind the anchal held no trace of sorrow or pain. Asha tried to leave, but

Binodini held her back and said, 'Tell me Behari-thakurpo, are you so repugnant to my Chokher Bali? Why does she want to run away the minute she sees you?'

Embarrassed, Asha poked at Binodini.

Behari laughed as he responded with, 'It's probably because my maker has not fashioned me to please the eye.'

Binodini said, 'Did you see that Bali dear, Behari-thakurpo knows the art of defence; he blamed his maker instead of your taste. You are so unlucky—you have such a gem of a brother-in-law and you don't know his worth.'

Behari said, 'If *you* are convinced of that Binod-bouthan, I have no regrets.'

Binodini said, 'Oh, the ocean stretches to the horizon, but the mariner thirsts for a drop of water.'

Asha could no longer be checked. She snatched her hand from Binodini's grip and ran out of the room. Behari also made to rise. Binodini asked, 'Thakurpo, can you tell me what's wrong with Mahendrababu?'

Startled, Behari stopped in his tracks and said, 'I don't really know; is something wrong?'

Binodini said, 'I don't know, Thakurpo, it doesn't bode well.'

Concerned, Behari sat down on a chair. He looked expectantly at Binodini, eager to hear the whole thing. Binodini continued with her darning without saying another word.

After some time, Behari asked, 'Has something about Mahin da struck you as odd?'

Binodini replied very casually, 'I don't know, Thakurpo, it doesn't look good to me. I just feel terribly concerned for my Chokher Bali.' She sighed, put her sewing away and made as if to get up.

Behari said, 'Bouthan, wait a minute.'

Binodini opened all the doors and windows of the room, stoked up the lamp light, picked up her sewing again and took a seat on the far corner of the bed. She said, 'Thakurpo, I cannot stay here forever. But when I am gone, please look after my Chokher Bali, see that no harm comes to her.' She turned away as if to hide an imminent onslaught of tears.

Behari spoke up impetuously, 'Bouthan, you cannot leave. You don't have anyone to call your own—you must take it upon yourself to safeguard this simple, innocent girl at all times. If you leave her and go, I don't see a way out.'

Binodini said, 'Thakurpo, you know the world as well as I do. If I stayed here forever, what would people say?'

Behari said, 'Oh, let them say what they will. You mustn't pay attention to that. You are divine—it is your responsibility to protect the helpless girl from all the stones and pellets hurled by the world. Bouthan, I misjudged you at first; please forgive me for that. Just like the narrow-minded, common man on the street, I did you injustice when I first met you. Once, I even felt that you envied Asha her happiness, that—anyway, it's a sin even to speak such thoughts aloud. Since then I have glimpsed your divine soul and because I have a deep respect for you, I felt I had to confess all my sins today.'

A stream of pleasure coursed through Binodini. Though her own show of concern was an act, she couldn't refuse this homage from Behari even in her own heart of hearts. She had never received such a gift from anyone. For an instant she truly believed she was chaste, noble—a vague sense of pity for Asha brought tears to her eyes. She didn't hide these tears from Behari—they gave her the illusion that she was indeed worthy of homage.

When Behari saw Binodini weeping, he was close to tears himself. He controlled himself somehow and went into Mahendra's room. Behari had no inkling why Mahendra had declared himself a scoundrel. On reaching his room he found that Mahendra wasn't there. He was told that Mahendra had gone for a walk. In the past Mahendra seldom left his room without reason. Away from his familiar people and places, he felt uncomfortable and fatigued. Behari started homewards, deep in thought.

Binodini fetched Asha to her own room, drew her into her bosom and with tear-filled eyes said, 'Dear Bali, I am very unfortunate, very ill-starred.'

Hurt and puzzled, Asha returned her embrace and said, 'Why, my dear, why do you say that?'

Binodini hid her face in Asha's bosom like a child close to sobbing and said, 'Wherever I go, bad things happen. Let go, my friend, let go of me—I will go back to my wilderness.'

Asha raised up Binodini's face by the chin and said, 'My sweet friend, don't talk like that. I cannot live without you. Why did these thoughts of leaving come to you today?'

Meanwhile Behari, having missed Mahendra, decided to go to back to Binodini on some pretext and thresh out the matter of Asha's and Mahendra's differences at greater length. He made up an excuse of requesting Binodini to ask Mahendra if he could have lunch with Behari the next day, and turned back to the house. From outside the room he called out,

'Binod-bouthan,' and immediately spotted, in the light of the kerosene lamp, the two teary-eyed women holding each other tight. His steps slowed to a halt. Asha noticed his hesitation; suddenly the thought crossed her mind that Behari may have said something unfair or unjust to Binodini and that was why she talked of going away thus. This was very wrong of Behari—he wasn't a good soul, she thought. Annoyed, Asha walked out of the room. Behari too left, with his heart overflowing with respect for Binodini.

That night Mahendra said to Asha, 'Chuni, I am leaving for Kashi by the morning train tomorrow.'

Asha's heart skipped a beat. She asked, 'But why?'

Mahendra said, 'It's been ages since I saw Aunty.'

At this, Asha felt mortified: she should have thought of this before. Filled with self-loathing she felt she was indeed hard-hearted to have forgotten her loving aunt in the midst of the ebb and flow of life, while Mahendra had recalled that loving soul living in a far-off land.

Mahendra said, 'She had left, entrusting her most precious jewel to my care—I cannot rest if I don't see her once.' Mahendra's voice quivered with unshed tears and his right palm stroked Asha's temple repeatedly in a gesture of silent blessing and unspoken good wishes. Asha couldn't make sense of this sudden onslaught of tenderness, but she felt overcome by emotion, and tears ran down her cheeks. She recalled Binodini's words of exaggerated affection earlier that evening. She didn't know if there was a link between these two incidents. But she did perceive that this was a watershed in her life. She couldn't figure out if it was benevolent or malevolent.

Distraught, she embraced Mahendra vigorously. He sensed her unspoken terrors and said, 'Chuni, you have the blessings of your devout Aunty, you have nothing to fear, nothing at all. She has sacrificed everything and gone away, for your good alone. No harm can ever come to you.'

Asha pushed away all her fears with determination and gathered her husband's blessings to her heart like a protective talisman. In her mind she touched her aunt's feet again and again and prayed fervently, 'Mother, may your blessings protect my husband at all times.'

The next day Mahendra went away without a word to Binodini. She said to herself, 'You make the mistake and then you take it out on me! What an impostor. These pretences won't last long.'

23

ANNAPURNA WAS NATURALLY DELIGHTED TO SEE MAHENDRA AFTER such a long time. But at the same time she feared that he had again fought with his mother over Asha and had come to Annapurna for sympathy. Even as a child, Mahendra had always run to his aunt in times of trouble. When he was hurt, Annapurna would console him, and when he was angry, she would advise him to deal with the situation calmly. But she was incapable of consoling him, let alone solving his problems, since his marriage. When she became certain that whatever she tried to do to help him would only serve to aggravate the domestic strife in Mahendra's life, she had walked out of the house. She had gone away like the helpless mother who goes to the next room when the sick child weeps for water and the doctor forbids it. In this far-off exile, away from the concerns of the house, busy with her religious duties and pious endeavours, she had forgotten the family to some extent. Now she feared that Mahendra had arrived with the intent of bringing up all those conflicts once again and upsetting her peace of mind.

But Mahendra said nothing about any friction with his mother about Asha. Now Annapurna feared other things: why would that same Mahendra, who was once incapable of leaving Asha long enough to go to college, suddenly come so far away to be with his aunt? Were the bonds of love between them wearing thin? Consumed with anxiety, Annapurna asked Mahendra, 'Tell me honestly, my son, I beg of you, how is Chuni?'

Mahendra said, 'She is fine, Aunty.'

'What does she do these days, Mahin? Are you two still as childish as ever or have you begun to take on some household duties?'

Mahendra said, 'No—the childlishness has stopped. Remember that alphabet book—the root of all evil? I don't know where it has vanished, but it simply cannot be found. If you were there, you'd be happy to see that Chuni is faithfully fulfilling the duties of a woman, in so far as it is advisable for a woman to neglect her education.'

'Mahin, what is Behari up to?'

Mahendra said, 'Everything but his own work. His finances are managed by his clerks and employees—I don't know with what intent. That is Behari for you. His own matters will be managed by others while he handles the affairs of others.'

Annapurna asked, 'Mahin, won't he get married?'

Mahendra smiled at that. 'I don't see any signs of it.'

This jolted Annapurna deep in her heart. She was aware that Behari had once agreed to get married, after seeing her niece and that enthusiastic desire had then been crushed unfairly. Behari had said, 'Aunty, please don't ask me to get married ever again.' Those words, full of hurt and anger, were still ringing in Annapurna's ears. She had left her much-loved and trusted Behari heartbroken and she hadn't even been able to offer him much consolation. With great trepidation and distress Annapurna wondered if Behari still yearned for Asha!

Mahendra brought her up to date on much of the news of their daily lives, with great wit and humour. But he did not mention Binodini at all.

Mahendra's college was in session and there was no reason for him to stay in Kashi for too long. But his visit to Annapurna was giving him the kind of pleasure that one gets while convalescing in healthy environs after a nerve-wracking and tedious illness. And so the days slipped by in quick succession. The conflict with his own self that he had been unable to resolve, disappeared gradually. The few days he spent in the company of the pious and loving Annapurna, made him so attuned to the duties and responsibilities of life, that his earlier fears began to seem almost ludicrous. He began to feel that Binodini was of no consequence. So much so that he could not recall her face clearly now. Eventually, with great force, Mahendra said to himself, 'I cannot see anyone on the horizon who has the power to dislodge Asha from her place in my heart.'

One day he said to Annapurna, 'Aunty, I have to go back to college—so I'll take your leave for now. Although you have cut yourself off from family ties, please allow me to come and visit you from time to time.'

Mahendra came back home and gave Asha the box of sindoor and the little pot made of white stone and glitter that were sent by her aunt with love. Asha wept copiously and when she recalled her aunt's unconditional love for them and the many ways in which all of them including Rajlakshmi had tormented her, she felt very unhappy indeed. She said to Mahendra, 'I really wish I could go to my aunt just once, touch her feet and beg forgiveness. Is that not possible?'

Mahendra understood her misery and he wasn't unwilling to let her go to spend a few days with Annapurna in Kashi. But he really didn't see how he could take leave from college once again, so soon after his previous trip.

Asha said, 'I believe my uncle's wife will go to Kashi shortly. Is it all right if I go with her?'

Mahendra went to Rajlakshmi, 'Mother, Asha wants to go to Kashi to visit Aunty.'

Rajlakshmi replied scathingly, 'Certainly, if her ladyship wants to go, she must go. Why don't you take her?'

She wasn't happy that Mahendra had re-established contact with Annapurna; at this request of Asha going there as well, she was quite displeased.

Mahendra said, 'I cannot go; I have classes. She can go with Anukulbabu.'

Rajlakshmi said, 'Oh, that's wonderful. They are rich people; their paths seldom cross ours, poor as we are. It would be an honour for her to go with them.'

Mahendra was sorely put out by this repeated derision from his mother. He hardened his heart and walked away, silently determined to send Asha to Kashi.

When Behari came to meet Rajlakshmi, she said, 'O Behari, have you heard—our daughter-in-law wants to go to Kashi!'

Behari said, 'What! Mahin da will take leave again to go with her?'

Rajlakshmi said, 'Oh no, why would Mahin do that! It wouldn't be the height of fashion, would it? Mahin will stay here and she will go with her uncle. Everyone is so modern these days.'

Behari felt concerned—not with the emerging signs of 'modernity' though; he wondered, 'What is going on—when Mahin da went to Kashi, Asha was here; now that she wants to go, he is staying back. Something must be seriously wrong between them. How long will this go on? As friends, can't we do something about this—should we just keep our distance?'

Mahendra was sitting in his room, thoroughly exasperated by his mother's rudeness. Binodini had not met him since he returned. Asha was pleading with her in the next room to come and meet him.

At this point Behari walked in and said, 'Is Asha-bouthan's trip to Kashi all fixed?'

Mahendra said, 'Why wouldn't it be fixed? What's the difficulty?'

Behari said, 'Who said anything about difficulty? But

what's behind this sudden idea?'

Mahendra said, 'Oh—wish to see her aunt—yearning for one's loved ones who are far away—it is not uncommon to human nature.'

Behari asked, 'Are you going with her?'

Behari's question made Mahendra feel that he had come to suggest that it wouldn't be right to send Asha with her uncle. He didn't want to flare up at Behari and so he answered brusquely, 'No.'

Behari knew Mahendra fairly well. He was fully aware that Mahendra was annoyed. He also knew that once Mahendra's mind was made up, there would be no way of bringing him around. So he didn't bring up the topic of Mahendra's going again. He found himself thinking, 'If poor Asha is stressed out over something and wants to leave with a burden on her heart, it'd help if Binodini accompanied her.' So he said very slowly, 'Wouldn't it be nice if Binod-bouthan went along with her?'

Mahendra roared in anger, 'Behari, why don't you say what's really troubling you? I don't see the need to beat about the bush with me. I am aware that you suspect I have fallen in love with Binodini. It's a lie. I haven't. You do not have to go about guarding me in order to protect me. Please protect yourself instead. If you were a genuine friend, you'd have told me the truth about your feelings long ago and kept yourself far away from your friend's inner chambers. I can say this to your face—you are in love with Asha.'

A speechless Behari stood up, ashen-faced, and advanced on Mahendra. He looked like he was about to lash out without a thought, like someone who had been wounded deliberately in his weakest spot. He stopped short just in time and spoke with great difficulty, 'May God forgive you—I must be gone.' He walked out unsteadily.

Binodini rushed out of the next room and called, 'Behari-thakurpo!'

Behari leaned on the wall and tried to smile. 'What is it, Binod-bouthan?'

Binodini said, 'Thakurpo, I will also go to Kashi along with my Chokher Bali.'

Behari said, 'No, no, Bouthan, that's impossible, absolutely impossible. I beg of you—don't do anything that I have said; I am nobody here, I do not want to interfere, the consequences won't be good. You are a virtuous soul—you must do what you think is right. I must go.'

Behari folded his hands and saluted Binodini politely as he left. Binodini muttered, 'I am no saint, Thakurpo—listen to me. If you leave, no one will be happy. Don't blame me then.'

Behari left. Mahendra sat there, stupefied. Binodini hurled him an angry look, spitting fire like a bolt of lightning, as she walked into the next room where Asha sat in utter mortification and shame. She couldn't bring herself to look up, after she had heard Mahendra say that Behari loved her. But Binodini felt no sympathy for her. If Asha had indeed looked up then, she'd have felt terrified. Binodini was livid, furious with the whole world. Lies indeed! Of course, no one loved Binodini! Everyone only loved this bashful, dainty china doll.

Ever since Mahendra had exclaimed to Behari, 'I am a scoundrel,' he had felt diffident in Behari's presence, ashamed of his confession, especially after his blood had stopped boiling. He felt that his heart lay exposed before his friend. He didn't love Binodini, but Behari felt that he did—this thought was eating away at Mahendra. After that day whenever he came face to face with Behari, he felt his friend was poking at him with amused interest. An irritation was piling up inside and today at the slightest provocation he had given vent to it.

But the manner in which Binodini rushed out of the adjoining room, begging and pleading with Behari to stay and agreeing to obey his wishes by accompanying Asha to Kashi, left Mahendra feeling shattered. He had claimed that he did not love Binodini; but what he saw and heard didn't give him a moment's peace—it taunted him in every way. And above all he felt deeply regretful that Binodini had heard him say he did not love her.

24

MAHENDRA KEPT THINKING, 'I HAVE UTTERED A LIE, THAT I DO NOT love Binodini. It was a harsh thing to say. While it may not be true that I love her, it is very cruel to say that I do *not* love her. Is there a woman in this world who wouldn't be hurt by this? How and when can I get a chance to retract what I said? I can't really go and tell her that I love her; but I must convey to her in a more mild and gentle way that I don't. I can't let Binodini go on believing something so wrong.' And so saying, Mahendra brought out the three letters from his box and read them over again. He thought, 'Without a doubt, Binodini is in love with me. But why did she plead that way with Behari? Was it just for my benefit? When I declared in so many words that I don't love her, I suppose she had to decline her love for me in some way in my presence. My rejection may even result in her falling in love with Behari on the rebound.'

Mahendra felt such deep remorse that his agitation worried and surprised himself. So, perhaps Binodini *had* heard Mahendra saying he did not love her—what was wrong with that? Perhaps this would lead to the indignant Binodini taking her affections elsewhere—would that be so terrible? Unable to make sense of his inner turmoil, Mahendra clung to Asha the way a wayward dinghy latches on to its anchor in a storm.

That night he held Asha's head on his bosom and asked her, 'Chuni, tell me how much do you love me?'

Asha thought, 'What kind of a question is that? Does he doubt me now that all those ugly words have been said with respect to Behari-thakurpo?' She felt she would die of mortification and said, 'For shame, why do you ask me that today of all days? I beg of you, tell me what's on your mind— have you felt anything lacking in my love for you?'

Mahendra enjoyed seeing her so tormented and said, 'Why do you wish to go to Kashi then?'

Asha said, 'I shan't go to Kashi, I shan't go anywhere.'

He said, 'But you did want to go earlier.'

Vexed, Asha said, 'You know why I wanted to go.'

Mahendra said, 'Perhaps you'll find greater happiness with your aunt, if you leave me and go.'

Asha said, 'Never. I didn't want to go for my pleasure.'

Mahendra said, 'I truly believe, Chuni, you'd have been

much happier married to someone else.'

Asha jerked away from Mahendra's grasp, dug her face into the pillow and lay there like a wooden doll—an instant later her tears were evident. Mahendra tried to pull her close to him in an effort to console her. But she refused to budge from the pillow. Mahendra felt wracked with guilt but at the same time he was filled with joy and pride at this evidence of his chaste wife's righteous anger.

This sudden articulation of a lot of things that had been running deep in their hearts threw everyone a little off balance. Binodini felt, 'Why didn't Behari protest against such blatant accusations?' She would have been happier had he put up even a token protest, however false. As it was, she felt he had got his just desserts from Mahendra. Why would a noble soul like Behari devote his heart to Asha? Binodini felt a sense of relief that this accusation had thrown Behari into confusion and removed him from the scenario.

But his face—Behari had looked ashen-faced and mortally wounded—began to haunt Binodini wherever she went. The nurturing woman within her heart wept at the remembered vision of anguish. She carried that image of suffering in her heart the way a mother carries about a sick child on her bosom. Binodini felt an impatient eagerness to nurse the image back to health, to see the signs of rejuvenation.

After a few days of this unmindful preoccupation, Binodini could hold still no longer. She wrote a consolatory letter that said:

Thakurpo,

Ever since I saw your anguished face that day I have prayed that you recover soon, and be your old self; when will I see that spontaneous smile again, hear those noble thoughts again? How are you? Drop me a line and let me know.

Your Binod-bouthan

Binodini dispatched the letter through the bearer.

Behari had never imagined in his wildest dream that Mahendra would be able to say such harsh words—that Behari loved Asha—he had never uttered such thoughts quite so clearly even to himself. At first he was thunderstruck. Then he stomped about in anger and hatred as he repeated to himself, 'Criminal, improper, baseless.'

But once the words had been uttered, their effect could not be erased completely. The grain of truth contained in them germinated and took shape in his mind. The face of that shy child-woman, whom he had glanced at just once in the falling light of the evening, as a fragrant breeze drifted in from the garden, haunted him now, and something seemed to grip his heart tightly even as a harsh pain rose all the way to his throat and threatened to choke him. He spent many nights lying on the terrace and many daytime hours pacing the path in front of his house. Gradually, what was hitherto implicit became a truth in his mind. What was repressed became uncontrolled. Mahendra's statement gave flesh and blood to an idea that had been formless henceforth and filled Behari inside out.

He perceived his own culpability and thought, 'It doesn't become me to be resentful. I must beg Mahin da's pardon and take leave of him. The other day I had stormed out as if he was guilty and I was sitting in judgement on him. I must accept that I was to blame.'

Behari knew that Asha had left for Kashi. One evening he approached Mahendra's room with hesitant steps. He met Rajlakshmi's distant uncle, Sadhucharan, and asked him, 'Sadhu da, I couldn't come earlier. Is everything all right here?' Sadhucharan informed him of everybody's well-being and Behari asked, 'When did Bouthan leave for Kashi?' Sadhucharan said, 'She hasn't gone to Kashi; that trip has been cancelled.' In spite of all that had happened, Behari yearned to rush indoors. He knew that he could no longer bound up the familiar stairs, make pleasant conversation with everyone without a thought, now it was all alien and forbidden to him—yet his heart craved for that very thing. He yearned to go inside, just once, like the member of the family that he once had been and speak a few words to Rajlakshmi, a few to Asha behind the veil, and call her bouthan. Sadhucharan said, 'Why are you standing here in the dark? Come inside.'

Behari took a few hurried steps towards the inner chambers, turned back and said to Sadhucharan, 'I have some work—I must go.' He left hurriedly.

The same night Behari undertook a journey. The bearer meanwhile took Binodini's letter to Behari and finding him gone, brought it back home. Mahendra was strolling in the garden. He asked, 'Whose letter is that?' The bearer told him everything. Mahendra took the letter from him. He was tempted to go and give it to Binodini—see her face turn red with shame—and come away without another word. He had no doubt that the contents of the letter would put Binodini to shame. He remembered that once before too such a letter had gone from Binodini to Behari. Mahendra could not rest without knowing the contents of the letter. He tried to tell himself that Binodini was living under his roof and as such he was responsible for her. Hence it was his duty to intercept such letters and read them, since Binodini should not be allowed to ruin herself.

Mahendra opened the short letter and read it. Written in simple language, the writer's genuine concern was quite palpable in it. He read it again and again and pondered on it, but could not figure out which way Binodini's thoughts flowed. He couldn't help feeling that Binodini was now trying to transfer her affections elsewhere because he—Mahendra— had declared that he did not love her. Angry with him, she had given up all hopes of ever gaining his affections.

Such thoughts made it very difficult for Mahendra to hold himself in check. The possibility that Binodini—who had once come to surrender herself to him—would slip from his hands for all time to come, thanks to a momentary lapse, drove him wild. Mahendra thought, 'If Binodini has feelings for me, it is good for her—her feelings would not be disrespected. I know myself, I shall never do anything to cause her harm. She can be quite safe in loving me. I am in love with Asha and Binodini will be safe from my attentions. But if she gives her heart to someone else, who knows what can come of it!' Mahendra decided he must get back Binodini's affections, without surrendering himself.

He stepped into the inner chambers and found Binodini standing in the corridor with an anxious look on her face, apparently waiting for something. Mahendra was instantly gripped by vicious jealousy. He said, 'You know, you wait in vain; he will not come. Here is your letter—it's come back.'

Binodini said, 'But it's open.'

Mahendra went away without answering her. Binodini assumed that Behari had opened the letter, read it and sent it back without a reply—and she went up in flames. She sent for the bearer who had carried the letter. He was busy elsewhere and so he didn't come. Behind closed doors, Binodini's tears fell from her burning eyes the way molten wax drips from a candle. She tore her letter to tiny bits and still wasn't satisfied—was there no way to erase those few lines from the past and the present, to nullify all of it? The irate bee stings whoever crosses its path; a thwarted Binodini was now ready to set fire to everything around her. Was she to lose everything that she ever desired? Could success never be hers? Since happiness was not to be hers, she decided she'd rest in peace only when she had dragged to the ground all the people who had hindered her happiness, posed an obstacle to her success and had deprived her of all possible joy.

25

THAT EVENING, AS THE FIRST BREEZE OF SPRING DRIFTED THROUGH the air, Asha laid out a mat on the terrace and sat there after ages. In the falling light, she was reading a serialized novel in a monthly magazine. The hero of the story was on his way back home after a whole year and was attacked on the way by robbers, setting Asha's heart aflutter; meanwhile, the unfortunate heroine had woken up at that very moment from a terrible nightmare. Asha could scarcely hold back her tears.

She was a generous reader of Bengali literature and she liked nearly everything that she read. She'd call Binodini and say, 'Dear Bali, I beg you to read this one—it's really good. I cried my heart out.' But Binodini would pick faults with the story and tear it to bits, leaving Asha crestfallen.

Today she decided she would make Mahendra read this story, as she shut the magazine, dewy-eyed. It was at this point that Mahendra appeared on the terrace. The look on his face made Asha tense, although he tried to affect an air of bonhomie and asked, 'Who is the fortunate soul you are thinking of, alone on the terrace?'

Asha forgot the travails of her hero and heroine completely and asked, 'Aren't you feeling too well today?'

Mahendra said, 'I feel just fine.'

Asha said, 'But you are lost in some thought, please tell me what it is.'

Mahendra picked up a paan from Asha's box, put it in his mouth and said, 'I was thinking that it's been ages since your aunt saw you. If you could go and visit her all of a sudden, she'd be so happy.'

Asha gazed at his face wordlessly; she failed to understand why this subject was being revived.

Seeing Asha silent, Mahendra asked, 'Don't you feel like going?'

This was difficult. Asha did want to visit Annapurna but she didn't feel like leaving Mahendra. She said, 'When your college closes, we can both go.'

Mahendra said, 'When my college closes, I won't be able to go. I'll have to prepare for my exams.'

Asha said, 'In that case, let it be—I don't have to go now.'

Mahendra replied, 'But why? Since you wanted to go, I think you should.'

Asha said, 'No, I don't want to go.'

Mahendra asked, 'Just the other day you wanted it and now you don't?'

Asha looked down silently. Mahendra wanted an unfettered space to claim his truce with Binodini and he felt impatience tugging at him. When Asha fell silent, he felt an unprovoked surge of anger. He said, 'Are you, by any chance, not sure of me? Do you want to guard me and keep me under surveillance?'

Suddenly, Asha's innate timidity, softness and uncomplaining nature struck him as unbearable. He thought, 'If you want to go to Aunty, you should say, yes I want to go, please arrange it somehow. Instead, it's yes, no, I don't know and then silence—what is all this?'

Asha was taken aback by this sudden, harsh outburst from Mahendra. She tried to think of an answer but nothing came to mind. She was at a loss as to why Mahendra was so affectionate at times and so cruel at others. But the more incomprehensible he grew to her, the harder Asha clung to him, with all the fears and affections of her trembling little heart.

Asha was suspicious of Mahendra and so she wanted to guard him day and night! What a cruel joke, what misplaced sarcasm. Should she take an oath and protest or should she brush it off in jest?

When a confused Asha remained speechless, Mahendra lost his patience, got up and stormed away. The hero and the heroine of the monthly magazine weren't given another thought. The last rays of the setting sun disappeared, the mild spring breeze of the early evening was replaced by a chilly nip in the air—Asha lay still on the mat.

Late that night Asha stepped into the bedroom and found Mahendra had already gone to bed without even calling her. She felt that Mahendra was repulsed by her indifference to her doting aunt. Asha got into bed, took Mahendra's feet in her hands, buried her face in them and lay still. Mahendra was overcome by pity and tried to pull Asha to him. But she refused to budge. She said, 'If I have done any wrong, please forgive me.'

Deeply affected, Mahendra said, 'You have done no wrong, Chuni. I am a great scoundrel to have hurt you so wickedly.'

Asha's tears drenched Mahendra's feet. He got up, held her in his arms and made her sit down beside him. Once her tears stopped flowing, she said, 'Do you think I don't want to visit Aunty? But I don't feel like leaving you and going away. That's why I didn't want to go—please don't be angry.'

Mahendra stroked her damp forehead gently and said, 'How can I be angry about this, Chuni? How can I be angry because you do not want to leave me and go anywhere? You don't have to go anywhere.'

Asha said, 'No, I shall go to Kashi.'

Mahendra said, 'But why?'

Asha said, 'Since the thought that I do not leave you because I don't trust you has crossed your mind, I must go away, even if for a few days.'

Mahendra said, 'But that was my sin, why should you pay for it?'

Asha replied, 'I don't know all that—but I must have sinned too, somewhere, somehow, or such impossible doubts would not have come to your mind. Why would I have to hear things that I cannot imagine in my wildest dreams?'

Mahendra said quietly, 'That is because you cannot imagine, even in your wildest dreams, what an appalling person I am.'

Asha was distressed. 'Not again! Don't say that. But my mind is made up—I will go to Kashi.'

Mahendra laughed. 'All right then, go. But what will you do if I fall to my ruin in your absence?'

Asha said, 'Don't you threaten me like that—as though I am quaking in my boots!'

Mahendra said, 'But it needs to be given a thought. If you allow such a great husband of yours to get ruined, who will you blame for it?'

Asha replied, 'I won't blame you, don't you worry.'

Mahendra said, 'Will you accept your part in it?'

Asha said, 'Most certainly.'

Mahendra said, 'All right. Then I'll go tomorrow, speak to Anukulbabu and make the arrangements.'

He added, 'It's very late now,' and turned over to sleep.

A little later he turned to her again and suddenly said, 'Chuni, forget it, don't go.'

Asha was desolate. 'Why are you saying this again? If I don't go just this once, your accusation will stare me in the face. Even if it's for a couple of days, please send me away.'

Mahendra said, 'Fine.' He turned over and went to sleep.

The day before she left for Kashi, Asha hugged Binodini and said, 'Bali, promise me one thing.'

Binodini pinched her cheeks and said, 'What is it, my sweet? You know I'd keep my word to you.'

Asha said, 'I'm not so sure, you have changed these days. You refuse to come in front of my husband.'

Binodini replied, 'Don't you know the reason for that? You heard what Mahendrababu said to Beharibabu the other day. After such words are spoken, do you think I should stand before him ever again—*you* tell me?'

Asha was aware that Binodini had a point. She herself had recently had a taste of how embarrassing such words could be. Still she said, 'Words come and go; if you cannot rise above them, what's love all about, my dear? You must forget all that.'

Binodini said, 'As you wish—I'll forget it.'

Asha said, 'Look, I leave for Kashi tomorrow. You must keep an eye on what my husband needs and see that he doesn't miss anything. You cannot hide from him the way you've been doing.'

Binodini was silent. Asha held her hands and said, 'For my sake, dear Bali, you must promise me this.'

Binodini said, 'Yes, I promise.'

26

WHEN THE MOON SETS, THE SUN RISES. ASHA HAD LEFT, BUT Mahendra still could not catch sight of Binodini. He walked around aimlessly, sometimes stepping into his mother's room on a slight pretext—but Binodini managed to give him the slip every time. From Mahendra's desolate, forlorn air Rajlakshmi thought, 'Now that his wife is away, Mahin doesn't seem to like being in this house any more.' She felt hurt that nowadays Mahendra's wife was more indispensable to his well-being than his mother. And yet, his lost and despondent air disturbed her. She sent for Binodini, 'Ever since that attack of flu I have developed asthmatic tendencies. I can't go up and down the stairs as easily as before. Child, you must look after Mahin yourself, whether he's eating properly or not. All his life he's been used to being pampered. Ever since Asha left, he's looking so lost. And speaking of the girl—I don't know how she could go, leaving him like this!'

Binodini curled her lip and scratched at the bedcovers. Rajlakshmi said, 'What is it, child, what are you thinking? There's nothing to think about; whatever anyone may say, you are no stranger to us.'

Binodini said, 'Aunty, let it be.'

Rajlakshmi said, 'Fine, let it go. Let me see what I can do myself.' She made as if to get up and climb the stairs to Mahendra's room on the second floor. Binodini hastily stopped her, 'You are unwell, you mustn't go. I'll go. Please forgive me, Aunty, your wish will be my command.'

Rajlakshmi never paid heed to what people said. Ever since her husband's death, with the exception of Mahendra nobody had meant anything to her. She didn't like Binodini hinting at social criticism where Mahendra was concerned. She had known him all his life—there wasn't a better man to be found anywhere! Criticism about *her* Mahin! If anyone dared to criticize him, may their tongue fall off! Rajlakshmi had a natural tendency to defy the entire world where something that she considered good was concerned.

That day Mahendra came back from college, went into his room and looked around in stunned disbelief. The minute he opened the door the scent of sandalwood and incense had filled his senses. The mosquito nets were adorned with pink tassels. The mattress on the floor glimmered with fresh sheets, and instead of the old cushions on it there were foreign-made, square cushions with embroidered silk and wool covers. The embroidery was the outcome of Binodini's hard labour of many months. Asha had often asked her, 'Who are you making these for?'

Binodini had laughed and said, 'For my deathbed. Death is my only intimate now.'

There were coloured yarns twisted decoratively into knots at the four corners of Mahendra's photo-frame and beneath it, on the floor on either side of a teapoy, were a pair of vases with fresh flowers, as though Mahendra's likeness had been worshipped by an unknown devotee. All in all, the room was transformed. The bed was shifted slightly from its old position; it was screened by the clothes rack and the clothes that hung on it, thereby dividing the room into two discrete spaces. The curio-cabinet which held all the little assortments, dolls and things that Asha held dear, was decorated with scrunched-up red fabric stuck on the inside of the glass panels, so that nothing within it was visible now. The deft touch of a new pair of hands had shrouded all that was reminiscent of the room's past.

Weary from his day's work, Mahendra lay down on the mattress and rested his head on the new cushions. Immediately, an aroma assailed his senses—the stuffing in the pillows were generously mixed with a fragrant pollen and some essence.

Mahendra's eyes drifted shut. He perceived the touch of the hands, light as a feather, that had done such subtle work on the pillows. Now the maid brought in fruits and sweets on a silver plate and iced pineapple juice in a glass tumbler. All this was different from the way things were done earlier. There was great attention to detail and novelty in every gesture. Mahendra's senses were dulled by this onslaught of freshness in every smell, every touch and every sight.

He finished his meal with great satisfaction. Binodini stepped into the room slowly with paan and mouth-freshner in a silver box. She laughed and said, 'Thakurpo, forgive me for not being present all these days, tending to your meals. For my sake, I beg of you, do not tell my Chokher Bali that you have been neglected. I try to do my best—but I have to look into all the household chores, you see.'

Binodini held the box of paan before Mahendra. Today the paan was scented differently—a new kind of lime paste had been used.

Mahendra said, 'It's good to slip up sometimes, even while tending so assiduously.'

Binodini asked, 'And why is that?'

Mahendra replied, 'Then later it can be held against you and greater penalties exacted.'

'So, Mr Shylock, what has the interest come to?'

Mahendra said, 'You weren't present when I had my meal. Now, after the event, you must stay longer and make up for it.'

Binodini laughed, 'Oh dear, you are so particular with

the accounts that woe betide anyone who falls into your trap.'

Mahendra said, 'Whatever the accounts say, have I succeeded in exacting payment?'

Binodini said, 'What is there to exact? You hold me a prisoner as it is.' She turned the jest into mock-seriousness by heaving a slight sigh.

Mahendra too grew sombre. 'Bali, is this a prison for you then?'

The bearer interrupted them, coming in to place the lamp on the teapoy.

Binodini shielded her face from the sudden glare of the lamp and answered with lowered eyes, 'I don't know. Who can beat you at wordplay? I must go now, there's work to be done.'

Mahendra grabbed her hand and said, 'Since you've admitted to being captive, where do you want to run?'

Binodini said, 'Oh for pity's sake, let me go—why try to imprison one who has nowhere to escape?'

She snatched away her hand and rushed out of the room.

Mahendra lay there on the scented pillows. The blood roared in his veins. The silent dusk, a room to themselves, spring in the air and Binodini's heart just within his reach— Mahendra felt he could hardly bear the intoxicating thrill of it all. Quickly, he blew out the lamp, bolted the door and went to bed long before his usual time.

It wasn't his old, familiar bed. A few extra mattresses had made it softer than before. Yet another aroma, he couldn't quite name the ingredient. Mahendra tossed and turned; he wanted to discover at least one marker of the past and cling to it. But nothing came to hand.

At nine o'clock there was a knock on his door. Binodini spoke from outside, 'Thakurpo, I have brought you dinner. Open the door.'

Mahendra sat up with a start and reached for the bolt. But he didn't open the door. He dropped down on the floor and said, 'Oh no, I am not hungry. I shan't have dinner.'

Binodini sounded concerned, 'Are you unwell? Shall I get you some water? What would you like to have?'

Mahendra said, 'I don't want anything, I don't need anything.'

Binodini said, 'For God's sake, don't play the fool. All right, even if you're not sick, just open the door.'

Mahendra shook his head vehemently. 'No, I won't, never. Go away.'

He got into the bed hastily. In that empty bed and in his restless state, he desperately groped for memories of the absent Asha.

When sleep eluded him till late at night, he lit the lamp again, sat at his desk and wrote to Asha.

Asha, please don't leave me alone for too long now. You are the goddess of my heart. When you are gone, I scarcely know how all my instincts run away with me and lead me astray. Where is the light that would light my way—it rests in the loving gaze of your eyes brimming with trust. Please come back soon, my innocence, my eternal, my only one. Make me strong, save me, fulfil my heart. Retrieve me from this nightmare of forgetting you for even an instant, of committing the blunder of sinning against you.

Thus Mahendra wrote, long into the night, goading himself towards Asha. Several clocks on church towers in the distance struck three. The roads of Kolkata were silent, devoid of traffic. At one end of the lane, a singer, invited to a house, had struck up a melody that had also now subsided into silence and slumber. Mahendra felt greatly relieved after meditating on Asha and pouring his heart out in a long letter. He lay his head on the pillow and was immediately claimed by sleep.

When he woke up, it was late in the day and sunlight was streaming into the room. Mahendra sat up with a start. A good night's sleep put the events of the night before in better perspective in his mind. He left the bed and looked at the letter on his desk, written to Asha the previous night. He read it over and thought, 'What have I done! Thank goodness I haven't sent it yet. What would Asha think if she reads this? She wouldn't be able to make sense of this.' Mahendra was embarrassed by the excess of his emotions the previous night; he tore the letter into tiny bits. Then he wrote another letter to Asha in simpler language—'Will you be away for much longer? If Anukulbabu has plans to stay longer, drop me a line; I shall go and fetch you. I don't like it here all alone.'

27

WHEN ASHA ARRIVED IN KASHI SOON AFTER MAHENDRA HAD LEFT, Annapurna was truly concerned. She began to interrogate

Asha, 'Chuni, didn't you tell me that this Chokher Bali of yours is the most talented and competent girl in the whole world?'

'It's true, Aunty, I am not exaggerating. She is as smart as she is pretty and efficient.'

'Well, she's your friend and so you're bound to feel that way about her. But what does everyone else in the house feel about her?'

'Mother is extremely fond of her. If she so much as mentions going back, Mother gets all worked up. There's no one like her when it comes to nursing someone. Even if a maid or a servant is sick, she nurses them like a member of the family.'

'What does Mahendra feel about her?'

'You know him well, Aunty. He doesn't take to anyone unless they are truly near and dear. Everyone is fond of my Chokher Bali; but he doesn't get on too well with her.'

'Why?'

'I worked so hard on getting them to meet. But now they hardly speak a word to each other. You know how reserved your nephew is—people think he's arrogant; but Aunty, except for a handful, he really doesn't like too many people.' The last few words had slipped out inadvertently and suddenly Asha was embarrassed. Her cheeks turned red. Annapurna was relieved and said, 'So that's the reason why Mahin didn't say a word about your Bali when he was here.'

Asha was miffed. 'That's the problem with him. If he doesn't love someone, she doesn't exist for him. He behaves as if he is not aware of their existence.'

Annapurna smiled serenely. 'But when he *does* love

someone, it's as if he has eyes only for her, doesn't he?'

Asha didn't answer. She looked at the ground and smiled. Annapurna asked, 'Chuni, tell me about Behari. Won't he ever get married?'

Asha's face fell in an instant. She didn't know what to say.

Asha's silence worried Annapurna and she asked, 'Tell me honestly, Chuni, is he in good health or is he unwell?'

For this childless woman with a golden heart, Behari had the honoured position of an ideal son. That she had left Kolkata without seeing him settled with a family bothered Annapurna every day in this far-off land. Her meagre demands from life had been fulfilled. The only thought that broke her concentration and stopped her from surrendering herself completely to an ascetic life, was of Behari, unsettled and drifting.

Asha said, 'Aunty, don't ask me anything about Behari-thakurpo.'

Taken aback, Annapurna asked, 'But why?'

Asha said, 'Oh, I cannot tell you that.' She left the room.

Annapurna sat in silence, thinking, 'How could that gem of a boy, Behari, change so much in this short while that the very mention of his name makes Chuni leave the room? It is destiny. If only his wedding hadn't been fixed with Chuni and if only Mahin hadn't snatched her away from him!'

After many months, Annapurna's eyes filled with tears again. She said to herself, 'If my Behari has done anything unworthy of him, he has done it from a lot of pain; he wouldn't do that unless pushed to it.' She imagined his pain, his sorrow and felt misery welling up in her heart.

In the evening, when Annapurna was at her prayers, a carriage came to a stop at the door. The coachman called out to open the door, and thumped on it loudly. Annapurna called out from the puja room, 'Oh dear, it had slipped my mind entirely—Kunja's mother-in-law and her two nieces were supposed to come here from Allahabad today. That must be them now. Chuni, could you please take the lamp and open the door?'

Asha held the lantern up and opened the door. She found Behari standing there. He said, 'Bouthan! But I was told you weren't coming to Kashi!'

Asha dropped the lantern in confusion. She ran upstairs as if she'd seen a ghost, and pleaded with Annapurna, 'Aunty, please tell him to go away.'

Annapurna started as she looked up from her puja, and asked, 'Who is it, Chuni?'

Asha said, 'Behari-thakurpo has come here too.' She rushed to the next room and slammed the door shut.

Behari had heard everything from the bottom of the stairs. He wanted to rush out immediately—but when Annapurna finished her puja and came downstairs, she found him sitting on the doorstep, ashen-faced and very stiff.

Annapurna hadn't brought the light. In the dark she couldn't see Behari's face and neither could he see her.

She called out, 'Behari.'

Alas, gone was that caring, mellow tone of the past. This voice held the thunder of judgement and punishment. Mother Annapurna, on whom were you raising your sword of justice? In this darkness, the unfortunate Behari was here to lay his weary head on your compassionate feet.

Behari started as if he had been whipped. He raised his numb body and said, 'Aunty, no more—don't say another word. I am leaving.'

Behari bent to the ground and bowed to her without touching her feet. Annapurna set him adrift into the dark night, the way unfortunate mothers cast their children into the Ganga; she didn't call him back. The carriage disappeared from sight.

The same night Asha wrote to Mahendra, 'Behari-thakurpo was here all of a sudden this evening. I don't know when my uncle plans to go back home—please come soon and take me away from here.'

28

AFTER STAYING UP HALF THE NIGHT, MAHENDRA WAS GRIPPED BY A strange lassitude the next morning. It was early March and the days were beginning to get warmer. On other days Mahendra sat with his books in a corner of his room. But today he leaned back on the pillows and lay flat on the mattress. The day wore on and he didn't go for his bath. The street-vendors called out as they peddled their wares in the street. The road echoed with sounds of traffic, of the people rushing to office. A neighbour was adding a new floor to his house—the artisans struck up a monotonous tune as they hammered away at their work. The delicate, warm breeze cast a languorous spell on Mahendra's senses. No harsh vows, intricate endeavours, or battles with the mind seemed worthy of this slack, lethargic spring day.

'Thakurpo, what's wrong with you—won't you have your bath? Your meal is ready. Why are you in bed still—are you unwell? Do you have a headache?' Binodini walked up to him and touched his forehead.

Mahendra answered in slurred mumbles, 'I don't feel too well today; I think I'll skip the bath.'

Binodini said, 'All right then, have a bite to eat.' She pleaded with him and dragged him downstairs where she personally attended to his meal with great concern and compassion. After the meal, when Mahendra returned to his mattress and lay down, Binodini sat by his side and pressed his head with gentle fingers. Eyes shut, Mahendra said, 'Bali, you haven't had lunch—why don't you go and eat.'

Binodini refused to go. On that lazy afternoon, the curtains flapped in the warm breeze and sounds of the meaningless fluttering of the coconut palm by the compound wall floated into the room. Mahendra's heart beat faster and faster and Binodini's balmy breath kept pace as it gently stirred the locks that lay across his temple. Not a single word emerged from either of them. Mahendra's thoughts went thus—we float through the endless river of life; how does it matter to anyone if the boat stops here or there? Even if it does matter, how long will it last?

As she sat by him, gently stroking his forehead, Binodini's head bent lower and lower, weighted down by the cumbersome, bemused passions of youth. Eventually, the loose strands of her hair rested on Mahendra's brow. The gentle brush of her hair as they stirred on his brow shook

Mahendra's entire body and his breath caught at his chest, nearly choking him. He sat up with a start and said, 'No-o, I must go to college.' He stood up without looking at Binodini.

Binodini said, 'Relax—I'll get you fresh clothes.' She brought out the clothes he usually wore to college.

Mahendra went off to college in a rush. But he was restless. After many vain attempts at concentrating on his books, he came back home earlier than usual.

He stepped into the room and found Binodini lying on her stomach, upon his mattress, reading a book. Her jet-black hair was strewn over her back. Perhaps she hadn't heard his footsteps. Mahendra tiptoed into the room and stood beside her. He heard her heave a great sigh as she read.

Mahendra said, 'Oh mother of all sad souls, don't squander your heart on fictitious characters. What are you reading?'

Startled, Binodini sat up straight and concealed the book in the folds of her sari. Mahendra tried to seize it by force. After many minutes of this game of catch, Mahendra managed to retrieve the book from a vanquished Binodini's hands—it was Bankim's *The Poison Tree*. Binodini turned away and sulked, even as her breath came faster from the just-lost tussle.

Mahendra's heart was clamouring in his breast. He tried to laugh and said, 'Shame on you, this is a comedown. I had expected something very clandestine and after all this effort I find it's only *The Poison Tree*.'

Binodini said, 'Pray tell me what can be clandestine about me?'

Before Mahendra could stop himself, the words had

slipped out, 'Say for example, if it was a letter from Behari?'

In an instant, lightning flashed through Binodini's eyes. The cupid that was cavorting around in the room was turned to ashes in a second. Binodini stood up, flaring like a flame that had been fanned. Mahendra gripped her hands. 'Forgive me, I spoke in jest.'

Binodini snatched away her hands. 'Whom do you mock? If you were worthy of his friendship I would have endured your mockery of him. You have a small mind; you are not strong enough to be a friend and you talk of jest.'

As she was about to leave, Mahendra reached out with both hands and grabbed her feet. At the same instant a shadow fell across the doorway. Mahendra let go of Binodini's feet and looked up—it was Behari.

It was as if Behari's steady, withering gaze burned up the two of them in turn. When he spoke, his voice was neutral and toneless, 'I'm afraid I have come at an inconvenient moment, but I shan't stay for long. I came to say one thing— I had gone to Kashi. I didn't know Bouthan was there. With no intent to do so, I have wronged her; there was no time to beg her pardon. So I have come to say sorry to you instead. I have one request to you—if I have ever sinned, even in thought, consciously or unconsciously, let that not result in any suffering for her.'

Mahendra felt helplessly angry because Behari had witnessed his moment of weakness. This wasn't the time for generosity. With a little laugh he said, 'You are like the proverbial man with the guilty conscience. I haven't asked you to beg pardon; why have you come to say sorry and act the martyr?'

Behari stood there like a wooden puppet for a few moments. When his lips trembled in an effort to speak, Binodini said, 'Behari-thakurpo, don't bother to answer him. Don't say a word. What this man has just said, taints only him—it doesn't touch you in any way.'

It wasn't clear if Binodini's words fell on Behari's ears— he turned away like one in a trance and walked out of Mahendra's room. Binodini ran after him and said, 'Behari-thakurpo, do you have nothing to say to me? If you want to reprimand me, please do so.'

Behari continued to walk away without saying a word. Binodini barred his way and gripped his right hand. Behari pushed her away with palpable revulsion. He didn't even notice that Binodini had lost her balance and fallen.

At the sound of Binodini's fall Mahendra came running. He found Binodini's left elbow had a bruise that was bleeding. He said, 'Oh no, that looks bad.' In an instant he ripped off a strip of his thin shirt and made as if to tie a bandage around the wound. Binodini drew away her arm and said, 'No, please don't. Let the blood flow.'

Mahendra said, 'Let me tie it up and I'll give you medication—that'll take away the pain and heal the wound quickly.'

Binodini moved aside. 'I don't want the pain to go—let this wound stay.'

Mahendra said, 'I lost my patience today and insulted you. Can you bring yourself to forgive me?'

Binodini said, 'Forgive you for what? You did nothing wrong; I am not afraid of people. I don't care about anyone. After all, what are they to me if they can hurt me and walk away? Instead, those who touch my feet and draw me towards them, should mean more to me.'

Ecstatic, Mahendra spoke fervently, 'Binodini, you will not reject my love then?'

Binodini said, 'I shall hold it to my heart. Since the day I was born, I have never experienced such an abundance of love that I can ever reject it.'

Mahendra held her hands in his and said, 'In that case, come to my room. I have wounded you today and you have returned the hurt. As long as that is not wiped away, I shall have no peace.'

Binodini said, 'Not today—let me go now. If I have hurt you, please forgive me.'

Mahendra said, 'And you will pardon me as well, or I shall not sleep a wink tonight.'

Binodini said, 'I forgive you.'

Mahendra impetuously wanted to receive a distinct sign of Binodini's forgiveness, right then and there. But he took a look at Binodini's face and stopped short. She ran down the stairs. Mahendra climbed the stairs back to the terrace and began to stroll there. He felt a sense of release in the fact that his feelings were exposed to Behari. The ignominy of smokescreens and camouflages was dispelled by this revelation to one person alone. Mahendra thought, 'No more grand delusions about myself—I am in love, I love and that is not a lie.' The new-found admittance of love made him conceited enough to feel proud of his own fall from grace. He cast a glance of scornful disdain at the entire universe, bedecked with the silent stellar constellations in the tranquil evening light, and said, 'The world may call me whatever they wish, but *I am in love.*' And he covered the whole world, the endless sky and all sense of duty with an image of Binodini that his mind conjured up. Behari's sudden arrival had acted as a force that upset the ink-bottle, uncorked it and spilled its contents all over—by and by, Binodini's black eyes and inky black hair fanned out and mussed up all the white sheets, and all that was ever written before.

29

THE NEXT MORNING, AS SOON AS HE OPENED HIS EYES, MAHENDRA'S heart was flooded with a sweet sensation. The morning sun spread a veneer of gold on all his thoughts and desires. What a lovely world, what a beautiful sky—the breeze seemed to lift his soul like pollen dust and set it adrift.

The Vaishnav mendicants played their one-string lute and sang on the street below. The watchman was about to shoo them off when Mahendra stopped him and found himself giving them one whole rupee. The bearer dropped the kerosene lamp as he was putting it away right in front of Mahendra. But the master smiled pleasantly and said, 'Hey you, see that you sweep it clean—bits of glass can pierce someone's feet.' Today, nothing angered him, no harm seemed too great.

Romance had been hidden behind a veil all these days. Today, the veil had been ripped away. It was as if a cover had been lifted off the face of a brave new world. Every banal detail of daily life had disappeared. The trees, birds, people on the streets, sounds of the city—they all seemed to look and sound new today. Where had this novelty been all this time?

Mahendra decided that today he would not meet Binodini in the usual way. It was a day fit for poetry and music. He wanted to turn this day into something out of the *Arabian Nights*, full of sumptuousness and beauty, unconnected to life and the mundane. It would be real and yet a dream, it would be devoid of material realism, duties, rules and norms of everyday living.

Mahendra was restless that morning; he couldn't go to college. There was no telling when the auspicious moment would arrive for that fateful union. All through the day Binodini's voice floated to his ears, sometimes from the kitchen, sometimes from the store room; she was busy with her household chores. He didn't like that—on this day he would have liked Binodini to be far beyond the reach of household duties.

Time hung heavy on Mahendra's hands. He had his bath and ate his meal. Finally, all household chores ground to a halt as the silence of the afternoon extended itself around him. But there was still no sign of Binodini. Mahendra was high-strung with sorrow and anticipated pleasure, impatience and hope.

The Poison Tree, rescued from the scuffle of the previous afternoon, lay on the mattress. Mahendra's eyes fell upon it and he felt a thrill coursing through his body as he remembered the tussle. He pulled out the pillow on which Binodini had lain, and laid his head upon it; he picked up the book and began to turn the pages. Mahendra wasn't aware when he lost himself in the book and the clock struck five.

Binodini entered the room with fruits and sweets on a plate and a bowl of iced melons with powdered sugar sprinkled on it. She placed it before Mahendra and said, 'What's wrong with you Thakurpo, it's past five o'clock and you still haven't freshened up or changed?'

Mahendra got a harsh jolt. Did she have to ask what was wrong with him? She should have known the answer to that. Was this day like every other day? Mahendra didn't dare to make any demands by harking back to the day before, for fear that he'd have to face something contrary to his expectations.

He sat down to eat. Binodini went to the terrace, gathered the clothes that were drying on the line and brought them in. She began to fold them deftly and arranged them in Mahendra's cupboard.

Mahendra said, 'Wait a minute. Let me finish eating and I'll lend you a hand.'

Binodini folded her hands and said, 'Oh pray do not try to help me, whatever else you may do.'

Mahendra finished eating as he said, 'Really! So you think I am hopeless with household chores? All right, let this be a test of my abilities.' He tried to fold the clothes, in vain.

Binodini snatched them from his hands and said, 'My dear sir, do let go. You will only pile up more work for me.'

Mahendra said, 'In that case, you carry on with your work while I watch and learn.' He sat down in front of the cupboard, beside Binodini. She began to air out the clothes on his back with a swish, before she folded them and put them on the shelf.

Thus began the first meeting of the day, without a hint of

the exclusivity that Mahendra had visualized and fantasized about all day long. Such a meeting did not befit poetry, music or even prose. But it did not upset Mahendra. In fact he felt a little relieved. He hadn't been able to decide how he would go about actualizing his fantasy, what to say, what to do and how to keep all predictability at a distance. The fun and jest that was native to this airing of clothes and folding them away, set him free of a self-induced, impossible ideal—and he breathed easier.

At this point Rajlakshmi walked into the room. She said to Mahendra, 'Mahin, Binodini is folding the clothes—but what are *you* doing there on the floor?'

Binodini said, 'You tell him, Aunty! He is teasing me and getting in my way.'

Mahendra said, 'Is that so! And here I thought I was lending you a hand.'

Rajlakshmi said, 'Rubbish! You and lend her a hand! Binodini, Mahin has always been that way. Always pampered by his mother and aunt, he has never learnt to do a thing for himself.' So saying, the mother cast a loving look upon her inept son. She felt all she had in common with Binodini was the concern that this adult, incompetent mother's boy should have all possible comfort. On the issue of tending to her son, being able to lean on Binodini gave Rajlakshmi great relief, great pleasure. She was also pleased by the fact that lately Mahendra seemed to understand Binodini's worth and worked towards making her feel at home. She made sure Mahendra was listening as she said, 'Binodini, today you've aired out Mahin's warm clothes. Tomorrow you must embroider his initials on his handkerchiefs. Ever since I brought you with me, I haven't been able to pamper you, child; I've only worked you harder and harder.'

Binodini said, 'Aunty, if you talk that way, I will feel that you are creating a distance between us.'

Indulgently Rajlakshmi said, 'Oh dear, who is dearer to me than you, my child?'

When Binodini had finished putting the clothes away, Rajlakshmi asked, 'Shall we start making the sugar syrup now or do you have other things to do?'

Binodini said, 'Oh no, I've finished everything. Let's go and make the sweets now.'

Mahendra said, 'Mother, you were just saying how hard you work her and again you are dragging her off to the kitchen?'

Rajlakshmi pinched Binodini's chin affectionately and said, 'This good little girl of mine loves to work.'

Mahendra said, 'I have nothing to do this evening. I'd planned to read a book with Chokher Bali.'

Binodini said, 'That's fine, Aunty. Let's both of us come and hear Thakurpo read?'

Rajlakshmi said to herself, 'My poor Mahin is feeling really lonely and we must all do our best to entertain him.' So she said, 'Why not! We shall come back later and hear him read, after we've finished cooking Mahin's meal. How about that, Mahin?'

Binodini threw an oblique glance at Mahendra's face. He said, 'Fine.' But his enthusiasm waned. Binodini left the room along with Rajlakshmi.

Mahendra muttered in frustration, 'I shall go out this evening and come back late.' He changed his clothes at once.

But having done that, he didn't execute his plan. He paced about on the terrace for many minutes, glanced towards the stairway a million times and finally came and sat in the room. He thought, 'I shall refuse to touch the sweets today and convey the message to Mother that if you boil the sugar syrup for too long, it loses its sweetness.'

At dinner time Binodini brought Rajlakshmi along. The latter was afraid to climb stairs these days, due to her asthma. Binodini's requests brought her upstairs today. Mahendra sat down to his meal with a very glum look.

Binodini said, 'Thakurpo, why are you pecking at your food today?'

Rajlakshmi was immediately concerned, 'Are you not well, my child?'

Binodini said, 'We worked so hard on the sweets, you must have some of it. Hasn't it turned out well? Oh, then leave it. No, no, don't eat it just because we asked you to— that means nothing. Leave it then.'

Mahendra said, 'Will you stop that! I liked the sweets the best and that's what I want to have—why should I listen to you?'

Mahendra finished the two sweets in their entirety; not a scrap, not a crumb was left on the plate. After the meal the three of them came into his room and sat down. Mahendra did not bring up the topic of reading. Rajlakshmi said, 'Didn't you say something about reading something?'

Mahendra said, 'Oh, but what I have doesn't have anything about gods or goddesses in it. You wouldn't like it.'

Not like it! Rajlakshmi was determined to like it, come hell or high water. Even if Mahendra read something in

Turkish, she would have to like it! Poor, dear Mahin—with his wife away in Kashi, he was so lonely; Mother must, absolutely *must* like whatever he liked.

Binodini said, 'Thakurpo, why don't you put your books aside and read some of the holy books that are there in Aunty's room? She would also like that and the evening would pass nicely.'

Mahendra threw a dismal look at Binodini. At this point the maid came with the news that the neighbour's wife had come visiting. This was a close friend of Rajlakshmi's and the latter loved talking to her in the evenings. Yet she said to the maid, 'Tell her I am busy in Mahin's room today and she should come back tomorrow.'

Mahendra spoke hastily, 'But why Mother, certainly you can go and meet her now?'

Binodini said, 'Oh no, Aunty, why don't you stay here and I'll go and talk to her.'

Rajlakshmi gave in to the temptation and said, 'No, you stay here—let me see if I can go and get rid of her. The two of you start reading, don't wait for me.'

The moment Rajlakshmi was out of the room, Mahendra burst out, 'Why do you torture me like this?'

Binodini seemingly didn't know what he was talking about. 'What! When did I torture you? Was I wrong to come into your room then? Fair enough, let me leave.' She made as if to get up with a crestfallen expression.

' Mahendra grabbed her wrist and said, 'This is precisely how you torment me.'

Binodini said, 'Really! I didn't know I had so much power. You are not too bad yourself; obviously you can take a lot. You don't look like you've been burnt at the stake.'

Mahendra said, 'Looks cannot tell you the whole story.' He grabbed her hand forcefully and pressed it to his heart.

Binodini screeched in pain and immediately he let go, saying, 'Did I hurt you?'

He saw that Binodini's wound from the previous day was bleeding once again. In abject apology he said, 'I was careless—how remiss of me. But now you must let me tie it and apply some ointment—please don't stop me today.'

Binodini said, 'No, it's nothing. I shall not put medication on it.'

Mahendra said, 'Why not?'

Binodini said, 'What do you mean "why not"! Don't put on your medical airs with me; let it be.'

Mahendra grew solemn and thought, 'Beyond me entirely—a woman's mind!'

Binodini rose to leave. Piqued, Mahendra didn't stop her this time. He merely asked, 'Where are you going?'

Binodini said, 'I have work to do.' She walked out slowly.

A few seconds later Mahendra got up, meaning to go and call her back. But he turned back from the stairway and began to walk about on the terrace instead.

Binodini drew him to her continuously, and yet she never let him get really close to her. Mahendra had recently surrendered the conceit that no one could have complete power over him. But would he also have to give up the conceit that he could have complete power over anyone if he so desired? Today he had to concede defeat as he failed to overpower Binodini. In matters of the heart Mahendra held

his head very high indeed. He didn't consider anyone his
equal. But today he had to lose that pride as well. And he
didn't gain anything in return. Like a beggar he stood empty-
handed at dusk, in front of a closed door.

In the months of March and April, Behari's farmlands yielded
honey from the mustard flowers. Every year he sent some to
Rajlakshmi and this year was no different.

Binodini took the pot of honey to Rajlakshmi and said,
'Aunty, Behari-thakurpo has sent honey.'

Rajlakshmi asked her to put it away in the store room.
Binodini did as she was told and then came and sat beside
Rajlakshmi. She said, 'Behari-thakurpo never fails to do his bit
for you. I suppose because he doesn't have a mother, he sees
her in you, doesn't he?'

Rajlakshmi was so used to seeing Behari as Mahendra's
shadow that she never gave him much thought. He was an
unpaid, uncared for, unthought of, loyal friend to the family.
When Binodini mentioned Behari as a motherless boy and
sited Rajlakshmi as his guardian, a tender, maternal spot was
touched in the latter's heart. Suddenly Rajlakshmi thought,
'That's true. Behari is motherless and he sees me as his
mother.' She recalled how Behari had always looked after her
in sickness and in health, without being sent for and without
any pretentiousness; Rajlakshmi had taken it all for granted,
just like the air she breathed. She had never considered being
grateful for it. But did anyone ever reciprocate any concern
for Behari? When Annapurna was around, she had looked
after him. Rajlakshmi had thought that she put on a great
show of affection to keep Behari tied to her apron-strings.

Today Rajlakshmi heaved a great sigh and said, 'True, Behari is just like a son to me.'

As she said it, she realized that Behari did more for her than her own son; he was devoted to her even without the promise of any returns. This thought provoked another sigh from the depths of her heart.

Binodini said, 'Behari-thakurpo really loves to eat food cooked by you!'

Rajlakshmi was full of maternal pride as she said, 'He doesn't like fish curry made by anyone else.' As she said it, she realized that Behari hadn't come around for many days. She asked, 'Why doesn't Behari come around these days?'

Binodini said, 'I was wondering about that myself. But then your son has been so busy with his wife ever since he got married—why would friends come round any more?'

Rajlakshmi felt the criticism was justified. For the sake of his wife, Mahendra had distanced all his near and dear ones. Behari was right in feeling hurt—why should he visit them? Rajlakshmi felt sympathy welling up for Behari once she saw him as neglected by Mahendra as she was. She began to narrate to Binodini, in great detail, how much Behari had done for Mahendra since their childhood days, how much he had sacrificed. Through this narration she rationalized all her own grievances against her son. Mahendra had done a grave injustice by alienating his childhood friend for the sake of a new wife!

Binodini said, 'Tomorrow, Sunday, why don't you send for Behari-thakurpo and cook for him? He'd be delighted.'

Rajlakshmi said, 'You are right. Let me send for Mahin and he can go and invite Behari.'

Binodini said, 'Oh no, Aunty, you invite him personally.'

Rajlakshmi said, 'I don't know to read and write, like all you youngsters.'

Binodini said, 'That's nothing—I can write the letter on your behalf.'

Binodini wrote out an invitation on behalf of Rajlakshmi and sent it off.

Sunday was eagerly anticipated by Mahendra. His fantasies went wild from the night before, although till that point nothing had really gone according to his fantasies. Yet, the morning sun seemed to pour honey on his eyes as Sunday dawned. The sounds of the city awakening were like a melodious tune to his ears.

But what was this—did his mother have a religious vow today or something? She wasn't resting like other days, leaving the household chores to Binodini. Today she was busy cooking in the kitchen.

Amidst all the hustle and bustle it was ten o'clock soon. In all that time Mahendra couldn't snatch a moment alone with Binodini. He tried to read but couldn't concentrate. His eyes were glued to an inconsequential advertisement in the newspaper for fifteen whole minutes. Finally he could take it no longer. He went downstairs and found his mother busy cooking in a corner of the veranda near her room. Binodini had her sari tucked firmly into her waist as she went about assisting Rajlakshmi.

Mahendra asked, 'So what are you two doing today? Why all these elaborate arrangements?'

Rajlakshmi said, 'Hasn't Binodini told you? I have invited Behari to lunch today.'

Behari invited to lunch! Mahendra felt vicious anger rise up to his throat. Immediately he said, 'But Mother, I shall not be here.'

Rajlakshmi asked, 'Why?'

Mahendra said briefly, 'I must go out.'

Rajlakshmi said, 'Go out after lunch—it won't take long.'

Mahendra said, 'But I have an invitation for lunch.'

Binodini threw a quick, veiled look at Mahendra's face and said, 'Aunty, if he does have an invitation, let him go. Let Behari-thakurpo have lunch alone today.'

But how could Rajlakshmi bear it if Mahin did not eat all that she was cooking with such great care? But the more she pleaded, the harsher was Mahendra's refusal: 'Very important lunch invitation, simply cannot refuse, you should have asked me before inviting Behari,' etc. etc.

This was Mahendra's way of punishing his mother. It had its effect. Rajlakshmi lost all interest in cooking. She felt like dropping everything and walking away. Binodini said, 'Aunty, don't you worry—Thakurpo may say all this; but he is going nowhere today.'

Rajlakshmi shook her head. 'No my child, you don't know my Mahin. Once his mind is made up, nothing can stop him.'

But apparently Binodini knew Mahendra no less than Rajlakshmi. Mahendra realized that Binodini was instrumental in this invitation to Behari. The more he burnt in envy at this revelation, the harder it grew for him to walk away. How could he go without seeing what Behari and Binodini were up to? It would be torture, but he *had* to see it.

After many days, Behari came into the inner chambers today as an invited guest. For an instant he stopped short at the doorway of the room where he had been a regular since his youth, where he had got up to all kinds of mischief as a child. A wave of emotion swelled in his heart, threatening to rise and crash with all its might. He suppressed it and walked in with a smile. Rajlakshmi had just finished her bath when Behari came in and touched her feet. When Behari used to come in almost daily, such a manner of greeting wasn't customary between them. Today it felt as though he was home after a long trip abroad. Rajlakshmi blessed him lovingly.

Rajlakshmi was full of affection and concern for Behari, out of a sense of heartfelt empathy. She said, 'O Behari, where were you all these days? Every day I felt sure you would come, but there was no sign of you.'

Behari laughed. 'If I came here every day, would you have spared me another thought, Mother? Where is Mahin da?'

Rajlakshmi replied glumly, 'Mahin had a lunch invitation; he couldn't stay here today.'

Behari's face fell. So this was the consequence of a lifelong friendship? Behari heaved a sigh, strove to drive away the dejection for the moment and asked, 'What's for lunch today?' He asked after his favourite dishes. Whenever Rajlakshmi cooked, Behari showed himself to be a little more eager and hungry. That was his way of stealing the love from the maternal Rajlakshmi's heart. On this day too, Rajlakshmi enjoyed Behari's eager craving for her food and reassured him with a laugh.

Suddenly, Mahendra arrived and greeted Behari in the most polite tones, 'Hello there, how are you, Behari?'

Rajlakshmi said, 'Mahin, didn't you go to your lunch invitation?'

Mahendra tried to mask his embarrassment as he said, 'Oh no, I was able to cancel it.'

When Binodini walked in, bathed and changed, Behari was lost for words at first. The scene he had witnessed between Mahendra and Binodini was still engraved on his mind. He couldn't bring himself to greet her.

Binodini stood quite close to Behari and spoke in low tones, 'Thakurpo, don't you know me at all?'

Behari replied, 'It's hard to really know someone.'

Binodini said, 'Not if you have good judgement.' She turned to Rajlakshmi, 'Aunty, lunch is ready.'

Behari and Mahendra sat down to eat; Rajlakshmi sat close by and tended to them while Binodini served the food.

Mahendra wasn't interested in the food. He noticed the special favours in the serving more keenly. He began to feel that Binodini was deriving a special kind of satisfaction while serving food to Behari. The fact that Behari got the largest piece of fish and the bigger portion of curds could easily be rationalized thus—Mahendra was family and Behari was the guest. But Mahendra burned with agonized spite simply because there was no cause to vocalize his complaint. A certain variety of delicious fish had been fetched specially from the market—it was unusual for this time of the year. One was stuffed full of roe and Binodini tried to serve it to Behari. He protested, 'No, no, give that to Mahin da; he loves it.'

Full of righteous indignation, Mahendra said, 'Oh no, I don't want it.'

Binodini didn't ask him a second time; she merely dropped it onto Behari's plate.

At the end of the meal the two friends came outside; Binodini came up to them and said, 'Behari-thakurpo, don't go home just yet. Let's go upstairs and sit and talk.'

Behari asked, 'Won't you have lunch?'

Binodini said, 'No, it's ekadasi, the three-quarter moon— the day we widows fast.'

A smile of cruel mockery touched Behari's lips; so even the fast must be kept! All rituals were adhered to!

That faint smile did not escape Binodini's notice. But she bore it the same way she had borne the gash on her arm. She pleaded, 'Please come and sit down for a while.'

Suddenly, Mahendra lost his temper and spoke out of turn, 'What's wrong with you all—drop everything you were doing, whether you like it or not, please come and sit for a while! I don't get the meaning of such excessive fondness.'

Binodini laughed out loud, 'Behari-thakurpo, just listen to your Mahin da talk. Fondness means just that, affection. The dictionary doesn't give another meaning.' She turned to Mahendra, 'I must say, Thakurpo, going by your childhood days there is no one who understands the meaning of excessive fondness better than you.'

Behari said, 'Mahin da, I have something to say. Could I talk to you alone for a moment?' Behari walked out with Mahendra without a backward glance at Binodini. She stood on the veranda, clinging to the railings, and stared into the void of the empty courtyard.

Behari came outside and said, 'Mahin da, I want to know—is this where our friendship ends?'

Mahendra was burning up with envy; Binodini's mocking repartee was splitting his head from end to end, like a searing bolt of lightning. He said, 'I suppose if we patch up, it will be to your benefit. But I do not see anything in it for me. I do not wish to admit strangers into my life, and I'd like to keep the inner chambers secluded from the world at large.'

Behari walked away without another word.

Green with envy, Mahendra vowed never to see Binodini again. Soon afterwards he restlessly paced the stairway and every room of the house in the hope of meeting her by chance.

30

ONE DAY ASHA ASKED ANNAPURNA, 'AUNTY, DO YOU EVER THINK OF Uncle?'

Annapurna said, 'I was widowed at the age of eleven. My husband is like a shadowy memory to me.'

Asha asked, 'Aunty, who do you think of then?'

Annapurna smiled. 'I think of Him who is now the keeper of my husband—of God.'

Asha asked, 'Does that bring you joy?'

Annapurna stroked her head lovingly and said, 'Child, what would you know of the matters of my mind? It is known only to me and to Him on whom my heart is fixed.'

Asha mulled over this as she thought, 'Does he know my heart—the one I think of day and night? Just because I cannot write well, why has he given up writing to me?'

It was a while since Asha had got a letter from Mahendra. She sighed and thought, 'If only Chokher Bali were with me, she'd have been able to pen down my thoughts faithfully.'

Asha couldn't ever bring herself to write to her husband for fear that her badly written prose would not be appreciated by him. The harder she tried, the more her scrawls went awry. The more she tried to express herself concisely, the further her thoughts scattered themselves. If only she could write the first 'Dearest' and then sign her name, such that an omniscient Mahendra would read between the lines all that she meant to write, Asha would have completed her letters with great success. Fate had gifted her with a great capacity to love, but with little verbal skills.

That evening Asha came back from the temple after the aarti, sat down at Annapurna's feet and began to stroke them gently. After many minutes of silence she said, 'Aunty, you always say that a husband should be worshipped and served like a god. But what can a wife do, if she is stupid, slow-witted and doesn't know how to serve him?'

Annapurna gazed at Asha's face for a few seconds and a covert sigh excaped her as she said, 'Child, I too am stupid, and yet I serve my God.'

Asha said, 'But He knows your heart and so He is pleased. But what if the husband is not satisfied with the dumb woman's devotion?'

Annapurna said, 'Not everyone has the capacity to satisfy everyone, my child. If the wife serves her husband and his family with the utmost devotion and genuine dedication, then even if the husband throws her service away as worthless, the Lord of the Universe will pick it up and treasure it.'

Asha sat in wordless silence. She tried very hard to take heart from these words spoken by her aunt. But she simply couldn't accept that a woman discarded by her husband can derive any solace even from the Lord of the Universe Himself. She sat with her head bent and continued to stroke her aunt's feet.

Annapurna held her hand and drew her closer. She kissed the top of her head. With great effort she cleared her choked voice and said, 'Chuni, the trials and tribulations of life are a great teacher—mere advice can't take their place. At your age, I had struck a give-and-take relationship with life. Just like you, I too thought that I should get recognition from whoever I served. But at every step I found that my expectation wasn't realistic. Eventually one day, I could take it no longer. I felt all that I had done had been in vain. The same day I left home. But today I find nothing has been in vain. My child, He who is the chief of this business called life, with Whom we have a constant give-and-take relationship, has been taking everything I have ever given. Today He rests in my heart and admits my worth. If only I knew it then! If I worked through life seeing it as work done for Him, if I poured my heart into life as if I was pouring it into Him, who would ever have had the capacity to hurt me?'

Asha lay in bed thinking hard, going back to Annapurna's words, although she couldn't make proper sense of them all. But she had immense respect for her pious aunt and in spite of not understanding all that she had said Asha gave credence to most of it. She sat up in bed, folded her hands and sent up a prayer in the direction of that God to whom her aunt had given her heart. She said, 'I am a child, I do not know You.

All I know is my husband; please don't blame me for that. Dear God, please tell my husband to accept the devotion that I place at his feet. If he chooses to reject it, I shall surely die. I am not as devout as my aunt; shelter at your feet alone cannot be my salvation.' Asha bowed again and again and prayed fervently before she got into bed.

It was time for Anukulbabu to go back home. The evening before Asha left, Annapurna sat her down by her side and said, 'Chuni, my child, I do not have the power to protect you from the sorrows, travails and hardships of life at all times. This is my advice to you: however anyone may hurt you, keep your faith, your piety intact; may your integrity always be uncompromised.'

Asha touched her feet and said, 'Bless me, Aunty, so that I can do that.'

31

ASHA RETURNED HOME. BINODINI REPROACHED HER PETULANTLY, 'Bali, you didn't write me a single letter in all these days!'

Asha said, 'As if you showered *me* with letters!'

Binodini said, 'Why should I write? You were supposed to write first.'

Asha hugged her and conceded defeat. She said, 'You know I cannot express myself too well. Especially writing to a learned person like you really makes me shy.'

Gradually, the two friends put aside their mutual

complaints and went back to their affectionate selves.

Binodini said, 'You have truly spoilt your husband by keeping him company day and night. He must have someone by his side at all times!'

Asha said, 'The precise reason why I left him in your care! You are better at keeping him company.'

Binodini said, 'In the day I'd be spared by sending him off to college; but the evenings were harder to escape—chat with him, read to him, endless demands!'

Asha said, 'Serves you right! Why would people spare you when you can entertain them so well?'

Binodini said, 'Watch out, my friend. The way Thakurpo behaves at times, I wonder if I have mesmeric powers!'

Asha laughed, 'You'd have to be the one! If only I had even an ounce of your charm.'

Binodini said, 'Why, who do you wish to ruin? Work on guarding the one you have—don't go after strangers; it's not worth the bother.'

Asha chided her with a push and said, 'Oh dear, what nonsense!'

The moment Mahendra met Asha for the first time after her return from Kashi, he said, 'I can see you've put on weight—the trip seems to have done you good.'

Asha felt mortified. She should not have looked so healthy—but nothing ever went right for poor Asha. Even while she was so miserable, her silly body had put on weight. On the one hand she didn't have the words to express herself, and on the other her body played truant.

Asha murmured, 'How have you been?'

In the past, Mahendra would have said, with mock

sorrow and some genuine emotion, 'I was only half alive.' But now he couldn't be playful; the words stuck at his throat. He said, 'I've been fine, not bad at all.'

Asha gazed at him and found he had lost weight—his face had a pallor and a bright flame burned in his eyes. A deep-seated hunger seemed to be licking away at his insides. Asha felt upset. 'My poor husband hasn't been well at all. Why did I leave him and go to Kashi?' She was outraged indeed, at her own health, at the fact that her husband had lost weight while she put it on.

Mahendra wondered what he should talk about next and slowly stumbled out with, 'I suppose Aunty is keeping well?'

He was reassured to that effect and thereafter he was lost for things to say. A tattered, old newspaper lay close by. He pulled it close and glanced through it absentmindedly. Asha stood there looking down as she thought, 'We meet after so long and he's not talking to me properly; he hasn't even looked at my face. Is he angry because I didn't write to him the last few days, or is he upset that I stayed back longer in Kashi at Aunty's request?' Desolate and miserable, Asha pondered over the possible sources of her own culpability.

Mahendra went to college and returned later in the day. While he had his snacks, Rajlakshmi waited on him and Asha stood at a distance with her anchal drawn over her head. But no one else was present.

Rajlakshmi asked with a concerned frown, 'Are you unwell today, Mahin?'

The question annoyed Mahendra. 'No Mother, why should I be unwell?'

Rajlakshmi said, 'But you have hardly eaten anything.'

Mahendra snapped back, 'I *am* eating, am I not?'

It was a summer evening. Mahendra wrapped himself in a light shawl and began to pace the terrace. He had great hopes that the regular reading session (with Binodini) would take place as usual. They were nearly through with Bankim's *Anandamath*, with just a couple of chapters to go. Binodini may be heartless, but she would surely come and read those out to him today! But the evening wore on, the hands of the clock moved on and Mahendra had to go to bed with a heavy heart.

Asha came into the bedroom, bashful and dressed up. She found Mahendra lying in bed. She didn't know what to do next. A long separation brought with it some coyness—both parties expected a fresh greeting from each other before they could become intimate with each other like before. How could Asha re-enter her old, familiar, pleasure-seat without being asked? She waited at the door for a few long minutes, but Mahendra did not say anything. She stepped into the room, one step at a time. If a bangle or an anklet made a sudden sound, she nearly died of shame. With heart aflutter she went up to the bed and realized that Mahendra was asleep. In that instant, all her finery seemed to strangle her and mock her cruelly. She wanted to hurl everything from her body and rush from the room, go anywhere else.

Asha got into bed as stealthily as possible. Yet, there were enough sounds and movement so as to wake Mahendra if he had truly been asleep. But tonight his eyes stayed shut because Mahendra wasn't asleep. He lay at one end of the bed and so Asha lay still beside him. It was clear to Mahendra, even with his back to her, that Asha was weeping silent tears in the dark. His own cruelty to her was tormenting him. But he simply did not know what to say, how to hold her or love her. He hurled abuses at himself and lacerated himself mentally—it hurt badly, but didn't resolve anything. He thought, 'In the morning I won't be able to pretend I'm asleep—what shall I say to Asha then?'

But Asha took care of his concern. At the crack of dawn she left the bed in her affronted finery; she couldn't face him either.

32

ASHA WONDERED, 'WHY DID THIS HAPPEN? WHAT HAVE I DONE wrong?' But she never considered the obvious. The very idea that Mahendra was in love with Binodini never crossed her mind. Asha was very naïve in worldly matters. Besides, she could never imagine that Mahendra could be anything other than the person she had known forever, ever since their marriage.

Mahendra left for college earlier than usual. As he left, Asha always came and stood at the window. Mahendra would glance up just once before he got into the carriage. This had been a routine with them for the longest time. Thus habituated, Asha drifted to the window mechanically the minute she heard the sounds of the carriage drawing up. Possibly by habit, Mahendra too shot a glance at the window. He found Asha standing there—she hadn't yet bathed, or changed her clothes; her face was pallid. Instantly Mahendra lowered his gaze and looked down at the books on his lap. Alas for that silent greeting as their eyes met, or that meaningful smile!

The carriage went its way; Asha dropped to the floor. The whole world turned to dust before her eyes. In the streets of Kolkata it was business as usual—carriages headed for offices, trams were chasing other trams—this lone, solitary, pained heart in a distant corner of the city was a misfit amidst the hustle and bustle of life.

Suddenly Asha saw the light. 'I know—he has heard that Thakurpo went to Kashi and he is upset about that. Nothing else has happened in the meantime that could cause him any displeasure. But—why blame me for that?'

As she mulled over this for a few seconds, Asha's heart skipped a beat. Suddenly she was gripped by the fear that Mahendra was under the misconception that Asha and Behari had colluded in his sudden arrival in Kashi. A conspiracy. Oh, shame! Such mistrust! It was bad enough that her name was linked to Behari, causing her such trauma; if Mahendra doubted her in this manner now, she'd surely die. But if there was really such a misgiving, if Mahendra felt she'd really gone wrong, why didn't he confront her with it? He should judge her and punish her to his satisfaction. She felt he was avoiding her without tackling the issue head-on. Asha was convinced that Mahendra was suffering from some misconception that he knew was intrinsically false and he was ashamed to admit it even to Asha. Why else would he walk around looking so guilty? The censorious husband would hardly look like this!

All day long Mahendra was haunted by that melancholy expression on Asha's face that he had glimpsed in an instant in the morning. Through the lectures in college, amidst the hordes of students, he could only see Asha, wan and dishevelled, her clothes in disarray, her eyes pained and aggrieved.

After college he went for a stroll around the circular lake. As he strolled, dusk drew close; he couldn't decide what he should do about Asha—sympathetic duplicity or harsh honesty—which did she deserve? Not once did he even consider letting Binodini go. He only wondered how he could honour both his loves at the same time.

Mahendra consoled himself with the thought that the love he still felt for Asha was rare in most women's lives. Asha should be grateful for that love and generosity. Mahendra's heart was large enough to carry both Asha and Binodini in it. His nuptial relationship wouldn't be affected in the least by the platonic, noble romance he had with Binodini.

Having thus convinced himself, Mahendra felt a weight lifting from his shoulders. He grew cheerful at the thought of spending his entire life like a planet with two moons, with both Binodini and Asha being where they belonged in his life. He decided to go to bed early that night and to caress and stroke away all the doubts that Asha was facing. Reassured by his own decision, he walked home hurriedly.

Asha was absent when he had his dinner. But he went to bed thinking that she'd have to come to the bedroom at some point. But in the silent room, in that empty bed, which were the reminiscences that flooded his heart? Were they the ones of the first days of his romance with Asha? No. All those memories had faded away from his mind the way moonshine melts before sunlight. A razor-sharp, accomplished young woman outshone the image of the naïve child-woman cloaked in shyness. Mahendra recollected his scuffle with Binodini over *The Poison Tree*. In the evenings, as Binodini had read out Bankim's *Kapalakundala* to him, the night crept up and the household fell asleep. In that solitary room, in that still silence, Binodini's voice grew softer and nearly disappeared as she read on. Suddenly, she came back to her senses, dropped the book and stood up to leave. Mahendra said, 'Let me come with you till the bottom of the stairs.' Mahendra reminisced about those evenings and felt thrilled anew. The night wore on and Mahendra began to dread Asha's arrival. But Asha did not come. Mahendra thought, 'I was ready to do my duty, but if Asha takes exception without reason and refuses to come here, what can I do?' And he gave himself up to more pleasurable meditations on Binodini and brought back even more of her.

When the clock struck one, Mahendra could hold still no longer. He went out to the terrace and found the mellow moonlight flooding the night. The mammoth silence of Kolkata felt as tangible as the waves in a speechless ocean—the breeze ambled casually amidst the row of edifices, shrouding them in thick layers of sleep.

Mahendra could not contain his craving: ever since Asha returned from Kashi, Binodini hadn't met him. The lonely night enchanted by moonlight propelled him relentlessly towards Binodini. Mahendra went down the stairs. He stood before Binodini's door and realized that it wasn't locked yet. He stepped into the room and saw that the bed was made, but there was no one in it yet. At the sound of footsteps, Binodini called out from the balcony to the south, 'Who's there?'

Mahendra replied in a voice drenched in emotion, 'Binod, it's me.' He walked straight out onto the balcony.

On this warm summer night Rajlakshmi happened to be lying there, on a mat, along with Binodini. She said, 'Mahin, what are you doing here so late at night?'

Binodini cast an angry, thunderous glance at him from under her thick, dark brows. Mahendra walked away without another word.

33

THE FOLLOWING MORNING WAS CLOUDY AND GLOOMY. THE SKY WAS laden with rain-clouds after days of scorching heat. Mahendra left early for his classes. His discarded clothes lay scattered on the floor. Asha counted them up as she handed them out to the washerman.

Mahendra was absentminded by nature. Hence Asha had instructions to check his pockets before handing his clothes over to the laundry. She fished into a pocket of his discarded shirt and came up with a letter.

If only that letter had turned into a poisonous snake and stung Asha's fingers before she could read it! If a potent poison spreads in the body, it can yield results in five minutes. But a poisoned mind only brings mortal torment, not death.

Asha fished out the open letter and saw it was written by Binodini. Asha's face turned ashen. She took the letter into the next room and began to read—

After what you did last night, I'd have thought you'll come to your senses. Why did you send me a clandestine note through Khemi, the maid? Shame on you! What must she think! Are you going to make it impossible for me to show my face to anyone in the world?

What do you want from me? Love? Why do you beg? You have received love since the day you were born, but still you crave for it.

In this world, I have no one to love and no one to love me. Hence I play at games of love and satisfy my craving for it. When you had the time to spare, you joined in the game. But all games must end some day. You have summons from the house—why do you still peep into the playroom? Shake off the dust and go back home now. I have no home. So I'll sit in a corner and play games in my head. I shall not call you.

You wrote that you love me. That may have worked while we were playing games—but if you want me to take it for the truth, I do not believe it. At one point in time you believed you love Asha—that was a lie too. Now you think you love me, this too is a lie. The only one you love is yourself.

Thirst for love has parched my heart and soul. You do not have the capacity to quench my thirst—I know that for a fact. As I keep telling you, let go of me, don't come after me. Don't be so shameless as to shame me. My desire for games has ended. Now, if you call me, I shall not answer. You have called me heartless in your note. That may be true. But I also have a soul and hence today I take pity on you and renounce you. If you dare answer this letter I shall be sure that the only way to escape you is to leave this house.

As she finished reading the letter, everything came tumbling around Asha. Her nerves gave way, she could scarcely breathe and the sun stole away the light from her eyes. Asha tried to hold on to the wall, then the cupboard and finally the chair as she crumpled to the floor. A little later she came back to her senses and tried to read the letter once again. But her shattered mind could hardly take it in. The black letters danced before her eyes. How did this happen? What was all this! What a terrible, earth-shattering disaster! Asha couldn't think of where to go, whom to call and what to do. Her heart fluttered like the fish that was hauled out of water and gasped for breath. Just as the drowning man reached up and groped for the sky over his head, deep down in her heart Asha desperately tried to get a hold of something firm, and finally she sobbed out, 'Aunty!'

The minute she took the name of her beloved aunt, tears sprang to her eyes and flowed relentlessly. She sat on the floor and wept her heart out. When the weeping subsided, she thought, 'What shall I do with this letter?' She cringed as she imagined Mahendra's severe embarrassment if he discovered that Asha had read the letter. She decided to put the letter back in the pocket of his shirt and hang it up on the shelf instead of sending it to the laundry.

With this thought she came back into her room. Meanwhile, the washerman had leaned back on his bundle of clothes and gone to sleep. Asha picked up the shirt and tried to put the letter back in its pocket when she suddenly heard, 'Bali dear!'

She dropped the shirt and the letter hastily on the bed and sat on it. Binodini came into the room and said, 'These days the washerman has been mixing up clothes. Let me take back the ones that haven't been marked yet.'

Asha couldn't bring herself to look at Binodini. She turned away and looked out of the window for fear that her face would give her away. She bit down hard on her lips so that the tears wouldn't escape her eyes.

Binodini stopped short and took stock of Asha's expression. She said to herself, 'I get it—so now you know all about last night. And I suppose I am the only one to blame!'

Binodini did not make any effort to speak to Asha. She just picked out a few clothes and walked away.

Asha was stung by the shame of having been friends with Binodini so naïvely for all these days. She wanted to compare the cruel letter just once more to the ideal of a friend that she carried in her heart.

She was opening the letter once again when Mahendra burst into the room. Apparently, he had rushed out in the middle of a lecture and run home for some reason.

Asha hid the letter in the folds of her sari. Mahendra also stopped short when he found Asha in the room. Then he cast anxious looks all over the room. Asha knew what he was looking for; but she couldn't think of a way to slip the letter back in its place and make good her escape from the room.

Mahendra picked up each discarded item and hunted through it. Asha couldn't bear to watch his pitiful attempts any longer. She hurled the shirt and the letter on the floor, gripped the bedpost with one hand and buried her face in the other. Mahendra picked up the letter in a flash. For a second he gazed at Asha. Then the sounds of his footsteps running down the stairs fell on Asha's ears. The washerman was

saying, 'Ma, how much longer for you to give all the clothes?
It's getting late and I live far away.'

34

SINCE MORNING RAJLAKSHMI HAD NOT SENT FOR BINODINI. WHEN
Binodini went into the storeroom as usual, Rajlakshmi did not
even look up.

This did not escape Binodini's notice. She said, 'Aunty,
are you unwell? I don't blame you, after what Thakurpo did
last night. He just barged in like a madman! I could hardly
sleep after that.'

Rajlakshmi merely sulked and didn't say a word.

Binodini said, 'He must have had a minor tiff with
Chokher Bali and that was that! He must drag me there to
resolve it or to hear them out. He couldn't wait for the
morning. I must say this, Aunty, and don't you blame me,
your son may have many qualities, but patience isn't one of
them. That's what all our spats are about.'

Rajlakshmi said, 'You are blabbering in vain—I am not in
the mood to listen to anything today.'

Binodini said, 'Neither am I, Aunty. If I criticized your
son I was afraid you'd be hurt and so I tried to pull the wool
over your eyes with a bunch of lies. But a time has come
when that's no longer possible.'

Rajlakshmi said, 'I know the good and the bad in my
son—but I didn't know what a temptress you could be.'

Binodini opened her mouth to say something and then closed it again. She said, 'That's true, Aunty—no one really knows anyone. One doesn't even know oneself. Wasn't it you who once wanted to tempt your son with this temptress, simply to avenge yourself on your daughter-in-law? Think about that and then answer me.'

Rajlakshmi flared up like a forest-fire, 'You wretched woman, shame on you for making such allegations about a mother where her son is concerned. May your tongue drop off for sinning so blatantly.'

Binodini replied calmly, 'Aunty, you know better than me whether I am a seductress or not and what enchantment I possess. Just so, I know the spell that you tried to cast, though you might deny it. But it must've been there or this wouldn't have happened. Both you and I lay the trap with some wilfulness and some ignorance. That's the way our breed goes—we are enchantresses.'

Rajlakshmi was so incensed that she could barely speak. She left the room in a huff.

Binodini stood a while in the empty room; her eyes burned with fire.

Once the morning chores were done, Rajlakshmi sent for Mahendra. He knew that the subject of last night's events would come up. He was already disconsolate with Binodini's response to his letter. As a consequence, his wayward heart was focused entirely on Binodini. A confrontation with his mother was beyond him right now. Mahendra knew that if his mother brought up Binodini and rebuked him, in defence he would be impelled to blurt out the truth; this would lead to terrible domestic strife. Hence it was imperative to leave the house for the moment, sit in solitude and sort out his thoughts. He instructed the servant, 'Go and tell Mother that I have urgent work at college today and I have to leave now. I shall talk to her when I come back.' He changed his clothes and scuttled away like a truant child without even eating. The terrible reply from Binodini that he had carried with him all morning and perused several times, stayed back in his discarded shirt pocket.

After a heavy shower, the sky remained overcast. Binodini was very distraught. Whenever she felt upset, she was given to working harder. So she had decided to gather all the clothes in the house and to mark them for the washerman. When she had gone to collect clothes from Asha and seen the latter's expression, her irritation knew no bounds. If she had to be held responsible for what had happened the previous night, why should she only get the humiliation and none of the pleasures of her crime?

The rain clattered away outside. Binodini sat on the floor in her room. The clothes lay in a heap in front of her. Khemi, the maid, was handing them to her one by one as Binodini stamped the initials onto them. Suddenly Mahendra barged into the room without warning. Khemi dropped her work, pulled the sari over her head and dashed away.

Binodini dropped the clothes she had in her hands, stood up in a flash and said, 'Go away, leave my room immediately.'

Mahendra said, 'Why? What have I done?'

Binodini said, 'What have you done! Coward! What *can* you do? You can neither love nor do your duty. Why must you drag my name into the mud?'

Mahendra tried to reason with her, 'How can you say I

do not love you?'

Binodini said in a scathing voice, 'That's exactly what I say. Stealth, camouflage, indecision—I am repulsed by your knavery. I hate it. Go away.'

Mahendra was miserable. 'You are repulsed by me, Binod?'

Binodini said, 'Yes.'

Mahendra said, 'There's still time for repentence, Binod. If I stop dithering and leave everything behind, will you come with me?'

Mahendra grabbed her with both hands and pulled her to him. Binodini said, 'Let me go, you are hurting me.'

Mahendra said, 'It doesn't matter. Tell me, will you come with me?'

Binodini said, 'No, never, not on your life!'

Mahendra said, 'But why? You were the one to ruin me—today you cannot turn your back on me. You have to come.'

Mahendra drew her to him forcefully and held her close. He said, 'Even your hatred cannot turn me away. I *will* take you along and somehow I shall make you love me.'

Binodini freed herself with a jerk.

Mahendra said, 'You have set fire all around you; now you cannot put it out and try to escape.'

Mahendra's voice rose as he shouted, 'Why did you play such games, Binod? Now you can't brush it all off as a game and get away. You and I have no choice but to die together.'

Rajlakshmi stepped into the room and said, 'Mahin, what do you think you are doing?'

Mahendra's delirious gaze turned just once at his mother

and came back to rest on Binodini as he said, 'I am leaving everything and going away. Tell me, will you come with me?'

Binodini looked at the infuriated Rajlakshmi. Then she stepped forward, took Mahendra's hand and said, 'I will.'

Mahendra said, 'In that case, wait just one more day. I am leaving this house. From tomorrow, you will be all I have left with me.'

Mahendra went away.

At this point the washerman came and said to Binodini, 'Ma, I cannot wait any longer. If you do not have the time today, I can come back tomorrow for the clothes.'

Khemi came and said, 'Bou-thakurun, the coachman says he's run out of hay.'

Binodini used to weigh out a week's feed and send it off to the stables. She would stand at the window watching as the horses ate.

Gopal, the servant, came and said, 'Bou-thakurun, the bearer has had a tiff with Sadhubabu. He says if you take the accounts for the kerosene from him, he will go to the head clerk, work out his pay and leave.'

Life went on as usual.

35

BEHARI WAS IN MEDICAL COLLEGE ALL THIS WHILE. BUT HE DROPPED out of college right before the exams. If anyone asked, he said, 'There's time enough to care for other people's health;

I must look after my own first.'

As a matter of fact, Behari had immense energy. He needed to be intensely involved with something at all times; but he did not need to work, to earn a living; nor did he seek fame. After he graduated from college, he'd gone to Shibpur first, to study engineering. He acquired as much knowledge as he wished, and as much skill as he thought was necessary, and left to join medical college. Mahendra had joined medical college a year before him. Among the students in college, their friendship was legendary. They teased them by calling them the Siamese twins. The previous year, when Mahendra failed his exams, the two landed up in the same year. But no one could understand why the pair broke up at this point. Behari couldn't bring himself to go to class where he was bound to run into Mahendra, but not meet him in the proper sense of the word. Everyone knew that Behari would pass the exams with flying colours, and win awards and prizes. But Behari didn't sit for the exams.

Behari's neighbour was a poor Brahmin, Rajendra Chakravarty. He worked in a printing press as a compositor and brought home twelve rupees a month. Behari said to him, 'Let your son live in my house, I shall teach him.'

The Brahmin heaved a sigh of relief. With a happy heart he surrendered his eight-year-old son, Vasant, into Behari's care.

Behari began to teach him in his own fashion. He said, 'I shall not give him a book to read before he's ten years old; I'll teach him orally until then.' Behari spent his days playing with the child, taking him to the park, the museum, the zoo and farmlands. Behari's entire day was taken up by teaching him English orally, telling him stories from history, testing his intelligence with various quizzes and games and riddles. He didn't have a moment to spare.

One evening, there was no way they could go out. Since noon, the rain had halted just once and had now begun again. Behari sat in his room upstairs with Vasant and played at a new game he had invented.

'Vasant, quick, tell me how many beams there are in this room—no, you cannot count them now.'

Vasant said, 'Twenty.'

Behari said, 'Wrong—it's eighteen.'

Suddenly he reached out, fingered the blinds and asked, 'How many rows in this blind?'

'Six.'

'Right. How long is this bench? What's the weight of this book?' In this way Behari was sharpening the boy's reflexes when the bearer walked in and said, 'Babuji, a woman—'

Before he had finished speaking, Binodini walked into the room.

Taken aback, Behari exclaimed, 'What is it, Bouthan?'

Binodini said, 'Do you have any female relatives who live here with you?'

Behari said, 'No relatives, no strangers, nobody. My aunt lives in the village.'

Binodini said, 'In that case, take me to your village and leave me there.'

Behari said, 'And what will be my excuse?'

Binodini said, 'Say that I am your maid. I shall do the housework there.'

Behari said, 'My aunt will be a trifle surprised. She has

not complained to me about a shortage of maids. First you must tell me how you came up with this idea. Vasant, go to bed now, child.'

Vasant left the room. Binodini said, 'If I tell you the events, you will not really understand what happened.'

Behari said, 'What's the harm—even if I misunderstand?'

'Fine, then misunderstand if you want to—Mahendra is in love with me.'

Behari said, 'That's not news and neither is it something that one would like to hear again and again.'

Binodini said, 'I have no wish to utter it again and again. That's the reason I have come to you—to seek refuge.'

Behari said acidly, 'You have no wish? And who, pray, caused this to happen? Who dragged Mahendra on to the path he now treads?'

Binodini said, 'I did. I cannot lie to you—this is my handiwork. I may be bad, or wrong, but do try to see things from my point of view just this once and understand me. The fire that burned in my heart caused me to set fire to Mahendra's home. Once, I did think that I loved Mahendra, but I was wrong.'

Behari said, 'If you loved him, would you have wreaked havoc like this?'

Binodini said, 'Thakurpo, these are sentiments straight out of your books. I am not yet ready to hear such sermons. Set aside your textbooks and peer into my heart just this once, free from your predisposed notions. Today I have come to tell you everything about me.'

Behari said, 'The books are there for a reason, Bouthan. I leave it to God to comprehend the heart by its own rules.

I must stick to the rules set out in the books or I will be lost.'

Binodini went on, 'Thakurpo, I will be shameless enough to admit to you—if you had wanted to, you could've pulled me back. Mahendra may be in love with me, but he is blind, he doesn't know me at all. Once, I did feel that you understand me; once upon a time you felt respect for me. Tell me the truth, don't hold back today!'

Behari said, 'It's true, I felt respect for you.'

Binodini said, 'You weren't wrong, Thakurpo. But if you did understand me, respect me, why did you stop there? Why couldn't you love me? I have abandoned shame and come to you, and so I say this to you—why didn't you love me too? It's my bad luck—you too had to lose your heart to Asha. Oh no, Thakurpo, you can't be angry. Sit down. I shall not hold back today. I knew that you loved Asha even when you didn't know it yourself. But I fail to understand what all of you see in Asha. Good or bad—what is there in that girl? Hasn't God given an ounce of insight to the male gaze? How little, and what stuff does it take to mesmerize you men! Fools, blind men!'

Behari stood up and said, 'I shall listen to everything you have to say today; but I beg of you, don't say that which must not be said.'

Binodini gave a wry smile and said, 'Thakurpo, I know exactly where it's pinching you. But please be patient and spare a thought for me—just think of the extreme agony that has dragged me here tonight, shedding all shame and fear, to appeal to the person who once respected me and whose love would have turned my life around. I can tell you very honestly, if you weren't in love with Asha, I wouldn't have wreaked such havoc on her life tonight.'

Behari turned pale. 'What has happened to Asha? What have you done to her?'

Binodini said, 'Mahendra has committed to going away with me tomorrow, leaving his family and everything behind.'

Behari suddenly snarled, 'That's impossible, this cannot happen!'

Binodini said, 'Impossible? And who is going to stop Mahendra today?'

Behari said, 'You can.'

Binodini was silent for a few minutes. Then she fixed her gaze on Behari and said, 'Why shall I stop him? For your Asha's sake? And I suppose I have no dreams and desires of my own? I am not so pious that I'd wipe out all my wishes from this life, for the sake of your Asha's well-being, for the sake of Mahendra's family—I have not studied the holy books so faithfully. If I give something up, what do I get in return?'

Gradually, the lines on Behari's face hardened as he said, 'You have tried to speak honestly, now let me be frank for a change. What you have done today, and the words you speak now, are all derived from the literature you're so fond of reading. Three-fourths of it is the language of dramas and novels.'

Binodini said, 'Dramas! Novels!'

Behari repeated, 'Yes, dramas and novels. And not of a very high standard, mind you. You believe this is all original—it's not. They are mere echoes of the printing press in your story. Had you been a silly, stupid, bumbling child, you'd still have got some sympathy from this world. But the heroine of the play is only fit for the stage, not the home.'

Where was Binodini's cutting sharpness, her famous pride? In response to Behari's words she bowed down in silence like the spellbound snake. Many minutes later she spoke calmly, without looking at Behari, 'What do you want me to do?'

Behari said, 'Don't try to work wonders. Let an ordinary woman's good sense prevail. Go back to your village.'

Binodini said, 'How can I go?'

Behari said, 'I can board you into the ladies' compartment and escort you to your destination.'

Binodini said quietly, 'Let me stay the night here then?'

Behari replied, 'No! Even I do not have so much faith in myself.'

Binodini slipped off the chair, dropped to the ground, held Behari's feet to her breast and said, 'Thakurpo, don't wipe out that tiny bit of weakness that you have! Don't be purer than the driven snow. Love the vile and be a little vile yourself.' She kissed his feet again and again. For an instant Behari lost control at this unexpected reaction from Binodini. His senses slackened their hold on sanity. Binodini sensed his moment of weakness and she let go of his feet; she raised herself on both knees and wound her arms around Behari who was seated on a chair and said, 'My dearest life, I know you are not mine forever; but do love me even if it's for this moment. After that I shall vanish into the forest where you cast me, I won't ask anyone for anything again. Give me something that can last me till my death.' She closed her eyes and offered her lips to him. For one second the two of them were still and the room seemed to hold its breath. Then, Behari heaved a sigh and unwound her arms from around his neck. He moved away to another chair and spoke in a voice that was nearly inaudible, 'There is a passenger train at one in the night.'

Binodini was mute for a few minutes and then she murmured, 'I shall take that train.'

Vasant walked into the room barefoot, bare-bodied and fair as the day; he stood by Behari's chair and stared solemnly at Binodini.

Behari asked, 'Didn't you go to sleep?'

Vasant didn't answer him and continued to stand there, looking grave.

Binodini stretched out her arms. Vasant hesitated a little and then went up to her slowly. She held him close to her heart as the tears flowed freely from her eyes.

36

THE IMPOSSIBLE CAN BECOME POSSIBLE AT TIMES AND THE UNBEARABLE can indeed be borne, or that night and the following day wouldn't have passed in Mahendra's house. After instructing Binodini to be prepared, that same night Mahendra mailed a letter to his house. This letter reached the following day. Asha was in bed. The bearer came to her with the letter and said, 'Ma, letter for you.'

Asha's heart leaped in her breast. In the flash of a heartbeat a thousand hopes and worries resonated in her mind. She picked up the letter hastily and found it was in Mahendra's hand, addressed to Binodini. Her head lolled back on the pillow instantly and she handed the letter back to the bearer mutely. He asked, 'To whom should I give this letter?'

Asha said, 'I don't know.'

It was around eight in the evening when Mahendra arrived at Binodini's room, charging in like a maelstrom. He found the room in darkness. He fished out a matchbox from his pocket, struck a match and found that the room was empty. Binodini wasn't there and neither were her things. He went into the balcony to the south and called out, 'Binod!' The balcony was empty and there was no answer.

'Fool! I'm a fool. I should've taken her with me. I'm sure Mother spoke such harsh words to her that Binodini was impelled to walk out,' Mahendra thought.

The moment the thought entered his head he was convinced of its veracity. He strode into Rajlakshmi's room impatiently. That room lay in darkness too, but Rajlakshmi was lying in bed; he could see even in the dark. In an angry tone, Mahendra asked, 'Mother, what have you said to Binodini?'

Rajlakshmi said, 'Nothing.'

Mahendra persisted, 'So where has she gone?'

Rajlakshmi said, 'How would I know?'

Mahendra was sceptical, 'You don't know? Fine, I am going to look for her. I shall find her, wherever she may be.'

Mahendra walked away. Rajlakshmi left the bed and tried to follow him, crying, 'Mahin, don't go, please Mahin, come back. Listen to me.'

Mahendra left the house like a madman. But he came back a moment later and asked the watchman, 'Where has Bou-thakurun gone?'

The watchman said, 'She did not tell us—we do not know.'

Mahendra roared in anger, 'You don't know!'

The watchman folded his hands and bowed low, 'No sire, we don't know.'

Mahendra decided his mother must have tutored them to supply these answers. He said, 'Fair enough!'

On the streets of the metropolis dusk had fallen; the ice-candy man was hawking his ice-candy and the fish seller was yelling out the names of the kinds of fish he carried. Mahendra waded into the throng of noisy people and disappeared in their midst.

37

BEHARI HAD NEVER SAT DOWN TO MEDITATE UPON HIMSELF. HE HAD never turned himself into a subject of analysis for his own mind. Books, chores and friends had kept him busy. He was happy to give the whole world around him more attention than he gave himself. But all of a sudden, one day, everything had crashed to pieces around him. Amidst the darkness and the destruction, he had found himself standing alone on the peak of the colossal mountain of anguish. Ever since, he had feared his own company; he had drowned himself in work and more work so that this unwanted companion of his, his own shadow self, wouldn't have access to him.

But on this particular day, Behari was powerless in

keeping his inner self at bay. The previous night he had taken
Binodini to her village. Since then, wherever he was and
whatever he tried to keep himself busy with, he felt his
agonized heart pointing him to his own immeasurable
loneliness.

Behari felt defeated by fatigue and heartache. It was
around nine at night; the south-facing terrace adjacent to
Behari's room was aflutter with a summer breeze. Behari sat
alone on the terrace, under a moonless sky. He hadn't been
able to teach Vasant that evening; he'd sent him to bed early.
His heart wept for the days of his old, familiar past like a
motherless child; arms outstretched, it searched for something
in the dark of the universe, yearned for consolation, for solace
of some sort. His determination, his control over himself, had
all washed away. He felt like running to the same people that
he had once vowed never to think of again. There was no way
of controlling his emotional turbulence.

Like a map marked in different colours for land, water,
hills and rivers, the various images of his long friendship with
Mahendra and its unfortunate conclusion unfolded before
Behari's eyes. He mulled over the precise moment at which
his world had come crashing down and all that he held dear
to him had been lost forever. Who had been the first to break
the charmed circle? The bashful face of Asha, coloured by the
rays of the setting sun, etched itself in the twilight. The
blowing of the conch shell, auguring good omens at dusk,
rang in his ears at the same time. Asha, Behari thought, was
something of a benevolent planet that had made its place
between the two friends, casting her influence on both. She
had brought with her a little conflict, and a strange kind of

pain that could neither be spoken of nor nurtured in the heart. And yet, this conflict, this pain were covered in a pleasant light, full of love and affection.

But then had come the malevolent planet and that had ripped apart the friendship, the romance, the peace and purity of the family. Behari tried to push away Binodini's image with great revulsion. But wonders never cease! The push was no more than a gentle thrust, barely touching her. That incredibly beautiful mirage with her dark eyes brimming with inscrutable mystery, stood still before him in the dense dark of the night. The fulsome breeze of the summer night touched him like her breath. Gradually, her still, steady gaze wavered; the dry, intense eyes overflowed with tears as emotion overcame them; like a flash the mirage dropped at his feet and grasped his knees to her breast with all her might. And then she wove herself around him like a human creeper and raised a pair of lips as fragrant as a flower, up to his own. Behari closed his eyes and tried with all his might to banish the image from his mind. But he felt powerless to hurt her in any way—an incomplete, fervent kiss hung on his lips, and he was suffused with a strange exhilaration.

Behari could no longer stay in the solitary darkness of the terrace. He rushed into his lamp-lit room in order to distract himself. In one corner, on a teapoy, was a framed photograph covered with a silk scarf. Behari uncovered it and sat down to gaze at it under the bright light.

It had been taken soon after Mahendra and Asha's wedding, with the couple smiling happily. Behind the photograph Mahendra had written his name and Asha had added hers in her childish scrawl. The sweetness of new-found romance still hung over the photo. Mahendra sat on a chair looking very pleased with his newly married status. Asha stood beside him shyly. The photographer had insisted on her dropping her veil, but he couldn't rid her of her shyness. Today, this same Mahendra was about to leave Asha in tears and go far away. But the Mahendra of the photograph still looked as much in love with her as ever—his emotions were frozen in time, ignorant of the irony of fate that time would unfold.

Behari tried to cast Binodini far away by hurling abuse at her, with the photograph on his lap. But those loving, youthful arms of hers still held on to his knees, strong as ever. Behari said, 'You went and destroyed such a loving, happy relationship!' But Binodini's face, raised for his kiss, silently told him, 'I have loved you. From all the men in this whole wide world I have chosen you.'

But was that an answer! Could these words obscure the pained shriek that arose from a household torn asunder? What a witch!

Witch! Was this only a rebuke or was there some indulgence mixed in the word? When Behari was left standing like a beggar, robbed of all the love he had ever counted on in his life, was he in a position to reject, from the bottom of his heart, such an outpouring of love that came unwarranted and unasked for? In comparison, what had he ever got? He had sacrificed his entire life in search of some crumbs of love. But when the goddess of love had sent him a golden plate replete with her blessings, how could he have the strength to turn his back on the feast?

He sat there with the photograph on his lap, lost in his thoughts. Suddenly a sound beside him made him look up—

Mahendra stood at his side. Startled, Behari stood up in a rush and the photo dropped to the floor—he didn't even notice.

Mahendra asked without any preamble, 'Where is Binodini?'

Behari stepped closer to Mahendra, took his hand and said, 'Mahin da, do have a seat. We can discuss everything by and by.'

Mahendra said, 'I don't have the time to sit and discuss things. Tell me, where is Binodini?'

Behari said, 'Your question cannot be answered quite so simply. You must calm down and have a seat.'

Mahendra said, 'Sermonizing, are we? Spare me the trouble. I have read the holy books when I was a child.'

Behari said quietly, 'I have neither the power nor the right to sermonize.'

Mahendra said, 'Perhaps it's reproach, then? I know I am a scoundrel, the worst kind, and whatever else you may choose to call me. But the point is, do you know where Binodini is?'

Behari replied, 'I do.'

Mahendra said, 'And you won't tell me?'

Behari said, 'No.'

Mahendra yelled, 'You have to. You have stolen her away and hidden her. She is mine; give her back to me.'

Behari stood in stunned silence for a while. Then he spoke with firm determination, 'She is not yours. I have not stolen her away; she came to me of her own free will.'

Mahendra barked, 'Liar!' He turned and banged on the closed door of the next room. 'Binod, Binod!' he yelled.

The sounds of weeping from inside the room made him

say, 'Don't be afraid, Binod! It's me, Mahin. I shall rescue you—no one can keep you locked away.'

Mahendra pushed hard and the door gave way. He rushed inside and found the room in darkness. He noticed a shadowy figure on the bed sobbing in fear and pressing the pillow to its chest. Behari stepped in hurriedly, picked Vasant up in his arms and consoled him gently, 'Don't worry Vasant, it's all right, everything's all right.'

Mahendra rushed out and searched all the rooms in the house. When he was back, Vasant was still crying out in fear even as he slept. Behari had the lights on in his room and was trying to stroke him gently to sleep.

Mahendra came and asked, 'Where have you kept Binodini?'

Behari said, 'Mahin da, do be quiet. You have needlessly terrified this child so much that he may be sick. I assure you, you needn't concern yourself with Binodini's whereabouts.'

Mahendra said, 'Brilliant! A saint! Spare me your homilies, you impostor. Which god were you meditating on, with my wife's photograph on your lap at this time of the night?' Mahendra hurled the photo to the floor and stamped on it with his boots. The glass shattered into tiny shards. He picked up the photograph, tore it into tiny bits and hurled it at Behari. His crazed behaviour made Vasant wail with fear again. Behari could barely speak as he pointed to the door and said, 'Leave!'

Mahendra ran out like a mad man.

38

THE GREEN FARMLANDS AND TREE-LINED VILLAGES FLASHED BY Binodini's window as she sat in a deserted train compartment. The sights brought back memories of the peaceful village life for her. She felt she'd be able to sit under the shade of those trees with her favourite books and have some respite from all the anger, sorrow and anguish of her sojourn in the city. As she took in the sun setting beyond the expanse of the barren fields of summer, she felt life was complete. She wished to drown in this green stillness and close its eyes, to take the boat away from the crashing waves of life, towards the shore, under the shelter of a banyan tree, and stay there, wishing for nothing else. The scent of green mango blossoms wafted in as the train hurtled on, and her heart came to terms with itself. She thought, 'This is for the best; I cannot tug and pull at myself any more. Now I'll forget, now I'll sleep. I shall be one with the village, live a quiet, rural life and spend my days peacefully and in joy.'

Binodini walked into her tiny home with a heart parched for peace and quiet. But alas for that rare commodity—emptiness and poverty were all she could find. Everything around her was worn, dirty and faded. She choked on the vapid air inside, the house not having been aired for many months. The little furniture that the room held was nearly ruined by dust, termites and rats. The house that evening was joyless and dark. Binodini managed to light an oil lamp and in that meagre light the dismal condition of the house was sadly exposed. All the things that hadn't bothered her before seemed to choke the very life out of her now and she muttered forcefully, 'This won't do for a single day.' A few old books and magazines were gathering dust on the shelf. But she didn't feel like touching them. Outside, in the still air the mosquitoes and insects struck up a dialogue that echoed through the night.

Binodini had an old aunt-in-law living with her earlier. She had gone to a distant village to visit her daughter, having locked up the house. Binodini went to visit her neighbours. They seemed to jump out of their skins when they saw her. My, my! Binodini's complexion had really cleared up, her clothes were well turned out, almost like a lady's. They nudged each other and gestured towards Binodini as they muttered among themselves: as though the rumours they'd heard were now confirmed.

At every step Binodini felt anew how distant she had become from her own village. She was exiled in her own home: there was not a moment's peace for her anywhere.

The old postman knew her since she was a child. The next morning when Binodini was about to go to the pond for a bath, she saw him walking up the street with his bag of letters and she couldn't control herself. She dropped her towel, rushed up to him and asked, 'Panchu-dada, any letters for me?'

The old man said, 'No.'

An anxious Binodini persisted, 'There may be one; will you please check?'

She took the five or six letters he had for that area and leafed through them carefully; not one was for her. When she returned to the pond looking glum, a friend spoke with mock curiosity, 'Bindi, why the rush for this letter?'

Another chatterbox butted in, 'Oh, this is good; how many of us are lucky enough to get letters by mail? We have husbands, brothers and brothers-in-law working in far-off places, but the mailman never has pity on us.'

Thus the conversation took off, the words got more blunt and the jibes sharper. Binodini had pleaded with Behari that he should write to her at least twice a week, if not daily, even if it was just a few lines. She couldn't really expect to have a letter from him so soon. But her craving was so strong that she couldn't let go of the hope, the distant possibility. She felt she'd left Kolkata many months ago.

Thanks to friends and foes, Binodini was left in no doubt as to how her name was being bandied about in every household in the village, linked to Mahendra's of course. Where was the peace!

She tried to distance herself from the people in the village. But the villagers took offence at that. They didn't want to be deprived of the pleasure of mocking and loathing the sinful woman.

In vain did Binodini attempt to hide herself from the public eye in that tiny rural community. There was no space here to nurse her wounded heart in a dark, lonely niche; curious glances poked and pried at her all the time and worsened the wound. The more she thrashed about like a fish in captivity, the more she lacerated herself by smashing against the narrow confines of her prison. There was no space to even indulge in one's own misery here.

On the second day, after the postman had gone his way

again, Binodini shut the door to her room and sat down to write:

> Thakurpo, don't worry—this is not a love letter. You are my judge and I bow before you. For my sins you have awarded me a harsh sentence. I have accepted it with full humility; my only regret is that you cannot see just how harsh the punishment is on me. I have been deprived of the pity you'd have surely felt, if only you could see my condition, or know of it. With your memories and with my head bowed at your feet, I shall take this in my stride. But my lord, even the prisoner deserves two square meals a day. Not fancy meals—but the bare minimum that is needed to survive. A few lines written by you would be a feast for me in this exile. Deprived of them, this isn't merely an exile; it's a life-sentence. Please do not test me so cruelly, my lord. My sinful heart was full of arrogance— I never thought I would have to bow before anyone so humbly. You have won, my lord. I shall not rebel. But please have mercy on me—grant me life. Give me the meagre bit necessary to survive this exile. It will give me the strength to stay on the path charted by you. This is my only request to you. The other things that my heart is prompting me to tell you, I have vowed never to speak of again. I shall keep my vow.
>
> Your Binod-bouthan

Binodini mailed the letter. Her neighbours continued their slander: 'She shuts the door of her house, writes letters, attacks the postman for letters she expects—this is how one is ruined if one spends a few days in Kolkata!'

The next day went without a letter as well. Binodini was

silent all day long and the lines on her face grew harsh. The torment and agony from within and without turned her defences—from the depths of the darkness in her heart—into a violent force that threatened to erupt. Binodini perceived the advent of that merciless brutality with fear and shut the doors to her house.

She had nothing of Behari—not a photograph, not a few lines on paper, nothing! She began to hunt for something in that barrenness. She wanted to hold something of his to her heart and bring tears to her arid eyes. She wanted to melt away the viciousness with her tears and place Behari's sentence on the throne of love, on the gentlest spot in her heart. But her heart continued to smoulder like the parched sky at noon; there was no sign of a single droplet in the distant horizon.

Binodini had once heard that if you contemplate on someone with all your heart and soul, he had to come. So she folded her hands, closed her eyes and called on Behari, 'My life is empty, my heart is empty, there is emptiness all around me—come unto this emptiness, even if for an instant, you have to come, I won't let go of you.'

She said these words over and over and began to feel heartened. She felt that the power of this love, this pleading, could not go in vain. But such tender bleeding of the heart at the roots of despair, such fierce concentration, made it weak and feeble. Still she felt stronger inside after this relentless meditation. She felt that her powerful yearning, neglecting all other worldly thoughts, by sheer will power alone could draw the desired one closer like a magnet.

When her lampless, dark room was suffused with thoughts of Behari, when the whole world, her village, her life and the entire universe lay in shambles before her, Binodini suddenly heard a hammering on her door. She stood up hastily, rushed to the door with heartfelt faith and trust, and opened it exclaiming, 'You have come!' She was convinced that no one other than Behari could stand on the other side of her door at that precise moment.

Mahendra replied, 'Yes, I've come, Binod.'

Binodini shouted with revulsion and distaste, 'Go. Go away from here. Leave right now.'

Mahendra stood there in stunned disbelief.

An elderly neighbour walked up to her door saying, 'Bindi dear, if your aunt-in-law comes back tomorrow—' As her glance fell on Mahendra, she stopped short, drew her anchal over her head and beat a hasty retreat.

39

THERE WAS AN UPROAR IN THE VILLAGE. THE ELDERS SAT AROUND the temple courtyard and said, 'This cannot be tolerated. It's possible to ignore whatever happened in Kolkata. But she has the audacity to ply him with letters, bring him into her house here and be so brazen about it all! We cannot allow such a fallen woman to stay in the village.'

Today Binodini was sure Behari would write to her. But no letters came. Binodini thought, 'What right does Behari have over me? Why should I obey him? Why did I give him the impression that I shall take his orders humbly and follow his instructions? All he cares about is saving his beloved Asha—he doesn't really care about me. I have no rights, no demands over him—not even two lines in a note—am I so insignificant, such an object of hatred?' The fumes of humiliation and hostility threatened to choke her; she said to herself, 'I would have taken this pain for anybody else, but not for Asha. Why do I have to tolerate this poverty, exile, denigration and this continuous denial of all my desires, merely for Asha's sake? Why did I have to accept such a farce? I should have stayed and fulfilled my promise of vengeance. Fool, I am a fool! Why did I have to love Behari?'

As Binodini sat in the room, still as a petrified statuette, her aunt-in-law returned from her trip, walked into the house and said, 'You wretch, what is all this I have heard!'

Binodini said, 'All that you have heard is true.'

Her aunt-in-law said, 'Why did you have to bring your shame into the house, why did you come back?'

Binodini was silent from suppressed misery. The old lady said, 'Child, let me tell you clearly, you cannot stay here. I am still living, even after fate has snatched away all my dear ones from me. I cannot tolerate this. Shame on you—you've disgraced us. Leave the house immediately.'

Binodini said, 'I shall go right now.'

At this moment Mahendra arrived again, unshaved, dishevelled. He looked wan and his eyes were bloodshot from lack of sleep. Earlier, he'd intended to try one last time at dawn, and make Binodini go with him; but Binodini's rudeness and vitriolic response the previous day had given rise to a host of doubts in his mind. Then, as the sun rose and the morning wore on, Mahendra saw that it was time for the train's arrival. He pushed aside all doubts and arguments in his mind, left the station, got into a carriage and arrived straight at Binodini's doorstep. When a person casts away all shame and embarks blatantly on a daring venture, he is imbued with a certain audacious strength; that power lent an abandoned thrill to Mahendra, sweeping away his earlier doubts and dithering. In his feral gaze the curious village folk looked like inanimate dolls in the dust. Mahendra didn't spare a second glance to any of them, walked right up to Binodini and said, 'Binod, I am not such a coward that I'll desert you in the face of public outrage. By hook or by crook, I must take you from here. After that, if you wish to cast me off, do so. I shall not stop you. I can swear by you on this day that nothing will happen without your wish or consent—if you wish to be with me, I shall be grateful. If you don't, I'll go far away from your life. I know I haven't been a model of trust, but please do not distrust me today. We are standing on the brink of devastation and this isn't the time for games.'

Binodini spoke naturally and without emotion, 'Take me with you. Do you have a carriage?'

Mahendra said, 'I do.'

Binodini's aunt-in-law came out of her room and said, 'Mahendra, you may not know me, but we are related. Your mother, Rajlakshmi, is from my village and in that sense I am your aunt. Let me ask you: what kind of behaviour is this? You have a wife at home, a mother, and you walk the streets in this half-crazed, brazen fashion! How can you show your face in civil society?'

Mahendra's world of impassioned madness got a severe jolt at these words. He had a mother, a wife and there was such a thing as civil society! This simple fact came home to him anew. There was a time when he would have trouble imagining that one day he'd have to hear these words from a stranger in an unknown, faraway village. It was a strange chapter in his life, indeed, that in broad daylight Mahendra was taking a virtuous widow by the hand and leading her away from her home. And yet, he had a wife, a mother and there was such a thing as civil society!

As Mahendra stood there dumbstruck, the old woman said, 'If you must leave, go right away. Don't dally at my doorstep—go away, right now!'

She walked into her room, slammed the door shut and bolted it from within. Binodini clambered onto the carriage, dishevelled, squalid, empty-handed and hungry. As Mahendra was about to board the carriage she stopped him, 'No, the station isn't far; you can walk.'

Mahendra said, 'But then everyone in the village will stare at me.'

Binodini said, 'Do you have a drop of honour left here to protect?' She shut the door of the carriage and instructed the coachman, 'To the station.'

The man asked, 'Isn't the gentleman coming?'

Mahendra hesitated a little and then decided to step back. The carriage drove off. Mahendra left the village road and took a roundabout route through the field as he headed for the station, head lowered and eyes to the ground. The village women had finished their bath and lunch; only a few hardworking old housewives, who got off work late, were walking through the mango-groves headed for the cool waters of the pond with their bowls of oil and towels.

40

RAJLAKSHMI WAS LOSING SLEEP AND HUNGER, WORRYING ABOUT Mahendra. Sadhucharan had hunted high and low for him but without any luck. Then, one day, Mahendra returned to Kolkata with Binodini. He dropped her off at his flat in Patoldanga and came home late at night.

Mahendra stepped into his mother's room and found it in darkness; the kerosene lamp was shaded so as to shield the glare of the flame. Rajlakshmi lay on the bed, looking ill; Asha sat at her feet, stroking them gently. At long last, the bride of the house had her place at the mother-in-law's feet. At Mahendra's advent, Asha looked up in surprise and left the room hurriedly. Mahendra cast away his diffidence forcefully and said, 'Mother, I cannot attend to my studies from here; I have rented a flat near college; I'll stay there.'

Rajlakshmi pointed to a corner of the bed and said, 'Mahin, sit down.'

Mahendra sat down awkwardly. Rajlakshmi said, 'Mahin, you are free to stay where you wish, but please, I beg of you, don't make my daughter-in-law suffer.'

Mahendra was silent. Rajlakshmi continued, 'I am so unlucky that I didn't know the worth of my darling daughter all these days.' Her voice broke as she spoke. 'But you have known her for so long, loved her so much; how could you cast her into such misery?' She began to weep openly.

Mahendra desperately wished to get up and leave, but something stopped him from doing so. He sat still in the dark, on one corner of his mother's bed.

Much later, Rajlakshmi said, 'Are you staying here tonight at least?'

Mahendra said, 'No.'

She asked, 'When will you leave?'

Mahendra said, 'Right now.'

Rajlakshmi sat up with great difficulty and said, 'Right now? Don't you wish to meet your wife just once and speak to her properly?'

Mahendra was silent. Rajlakshmi said, 'Can't you even guess how she has spent the last few days? Oh you shameless wretch, it breaks my heart to see just how cruel you can be.' Rajlakshmi fell back on the bed like a felled branch.

Mahendra rose and walked out. He tiptoed stealthily up the stairs towards his bedroom. He had no wish to run into Asha. But there she was, lying down on the covered terrace adjacent to his room. She hadn't heard his footsteps. When he stood in front of her, she sat up in confusion and began to arrange her clothes hurriedly. At that moment if he had called out just once, 'Chuni,' she would have taken his transgression upon her own head, fallen at his feet in remorse and guilt, and wept all the tears she could ever weep. But Mahendra couldn't bring himself to utter that beloved name. However hard he tried and wished with all his might that he could be intimate with her again, though he felt sorrier than ever, he couldn't forget that caressing Asha today would be nothing but an empty gesture on his part. What would be the use of consoling her, when he had closed out all options of renouncing Binodini?

Meanwhile, Asha was flooded with shame as she sat there. She was too embarrassed to stand up, walk away or try to move in any way at all. Mahendra began to pace the floor slowly without uttering a single word. The sky was moonless tonight. In a corner of the terrace a tuberose plant yielded two stems of flowers in an earthen pot. In the dark sky overhead, the same stars that had once been witness to many scenes of impassioned love being enacted between these two, now twinkled mutely.

Mahendra wished he could wipe out the devastating events of the last few days in the dark of the night, and take his accustomed place beside Asha on the mat, on that terrace. No questions, no explanations, just the same trust, the same love and that pure, simple joy. But alas, there was no way of going back to that space ever again. On this terrace, that little space beside Asha upon the mat was lost to Mahendra forever. Until now, his relationship with Binodini had no ties. There was the unfettered pleasure of loving, but none of its ancillary bindings. But now that he had ripped her apart from society with his own hands—now that there was no place to keep her, or to send her back to, Mahendra was her sole recourse. Now, whether he liked it or not, he was bound to shoulder all responsibility for her. This thought weighed heavy on him. All of a sudden, he found great solace in this room on the terrace, in the memory of the peace, the sweet romancing of lovers at night that came with it. But this solace, to which he had full rights once, was out of his reach today. Not even for a day would he be allowed to put aside the burden he had promised to shoulder all his life and catch a moment's peace for himself.

Mahendra heaved a sigh and glanced at Asha. She sat in still silence, holding back her mute tears. The dark of the night shielded her mortification and pain, like a protective mother.

Mahendra paused in his pacing and walked up to her, as if to say something. Asha's blood roared in her veins and she closed her eyes. Mahendra lost track of what he had wanted to say and couldn't figure out what he should do. But he couldn't step back without saying something at least. So he asked, 'Where are the keys?'

They were under the mattress. Asha got up and went into the room—Mahendra followed her. Asha took the bunch of keys from under the mattress and placed them on the bed. Mahendra picked them up and began to insert them one by one, to unlock his clothes-cupboard. Asha couldn't check herself; she spoke softly, 'Those keys are not with me.'

She couldn't bring herself to say who had those keys, but Mahendra understood. Asha left the room in a hurry, fearing she'd be unable to hold back her tears any longer. In the dark, she stood in one corner of the terrace and sobbed her heart out, trying very hard to keep the noise down.

But she didn't have much time in hand. Suddenly she remembered it was time for Mahendra's dinner. Quickly, she ran downstairs.

Rajlakshmi asked her, 'Bou-ma, where is Mahin?'

Asha said, 'He is upstairs.'

Rajlakshmi said, 'Then why have you come down?'

Asha lowered her eyes. 'His dinner—'

Rajlakshmi said, 'I will take care of that. Why don't you freshen up, Bou-ma. Wear your new sari from Dhaka and come to my room—I shall do your hair.'

Asha couldn't refute Rajlakshmi's affection, but all this

talk of dressing up made her wish she could sink through the floor. She bore Rajlakshmi's ministration patiently, in tortured silence.

Decked up to the full, Asha went upstairs slowly. She peeped in and saw that Mahendra was not on the terrace. Quietly, she walked up to the room and found it empty. His dinner lay untouched.

Having given up on the keys, Mahendra had wrenched open his cupboard, taken some essential clothing and medical textbooks, and left.

The following day was ekadasi, the three-quarter moon fast; Rajlakshmi lay on her bed, weak and fatigued. Outside, the wind blew fiercely, brewing up for a storm. Asha stepped into the room gently. She sat at Rajlakshmi's feet, stroked them softly and said, 'I have brought you milk and fruits; come and eat.'

Rajlakshmi's parched eyes flooded with tears at this diffident attempt at nursing by her sad-eyed bride. She sat up, drew Asha to her heart, kissed her tear-soaked temple and asked, 'Bou-ma, what is Mahin doing?'

Asha felt embarrassed as she said softly, 'He has gone.'

Rajlakshmi said, 'When did he leave—I wasn't even told?'

Asha bowed her head as she replied, 'He went away last night.'

Immediately, all trace of gentleness vanished from Rajlakshmi's face and her touch lost its tenderness. Asha sensed a silent rebuke, and walked away slowly with her head bowed.

41

WHEN MAHENDRA HAD GONE HOME ON THAT FIRST NIGHT, BINODINI sat alone in the Patoldanga flat in the midst of the ceaseless commotion of Kolkata, thinking about herself. She had never been blessed with a lot of spaces to turn to; but there had always been enough room to turn over and lie on the other side, if the bed felt too uncomfortable. But today the space left to her was very restricted indeed. Her boat would pitch her straight into the water if it so much as tilted a little to one side. Hence, she had to steer it very carefully now—there was no room for a single error or even a little bit of dithering. It was a daunting prospect for any woman. Where was the space, in these narrow confines, for those little hide-and-seek games so necessary to keep a male mind in thrall? She'd have to spend all her life face-to-face with Mahendra, without any veils. The difference was that if the boat did overturn he had the means to scramble to the shore, but she had none.

As Binodini's vulnerable position became very clear to her, she began to gather strength within herself. She had to find a way out—this wouldn't work for her.

The day she had admitted her love for Behari, she had reached the end of her tether. The lips that she had raised for his kiss, and had been forced to draw back, were suspended in an incompleteness of desire—unable to find their place in this world and carried from place to place like the flowers preordained for a certain deity but never used in worship. Binodini's heart was unfamiliar with the concept of despondency—under no circumstances did she usually let go of hope. Her heart still claimed, every minute of every day, with great vehemence, 'Behari will have to accept my appeal one day.'

To this unrestrained ardour was added her strong desire for self-defence. Behari was her only way out. Binodini knew Mahendra very well indeed—if she leaned on him, he'd not be able to take the pressure. He could be attained only if he was allowed to go—if he were clung to, he would wish to run. Behari alone was capable of giving her the tranquil, reliable, safe haven that a woman needed. Today, she couldn't let go of Behari at any cost.

The day she left the village, Binodini had made Mahendra go to the post office adjacent to the station and leave firm instructions for all letters in her name to be forwarded to her new address in Kolkata. She couldn't bring herself to accept that Behari wouldn't answer even a single one of her letters. She said to herself, 'I shall be patient and wait for seven days—after that I'll decide what to do.' She then opened the window and sat there in the dark, staring out unmindfully at the streets of Kolkata lit by gaslamps. On this dark night, Behari was somewhere in this very same city—a few roads and lanes lay between her and his house, with the same tiny courtyard that had a tap in it, those stairs, that same well-arranged, brightly lit, secluded room—Behari sitting alone on his armchair, amidst tranquil peace; perhaps Vasant, the fair, healthy and handsome boy with large eyes, sat beside him turning the pages of his book. As she conjured up this image bit by bit, Binodini's heart was flooded with love and affection. If she wanted to, she could go there immediately. Binodini's heart picked up this thread of thought and played with it; in the past she would have rushed to fulfil her desires. But now she had to think before taking such steps. Now it was no longer about fulfilling a desire but about accomplishing a mission. Binodini said, 'Let me first see how Behari responds and then I can decide on my course of action.' She did not dare to go and disturb Behari without first understanding his reactions.

As she sat lost in her thoughts, the clock struck ten and Mahendra returned. The last few sleepless nights and fitful days had taken their toll on him; now, when he was finally successful in bringing Binodini to his home, he seemed overwhelmed by fatigue and exhaustion. He had no strength left to fight with himself or with his state in life. Today, he was bent low with the unwieldy burden of his future life.

Mahendra was too embarrassed to stand before the closed door and bang on it. Where now was that ardour that had helped him to overlook the entire world? Even the eyes of a complete stranger on the road were enough to make him cringe in shame.

The new servant was fast asleep inside. It took a while to get the door opened. As he stepped inside an unfamiliar, new home in the dark, Mahendra's heart plummeted. The apple of his mother's eye, Mahendra was used to certain comforts, hand-pulled fans and decorative furniture, and the lack of it all struck him anew this particular evening. Mahendra would have to fill in the requirements himself, he had the sole responsibility of this household. He had never given much thought to someone else's comforts. But from this day, the burden of a new, unfinished household with all its minute details, rested on his shoulders alone. A kerosene lamp on the staircase emitted smoke continually—it needed to be replaced by a proper lamp. The area between the corridor and the stairway was damp and soggy from its proximity to the tap. He must call the mason and get it fixed. He would have to fight with the landlord about the two shops in the front of the house that were occupied by shoe sellers who were yet to vacate the property. In a flash he realized that each of these things could only be done by him, and it merely served to increase the weight of his burdensome fatigue.

Mahendra stood below the stairs for some time, trying to compose himself. He tried to stoke the embers of the love he felt for Binodini. He tried to tell himself that eventually he had got the person he had wanted above all else in the world; today nothing stood between the two of them—it was a day of great joy for Mahendra. But perhaps the fact that nothing stood between them was the greatest barrier—today Mahendra was his own hurdle.

Binodini, spotting Mahendra at the door, left her meditative pose, got up and lit a lamp. She picked up her sewing, lowered her eyes and immersed herself in the needlework. This sewing was her shield, she felt safe behind it.

Mahendra stepped into the room and said, 'Binod, you must be terribly uncomfortable here.'

Binodini carried on with her sewing as she said, 'Not at all.'

Mahendra said, 'I'll arrange for all the furniture to be delivered within the next couple of days; but until then you must bear with the discomfort.'

Binodini said, 'Oh no, you cannot do that—you will not

bring in another piece of furniture into this house. The ones that are there are already excessive.'

Mahendra said, 'And am I included in that list?'

Binodini said, 'It's good to have some humility—don't think of yourself as "excessive".'

As he gazed at Binodini, lost in her work with her head bent low, in that furtive lamplight Mahendra felt the thrill of the romance course through his veins once again.

If he had been at home, he would have thrown himself at her feet—but this was not home and so he couldn't do that. Binodini was vulnerable, very much within his reach and if he did not restrain himself now, it would be the worst kind of baseness.

Binodini said, 'Why have you brought your books and clothes here?'

Mahendra said, 'I happen to consider them essentials—they don't exactly belong to the category of "excessive".'

Binodini said, 'I know, but why here?'

Mahendra said, 'You're right—essential things are a misfit here. Binod, if you throw the books out on the street, I shan't say a word. But please don't throw me out as well.' He used this pretext to move a little closer to Binodini and place the bundle of books at her feet.

Binodini didn't look up from her sewing as she replied gravely, 'Thakurpo, you cannot stay in this house.'

Mahendra grew impatient as his renewed enthusiasm was thwarted; he spoke ardently, 'Why Binod, why do you wish to push me away? I have left everything for you and is this what I get?'

Binodini said, 'I will not allow you to leave everything for my sake.'

Mahendra exclaimed, 'Now it is no longer in your hands—my life, my family have gone away from me—only you remain, Binod! Binod—Binod—' Mahendra lay flat on the ground, gripped her feet and covered them with innumerable kisses.

Binodini snatched her feet away and stood up as she said, 'Mahendra, don't you remember your promise?'

Mahendra exerted immense will power and checked himself. 'I remember. I promised I shall only do as you wish and never cross your wishes. I shall keep my word. Tell me, what should I do?'

Binodini said, 'You must go and stay in your own home.'

Mahendra said, 'Am I the only surplus object here, Binod? If that is so, why did you drag me here? What is the point of hunting that prey which you do not like to devour? Tell me honestly—have I surrendered to you of my own free will or have you hunted me down at your will? Why should I endure you playing such games with me? Yet, I shall keep my word—I will go back and stay in that house where I have crushed my own place underfoot so callously.'

Binodini sat on the floor and carried on with her sewing without saying a word.

Mahendra fixed her face in an unwavering glance for a while and said, 'Heartless, Binod, you are heartless. I am unfortunate indeed to have loved you so.'

Binodini made a wrong stitch, held it up to the lamp and began to undo it with great care. At that moment, Mahendra wanted to grab her pitiless heart in his callused fist and crush it to death. He wanted to confront this silent cruelty and unyielding disregard with sheer brute force and bring it to heel.

He walked out of the room and came back immediately to say, 'If I go away, who will look after you, all alone here?'

Binodini said, 'Don't worry about that. Aunty has sacked Khemi, the maid, and she has joined me here today. The two of us will lock the door and be quite safe inside.'

With his anger, Mahendra's attraction for Binodini intensified. He longed to crush her body to his bosom with all his might and wreak havoc on it. In order to escape this terrible urge, Mahendra rushed out of the house.

As he walked the streets, Mahendra vowed to retaliate with equal disregard against Binodini's indifference. Even at her most vulnerable, when Mahendra was her sole recourse, she chose to show him such patent indifference so coolly and fearlessly—such humiliation was perhaps seldom meted out to a man. Mahendra's pride lay shattered and yet it refused to die; it only continued to feel tormented and battered. Mahendra said, 'Am I so pathetic? How dare she treat me thus! Who does she have to call her own, except me?'

Suddenly he remembered—Behari. In the flash of a second his passion turned to ashes. So Binodini had placed all her faith in Behari! He was just a pretext, he was the stepping-stone on which she placed her feet, only to crush it underfoot every single moment. That was what gave her the strength to insult him! Mahendra became convinced that Binodini was in touch with Behari through letters and had received his reassurance.

So, he set off for Behari's house. When he finally banged on Behari's door, the night was all but over. After much banging and shouting the bearer opened the door and announced that his master was not at home.

Mahendra was shell-shocked. He thought, 'All the time that I was walking the streets like a madman, Behari was with Binodini. This is the reason why Binodini humiliated me so heartlessly and I, fool that I am, stormed out in a huff and left her alone, just as she wished.'

Mahendra asked of the old, familiar bearer, 'Bhoju, when did your master leave the house?'

Bhoju replied, 'Oh, about four or five days ago; he has gone somewhere to the west.'

Relief flooded through Mahendra and he thought, 'Now I must lie down and rest a bit—I am too tired to walk any more.' He walked up the stairs, went into Behari's room, lay upon the couch and promptly fell into a deep sleep.

The same night that Mahendra had come and kicked up a ruckus in Behari's house asking after Binodini, Behari had decided to leave for the west without having a particular destination in mind. He felt that if he stayed on, his conflicts with his old friend would take such an ugly turn that he would regret it all his life.

The next day when Mahendra woke up, it was nearly eleven. His glance fell upon the teapoy before him and he saw that a note to Behari, addressed in Binodini's hand, lay on it, a marble paperweight holding it in place. He picked the note up hastily and saw that it was unopened. It was awaiting Behari's return. Mahendra opened it with trembling hands and read the letter. This was the same letter that Binodini had written to Behari from her village, to which she hadn't received a reply.

Every alphabet in the letter bared its teeth at Mahendra. Ever since their childhood, Behari had always stood in

Mahendra's shadow. In terms of love and affection, he only received the stale leftovers from the godly Mahendra's plate. Today, Mahendra himself was the seeker and Behari was indifferent; and yet, Binodini had pushed Mahendra aside and chosen this undeserving oaf of a Behari over him! Mahendra had also got a few letters from Binodini. But compared to this letter to Behari, those were mere artifice, a vain and vacuous attempt to pacify the gormless.

Mahendra recalled Binodini's eagerness to send him to the post office to update her present address there, and he now knew why. Binodini was waiting for a reply from Behari, with her heart and soul fixed upon it.

In keeping with the past, Bhoju brought him tea and breakfast from the shop around the corner despite his master being absent. Mahendra forgot all about his bath. His eyes drifted over Binodini's inciting letter with compulsive haste, just as the traveller covers the flaming hot desert sands in hurried steps. Mahendra made promises to never set eyes upon Binodini again. But he realized that if a few more days passed without a response, Binodini would arrive at Behari's house and she would be relieved to know the truth of the matter. That prospect was anathema to him.

So Mahendra pocketed the letter and just before dusk he arrived at the flat in Patoldanga.

Binodini took pity on Mahendra's deplorable condition. She realized that he must have spent the night walking the streets, without a wink of sleep. She asked, 'Didn't you go home last night?'

Mahendra said, 'No.'

Binodini got worked up. 'Haven't you eaten all day?' The

nurturing heart in Binodini prompted her to go and arrange a meal for him.

Mahendra said, 'Forget it—I have already eaten.'

Binodini pressed him, 'Where have you eaten?'

Mahendra said, 'At Behari's.'

In an instant Binodini's face turned pallid. After a moment's pause she controlled her emotions and asked, 'Is everything all right with Behari-thakurpo?'

Mahendra said, 'Quite so. He has gone west.' The way he said it implied that Behari had left that very day.

Binodini's face fell once again. But she composed herself valiantly and said, 'I have never seen such a restless soul before. Has he heard all about us? Is Thakurpo very angry?'

Mahendra said, 'Why else would someone go away to the west in this desperate heat?'

Binodini asked, 'Did he say anything about me?'

Mahendra said, 'What is there to say? Here's the letter.'

Mahendra handed the letter to Binodini and began to scan her face with eagle eyes for every reaction.

Binodini took the letter hastily and found that the envelope was open and the writing on the envelope was hers, addressed to Behari. She took it out of the envelope and found that it was her letter. She turned it this way and that and failed to find even a line of reply from Behari.

After a few moments' silence Binodini asked Mahendra, 'Have you read the letter?'

The look on her face frightened Mahendra and the lie slipped out easily, 'No.'

Binodini tore the letter into tiny bits and threw it out of the window.

Mahendra said, 'I am going home.'

Binodini did not answer him.

Mahendra said, 'I shall do exactly as you wish. I will stay at home for seven days. On my way to college every day I'll look into the matters here and leave the rest in Khemi's hands. I shall not disturb you by seeking an audience.'

It was hard to tell if Binodini heard a single word Mahendra spoke; there was no answer. She stared out of the open window, into the dark sky.

Mahendra collected his things and left the house.

Binodini sat in the deserted house, alone and immovable— until finally, perhaps to revive her senses forcibly, she tore off her sari and began to whip herself with it ruthlessly. Khemi heard the sounds and came running, 'Bou-thakurun, what are you doing?'

Binodini snarled, 'You get out of here,' and shooed Khemi out of the room. Then she slammed the door noisily, bunched up her fists, threw herself on the ground and howled like a wounded animal. Eventually, she wore herself out and lay in a faint under the open window all night long.

When the sun rose the next morning, she was gripped by suspicion: suppose Behari hadn't left the city and Mahendra had said that to her merely to delude her? Binodini summoned Khemi immediately and said, 'Khemi, go to Behari-thakurpo's house immediately and find out how they are doing.'

Khemi returned an hour later and said, 'All the doors and windows of Beharibabu's house are firmly shut. When I banged on the door the bearer said from within that the master wasn't at home—he had gone west.'

Now Binodini's doubts were laid to rest.

42

WHEN RAJLAKSHMI HEARD THAT MAHENDRA HAD LEFT HOME THAT
same night, she was displeased with her daughter-in-law.
Rajlakshmi thought Asha's condemnation must have driven
her son away. So she asked Asha, 'Why did Mahendra go
away last night?'

Asha looked at the floor as she said, 'I don't know,
Mother.'

Rajlakshmi thought this was merely Asha's wounded ego
speaking. Disgruntled, she said, 'If you don't know, who
would? Did you say anything to him?'

Asha merely said, 'No.'

Rajlakshmi didn't believe her. This was impossible. She
asked, 'What time did Mahin leave last night?'

Asha cringed in discomfiture and said, 'I don't know.'

Rajlakshmi was furious. 'You don't know anything! My
little china doll! Very smart, aren't you?'

Rajlakshmi blamed Asha's behaviour and inadequate
personality for Mahendra's actions and spoke her mind
vehemently. Asha accepted the insult with her head bowed,
went away to her room and began to cry. She thought, 'I
scarcely know why my husband loved me once upon a time
and now that he doesn't, I don't know how to win his love
back.' When you were loved, your heart told you how to
please him. But how would she know how to win the heart
of someone who didn't love her? How on earth was she
supposed to make a brazen attempt at winning back the

affections of someone who loved another woman instead?

At dusk the family priest and his sister, Acharya-thakurun, came to the house. Rajlakshmi had sent for them in order to conduct some prayers to a favourable constellation for her son. Rajlakshmi requested the priest to read her daughter-in-law's palm, but that was just a pretext for her to present the unfortunate Asha to the priest. The poor girl cringed in shame when her disgrace was being discussed in public. She sat down, palm extended and eyes lowered. Suddenly, Rajlakshmi heard the soft tread of shoes outside the room, along the dark veranda. Someone was trying to sneak past the door. Rajlakshmi called out, 'Who is it?'

At first there was no response. When she called out again, 'Who goes there?' Mahendra stepped in silently.

Far from being thrilled, Asha's heart brimmed over with sadness for Mahendra. He now had to walk into his own house in stealth. Asha was all the more embarrassed because the priest and his sister were seated there. For her, the censorious gaze of the whole world actually seemed greater than her own personal sorrow. Rajlakshmi murmured to Asha, 'Bou-ma, tell Parvati to bring Mahin's dinner upstairs.' Asha replied, 'I'll get it, Mother.' She wanted to shield Mahendra even from the gaze of the servants.

Meanwhile, Mahendra was quite upset when he found the family priest and his sister in the room. He couldn't bear the thought that his mother and his wife were conniving with these illiterate oafs in order to control him by occult methods. To add to it, when Acharya-thakurun asked him in a honeyed voice, 'How are you, my son,' Mahendra was hard put to sit there any longer. He didn't respond to the question and spoke to Rajlakshmi, 'Mother, I'm going upstairs.'

Rajlakshmi thought he wanted to go up and have a few words in private with his wife. Delighted at the prospect, she rushed to the kitchen and said to Asha, 'Go on, go upstairs quickly—I believe Mahin wants something.'

Asha went upstairs with a beating heart and faltering steps. From what Rajlakshmi had said, Asha had thought that Mahendra had sent for her. But she simply couldn't walk into the room uninvited. Instead she stood at the threshold, in the dark, and gazed at Mahendra.

He was lying on the mattress upon the floor, staring desolately at the beams on the ceiling. This was the same Mahendra she had known, everything about him was the same, yet what a change there was! There was a time when Mahendra had turned this tiny room into heaven for Asha. Why then was he insulting the same room, drenched as it was in happy memories? If you are so sad, so restless, and so piqued, please do not sit upon that bed, Mahendra! If you do not remember those fulfilling, profound nights, the intense afternoons, the fancy-free monsoon days, the overpowering spring evenings swept by a mild breeze, the endless, unlimited, countless conversations that you have had in this room, there are many other rooms to choose from in this house—but do not tarry here a moment longer.

The longer Asha stood there staring at Mahendra, the more she felt that he had just come from Binodini's arms—her touch clung to his body, his eyes held her image, her voice rang in his ears and his heart was filled with desire for her. How could Asha gift her chaste devotion to this Mahendra, how could she say, 'Come unto my steadfast heart, come and place your feet upon the spotless lilies of my chaste wifely devotion'? She couldn't bring herself to follow her aunt's advice, the words of the holy texts and religious sermons. She no longer perceived this Mahendra—dispossessed of conjugal loyalties—as her god. Today, Asha immersed her deity and let go of her devotion in Binodini's oceans muddied by sin; in the dark of that loveless night, the drums of farewell echoed in solemn and sombre tones in her ears, in her heart and mind, in her veins, all around her, in the stars of her sky, in her very own terrace, in her own room, on her own bed.

Binodini's Mahendra was like a strange man for Asha, or something even worse—even with a stranger she wouldn't feel such terrible shame. She simply couldn't bring herself to enter the room.

At one point Mahendra's careless eyes slid down from the ceiling and came to rest on the wall in front of him. Asha followed his gaze and found her own photograph adorning the wall, right beside Mahendra's. She wanted to cover it, tear it off the wall and take it away. She began to curse herself for not noticing it earlier; she should have thrown it away. Asha felt Mahendra was laughing at it and along with him, the image of Binodini that he held in his heart, was also casting an oblique glance at the photograph through her arched brows and smiling in cruel mockery.

Finally, Mahendra's gaze dropped from the wall and roamed around the room. These days whenever Asha had the time to spare from attending to her mother-in-law, she studied until late in the night, wishing to rid herself of her ignorance. Her textbooks and notebooks were neatly arranged in a corner of the room. Suddenly, Mahendra picked out one idly and began to glance through it. Asha wanted to scream and snatch it away from him violently. She could barely stand still as she visualized Mahendra's contemptuous gaze taking in her childish scrawls. Quickly she walked towards the stairs, without making any attempt to hide her presence.

Mahendra's dinner was ready. Rajlakshmi was under the impression that he was busy talking to Asha and so she didn't feel like disturbing him by calling him for his meal. But when she saw Asha coming downstairs, she laid out the dinner and sent word to Mahendra. The minute he went down to eat, Asha ran into the bedroom, tore her own photograph into bits and threw it over the terrace wall, picked up her books and took them away with her.

After the meal Mahendra went and sat in his room again. Rajlakshmi couldn't find Asha anywhere. Eventually, she went down to the kitchen and found Asha boiling the milk for Rajlakshmi. There was no need for this because the maid who usually did this chore stood close by, protesting at this undue interest from Asha. The maid was quite upset about losing her chance of stealing the little bit of milk that she replaced every night with water.

Rajlakshmi said, 'Bou-ma, what's this! Go upstairs.'

Asha went upstairs and took refuge in Rajlakshmi's room. Rajlakshmi was vexed at this behaviour as she thought, 'If Mahendra has come home for a short while, disentangling himself from that siren's clutches, Asha will send him back to her with tantrums and ego tussles like this. After all, it was Asha's fault that Mahendra was caught in Binodini's snares. A man, by nature, is bound to go astray. It is the wife's duty to keep him on the straight and narrow path, by fair means or foul.'

Rajlakshmi spoke to Asha in harsh and unsparing tones, 'What kind of behaviour is this, Bou-ma? You're fortunate enough that your husband has come home; why are you skulking around corners with a sullen face?'

Asha felt she was really at fault and so she ran upstairs in deep distress; without giving herself a chance to think twice, she took a deep breath and stepped into the bedroom. It was past ten o'clock now. Mahendra was standing in front of the bed with a thoughtful expression on his face, dusting the mosquito net slowly. He was beset by a strong sense of indignation against Binodini as he thought, 'Does she take me for such a worthless knave that she didn't feel a moment's fear when she sent me to Asha? From this day on if I revert to abiding by my duties towards Asha, who in this world will be there for Binodini to lean on? Am I such an oaf that this course of action is unthinkable for me? Is that how Binodini sees me? I have lost her respect, failed to win her heart—and been humbled by her.' As he stood before the bed, Mahendra vowed to protest against this disregard from Binodini—by hook or by crook; he'd incline his heart towards Asha once again and take his revenge on Binodini.

When Asha stepped into the room, Mahendra's careless dusting of the mosquito net came to an abrupt halt. He was faced with the insurmountable problem of finding something to say to Asha.

Mahendra tried to smile, failed miserably and said the first thing that came to his mind, 'I see that you have also taken to studies, like me. Where are the books that I saw here some time back?'

The words were not merely out of place, but they also

seemed like a whiplash to Asha. The fact that the illiterate Asha was trying to educate herself, was a matter she was very sensitive about. Asha was convinced that it was a laughable thing to do. And if there was one person whose derision and mockery she was determined to shield this matter from, it was Mahendra. When Mahendra, after all these days, chose to begin his conversation with a reference to that very subject, Asha cringed in pain like a small child cringes before the cruel lashes of the schoolteacher's cane. She didn't say a word as she looked away and stood there holding on to the edge of the teapoy.

Mahendra too realized, the minute the words were out, that it wasn't the most apt and opportune thing to bring up. But he simply couldn't think of anything else to say under the circumstances. After the hurricane that had swept their lives, simple words from the past would sound awkward; the heart too was silent, unprepared with new words to say. Mahendra thought, 'If we get into bed, it may be easier to find words within that enclosed, confined intimacy.' With that notion Mahendra began to dust the outside of the mosquito net once again. He began to go over his dialogue and his performance in the manner of a new actor standing in the wings and nervously memorizing his lines just before he has to walk on to the stage. Suddenly, a mild sound made him turn around, and he found Asha had left the room.

43

THE FOLLOWING MORNING MAHENDRA SAID TO RAJLAKSHMI, 'MOTHER, I need a room of my own for my studies. I'd like to stay in Aunty's old room.'

Rajlakshmi was thrilled as she thought, 'So then, Mahin will stay at home now. He must have resolved everything with Bou-ma. How could he possibly neglect my darling daughter-in-law for too long? And how long can one be spellbound by that siren, neglecting such a chaste wife?'

She replied in haste, 'Why, certainly Mahin!' She unlocked the room and set about dusting it and cleaning it with great ceremony. 'Bou, oh Bou, where is Bou?' she kept enquiring. After hunting high and low, a tentative Asha was dragged out of a corner of the house. 'Lay a fresh mattress here. There is no desk here—bring one and put it here. This lamp will not do; send the one from upstairs.' In this manner, between the two of them, they prepared a princely seat for the monarch of the house in Annapurna's old room. Mahendra didn't spare a second glance at his willing slaves, moved into the room with his books and notes, and without wasting a single moment, sat down to study.

In the evening, after his dinner, he went back to his books. No one could tell if he would go up to his bedroom to sleep or if he'd sleep in his room downstairs. Rajlakshmi decked a stiff, doll-like Asha in all her finery and said, 'Go on, Bou-ma, ask Mahin if his bed should be made upstairs?'

Asha's feet refused to budge. She stood in silence with

her head bent low. An irate Rajlakshmi began to hurl cruel accusations at her. Asha dragged her feet up to the door but simply couldn't go any further. Rajlakshmi looked at Asha from a corner of the corridor and gestured wildly for her to go on inside.

In desperation, Asha walked into the room. Mahendra heard her footsteps behind him and spoke without turning his head, 'I'll be here for some more time—tomorrow I have to wake up early to study—I shall sleep here tonight.'

Oh, the shame of it! Was Asha here to persuade Mahendra to go and sleep upstairs?

As she stepped out of the room, Rajlakshmi asked her eagerly, 'What's the matter, what happened?'

Asha said, 'He is studying, he'll sleep downstairs.' She went into her own dishonoured bedroom. There was no peace to be had anywhere—every little inch of this earth flamed like the desert under an afternoon sun.

A little late in the night there was a banging on Asha's closed door. 'Bou, Bou, open the door.'

Quickly, Asha held the door open. Rajlakshmi had braved the stairs despite her asthma and now she stood there gasping for breath. She tumbled into the room and flopped down on the bed. When she recovered her breath, she spoke in hoarse tones, 'Bou, what are you up to? Why have you come up and shut the door? Is this a time for petty tantrums? Your misery should teach you a few lessons! Go on, go downstairs.'

Asha spoke softly, 'He wishes to be alone.'

Rajlakshmi said, 'And that is that? He may have spoken in anger, without thinking twice, but you don't have to take him up on his word. You cannot afford to be so arrogant. Go now, go quickly.'

In times of trouble, the mother-in-law had no secrets from the daughter-in-law. She wanted to use the only weapons she had to bind Mahendra irrevocably.

As she spoke fervently, Rajlakshmi again had trouble breathing. She calmed herself a bit and rose. Without a word Asha held her and walked downstairs with her. She took Rajlakshmi into her bedroom, sat her down on the bed and began to plump up the pillows and cushions behind her. Rajlakshmi said, 'Let it be for now, Bou-ma. Send Sudho, the maid, to me. You go on, don't linger here.'

This time Asha did not hesitate. She walked out of her mother-in-law's room and headed straight for Mahendra's room. The book lay open in front of Mahendra—he sat with his feet hoisted on the desk and his head resting on the backrest, thinking intently. When he heard her footsteps, he looked up in surprise and turned his head, as if wishing the fleeting appearance of the one in whose thoughts he was lost. When he saw Asha he composed himself, put his feet down and pulled his book to him.

Mahendra was quite stunned today. Usually Asha never appeared before him thus, so boldly. If their paths ever happened to cross, she moved away immediately. But today, at this late hour, her sudden entry into his room was really quite incredible. Without lifting his head from his book, Mahendra sensed that Asha showed no signs of leaving. She came and stood in front of him, still and silent. Now he could no longer pretend to go on reading. He looked up. Asha spoke in clear, ringing tones, 'Mother's had an asthma attack. Could you please take a look at her?'

Mahendra asked, 'Where is she?'

Asha said, 'In her bedroom; she's not able to sleep.'

Mahendra said, 'Come on then, let me go and take a look.'

After ages, this tiny communion with Asha made Mahendra feel very buoyant. Silence had stood between them like an impregnable fortress. Mahendra had no weapons to tear the barrier down. Asha had suddenly opened a door to the fort with her own hands.

Asha waited outside Rajlakshmi's room, while Mahendra went in. Rajlakshmi viewed this inopportune arrival of Mahendra with anxiety—she feared he had sparred with Asha once again and was ready to leave the house. She said, 'Mahin, haven't you gone to bed yet?'

Mahendra said, 'Mother, is your asthma troubling you?'

This question, long awaited and coming so late, piqued the mother deeply. She realized that Mahin had come to ask after her health today only at Asha's insistence. This anxious agony only augmented her trouble and she spoke with difficulty, 'Go on, go to bed—my asthma is nothing.'

Mahendra said, 'No, Mother, it's best to do a check-up; this isn't something one should ignore.'

Mahendra knew that his mother had a weak heart and the look on her face was not too reassuring—he was anxious.

Rajlakshmi said, 'There's no need for a check-up; my ailment is beyond cure.'

Mahendra said, 'All right, let me get you a sleeping pill for tonight and tomorrow we shall examine you thoroughly.'

Rajlakshmi said, 'I've had enough of pills; they don't work on me. Go on, Mahin, it's very late—you go and sleep.'

Mahendra replied, 'I'll go as soon as you feel a little better.'

Miffed and hurt, Rajlakshmi addressed Asha, concealed behind the door, and said, 'Bou, why did you bother Mahin so late at night and fetch him here?' As she spoke she could scarcely breathe.

Asha stepped into the room now and addressed Mahendra in soft yet firm tones, 'Go on, you go to sleep. I'll stay with Mother.'

Mahendra called Asha out of the room and said to her, 'I am sending for some medicine; there'll be two doses in the bottle. Give her one dose first and if she still cannot sleep, administer the second dose after an hour. If it gets worse in the night, don't forget to send for me.'

Mahendra went back to his room. This new face of Asha was a novelty to him. This Asha had no diffidence, no inadequacy; this Asha was confident of what she was doing and she wasn't begging for protection from him. Mahendra may have rejected his wife, but he felt a growing respect for the daughter-in-law of the house.

Rajlakshmi was secretly pleased that Asha had fetched Mahendra out of concern for her health. What she said, however, was, 'Bou-ma, I sent you to sleep—why did you drag Mahendra here?'

Asha didn't answer her and simply began to fan her as she sat behind her on the bed.

Rajlakshmi said, 'Go to bed, Bou-ma.'

Asha spoke softly, 'He has asked me to stay here.' Asha knew that Rajlakshmi would be pleased to hear that Mahendra had instructed her to serve his mother.

44

WHEN IT BECAME OBVIOUS TO RAJLAKSHMI THAT ASHA WASN'T ABLE to hold on to Mahendra, she felt, 'If my illness is the pretext needed to hold Mahin back, so be it.' She was afraid that she might be completely cured soon. She began to pull the wool over Asha's eyes and to throw her medication away.

Mahendra, in his preoccupation, didn't notice anything. But Asha perceived clearly that Rajlakshmi's ailment had worsened. She thought that perhaps Mahendra wasn't giving enough thought to his choice of drugs and treatment; so lost was he in his own confusions that even his mother's illness couldn't prod him out of his daze. Asha couldn't help feeling disgusted at the extent of Mahendra's downfall. If a man was ruined in one way, did he have to let everything go in this manner?

One evening, as she was in the throes of pain, Rajlakshmi suddenly recalled Behari. It was ages since he had visited them. She asked Asha, 'Bou-ma, do you know where Behari is right now?' Asha realized that it was Behari who had always nursed Rajlakshmi when she was sick and that's why she was thinking of him now. But Behari, once the bulwark of the household, had also been thrown out. Had he been here, Asha thought, Rajlakshmi would have received proper treatment— he wasn't as heartless as Mahendra. She heaved a sigh.

Rajlakshmi said, 'Has Mahin had a fight with Behari? That's very wrong, Bou-ma. Mahin doesn't have a greater well-wisher, a better friend than him.' As she spoke tears gathered in her eyes.

Many memories flitted slowly through Asha's mind. She recalled how many times, in various ways, Behari had tried to warn the stupid and unseeing Asha, thereby earning her displeasure; today she cursed herself for it. Why should fate spare a foolish woman who had hurled abuses at her true ally and drawn to her bosom her one and only foe? The poignant sighs that Behari had heaved as he left the house were bound to echo between the walls and have an effect someday.

Rajlakshmi was silent and thoughtful for a while before she spoke again, 'Bou-ma, if Behari had been here, he could have saved us in these times of trouble—things wouldn't have gone so wrong.'

Asha sat mutely, lost in her thoughts. Rajlakshmi sighed and said again, 'If he hears I am sick, he won't be able to stop himself from coming over.'

Asha realized that Rajlakshmi wanted this news to reach Behari. She was evidently feeling quite helpless in his absence.

Mahendra was standing by the moonlit window in silence, with the room in darkness. He was tired of studying. The house did not provide him any happiness. When you are estranged from your closest ones, it is not possible to discard them like strangers; neither can you draw them to your bosom comfortably. This weighs heavy on the heart and constricts one's breath. Mahendra hesitated nowadays before going to his mother; if she ever saw him approach, she looked at his face with such anxious panic that he felt wounded. If Asha ever came anywhere close to him, he had trouble finding words to say; but the silence between them was equally troubling. His days had turned into a living nightmare.

Mahendra had vowed that he wouldn't set eyes on Binodini for at least seven days. Two days were left for the week to be over—how would he endure those two days?

Mahendra was lost in these thoughts when he heard footsteps behind him. He knew Asha had entered the room. He stood still, pretending not to have heard her. Asha realized his pretense, but she didn't leave the room. She stood behind him and said, 'There's something I have to say—I'll finish saying it and then I'll leave.'

Mahendra turned around and said, 'You don't have to leave—why don't you sit for a while?'

Asha paid no heed to this courteous offer and continued, 'Behari-thakurpo needs to be told about Mother's illness.'

The very mention of Behari was like adding insult to injury for Mahendra. He composed himself and said, 'But why? Don't you have faith in my treatment?'

Asha was already too upset at the thought that Mahendra wasn't working hard enough on his mother's treatment and so she blurted out, 'Well, Mother's ailment hasn't abated one bit! It seems to get worse every day.'

The covert criticism cloaked in this simple statement of fact hit Mahendra hard. Never before had Asha hurled such masked allegations at him. His ego was wounded and he spoke in bemused derision, 'I suppose now I'll have to take medical lessons from you.'

Asha's deep feeling of hurt got a fresh jolt at this disparagement. The room was in darkness; the ever-silent Asha gathered her courage and spoke with resolute vigour, 'Perhaps not medical lessons, but you can surely take lessons on caring for your mother.'

Such a riposte from Asha left Mahendra gasping for words. The unfamiliar harshness of Asha's words made Mahendra turn vicious and he said, 'You are well aware why I have forbidden your Behari-thakurpo to enter this house— I suppose you've begun to miss him again!'

Asha stormed out of the room. She felt impelled to leave because of an onrush of shame. The shame wasn't for herself. How could the person who was himself neck-deep in culpability utter such baseless allegations? Such brazenness could not be covered over even by mountains of mortification.

The moment Asha left, Mahendra perceived his total defeat. He had never imagined that Asha would, in any situation, ever be capable of reprimanding him thus. He realized that his status had now been dragged down from the throne to the ground. He was suddenly gripped by a fear lest Asha's anguish turned into disgust.

Meanwhile, the very mention of Behari filled him with anxious qualms about Binodini. He didn't know whether Behari was back from his trip. In the meantime, Binodini may have found him and the two may even have met up. Mahendra could scarcely honour his vow now.

That night Rajlakshmi's ailment took a turn for the worse and she sent for Mahendra. She spoke with great difficulty, 'Mahin, I would dearly love to see Behari—he hasn't come around for ages now.'

Asha was fanning her mother-in-law as she sat with her eyes lowered to the ground. Mahendra said, 'He is not here; he left on a trip to the west or somewhere.'

Rajlakshmi said, 'I feel certain he is right here and he's just staying away because he is upset with you. For pity's sake, please go and look him up tomorrow.'

Mahendra said, 'All right, I will.'

Today everyone was reaching out for Behari. Mahendra felt that no one in the whole wide world wanted or desired him.

45

THE VERY NEXT MORNING MAHENDRA LANDED UP AT BEHARI'S house. He found the servants at the gate, loading furniture onto several bullock carts. Mahendra asked Bhoju, 'What's up?'

Bhoju said, 'The master has acquired a farmhouse by the river Ganga in Bally and everything is being moved there.'

Mahendra asked, 'Is the master at home?'

Bhoju said, 'He spent just two days in Kolkata and yesterday he went back to Bally.'

Mahendra's heart sank. He was sure that Binodini and Behari had met in his absence. In his mind's eye he could see a similar queue of bullock carts at Binodini's door, and furniture being loaded onto them. He felt certain that for this very reason Binodini had made him, the senseless fool, stay away from her house.

Without a second's delay, Mahendra leaped onto his carriage and barked orders at the coachman. He swore continuously at the coachman for the tardiness of the horses. Once inside the lane at Patoldanga, he found that there were no preparations for a move or transfer. He was afraid that it had all been accomplished already. He banged on the door loudly. The minute the old servant opened the door, Mahendra asked, 'Is everything all right?' He replied, 'Yes sir, everything's fine.'

Mahendra went upstairs. Binodini was in the bathroom. Mahendra stepped into her bedroom and threw himself on Binodini's unmade bed. He gripped the soft mattress with both hands, buried his face in the pillow and took in the scent with a deep breath as he said, 'Heartless! Heartless!'

Thus he emptied his heart of its turbulent emotions, left the bed and began to wait impatiently for Binodini. As he paced the floor he noticed a Bangla daily lying open upon the mattress on the floor. He picked it up casually to pass his time. But from the first spot on which glance fell, Behari's name leaped out at him. In an instant his whole being was concentrated on the newspaper. A report said that Behari had acquired a property in Bally, beside the Ganga, where he proposed to provide free treatment to poor and needy gentlefolk—the clinic could accommodate five people at a time, etc. etc.

Binodini had obviously seen this piece of news. What did she feel? Mahendra felt sure that Binodini yearned to go away to Bally. He was further agitated at the thought that this new step taken by Behari would only enhance Binodini's respect for him. As for himself, Mahendra labelled Behari a 'humbug' and his new venture a 'vagary'; he thought, 'Behari has always had a penchant of making a show of doing good.' As opposed to Behari, Mahendra tried to laud himself as a very spontaneous and genuine person, thinking, 'I abhor the attempt to con simple folk under the guise of philanthropy and altruism.' But alas, perhaps people, and one person in particular, would not really appreciate the worth of his sincerity and lack of subterfuge. Mahendra began to feel this was another way in which Behari had unfairly scored over him.

As he heard Binodini's footsteps, Mahendra folded up the newspaper and sat upon it. When a freshly bathed Binodini entered the room Mahendra looked up at her—and reeled in shock. What a change had come over her—she seemed to have endured austere penance through fire in the last few days. She had grown thin and a strange glow emanated from behind her pallid face.

Binodini had given up all hopes of hearing from Behari. Imagining Behari's obvious indifference towards her, she had suffered in silence every minute of the day. She knew no ways of liberating herself from this torment. She felt Behari had gone away after rejecting her and she had no way of reaching him any more. Binodini, who loved to do the housework to perfection, felt stifled in the walled confines of this house where she had nothing to do—all her energies turned inwards and lacerated her instead. When she imagined her entire future within the confines of this loveless, joyless, activity-less house, when she contemplated this narrow lane and thoughts of living there forever, her rebellious nature made vain attempts at battering away at the sky in mute frustration against providence. Binodini felt relentless hatred and disgust for Mahendra, the senseless fool who had closed out all her escape routes and constricted her life thus. She realized that she would no longer be able to keep Mahendra at arm's length. In this tiny house, Mahendra would inch relentlessly closer to her—every day he'd edge closer, propelled by an invisible attraction; she knew that disgusting battles would be fought within this black hole, on this grimy bed of an immoral life, between hatred and attraction. How could she protect herself from the deadly whiplash of the dragon's tail when she had dug out with her own hands, this drooling, lusting, filthy beast from the depths of Mahendra's heart? On the one hand was her anguished heart, on the other was her entrapment in this tiny house and added to that the waves of Mahendra's desire crashing away at the door—Binodini's soul recoiled in fear. Where would all this end? When would she be free of it all?

The sight of Binodini's gaunt, pallid face lit the fires of jealousy in Mahendra's heart. Did he have any powers by which he could, forcefully, uproot all thoughts of Behari from this woman's heart? The eagle flies down and snatches away the lamb in one fell swoop and flies back to its nest atop the insurmountable mountain. Wasn't there one such spot, shrouded in the clouds and beyond all memories, where a lone Mahendra could hold his gentle, pretty captive to his bosom? The heat of envy augmented the force of his desire. Now he could no longer let Binodini go out of his sight, even for an instant. He must keep the nightmare of Behari at bay; he didn't dare to give Behari even an inch of opportunity hereafter.

Mahendra had read in Sanskrit poetry that the anguish of separation lent a softness to a woman's beauty. Today, the more he looked at Binodini he realized the truth of it, and his heart was astir with a cavernous sorrow tinged with pleasure.

After a few moments of silence Binodini asked Mahendra, 'Have you had tea?'

Mahendra said, 'I may have, but please don't let that stop you from making me another cup with your hands—fill my cup, oh beloved!'

Perhaps quite deliberately, Binodini chose to cruelly lash out at this burst of passion from Mahendra, asking abruptly, 'Do you happen to know where Behari-thakurpo is right now?'

Mahendra lost colour in an instant as he replied, 'He is not in Kolkata now.'

Binodini said, 'What is his new address?'

Mahendra replied, 'He doesn't wish to disclose that to anyone.'

Binodini said, 'Is it possible to look for him and locate it?'

Mahendra said, 'I have no urgent need to do that.'

Binodini said, 'Need is not everything. Isn't a friendship as old as this worth something?'

Mahendra said, 'Behari may be a very old friend of mine, but you have known him for a very short while—yet I sense that you have a greater urgency to find out where he is.'

Binodini retorted, 'That should tell you something; hasn't a friend like that taught you the meaning of the word friendship?'

Mahendra replied, 'No, and that's no great loss to me. But if I had learnt the art of stealing a woman's heart by deception, it would have stood me in good stead now.'

Binodini said, 'That particular art requires skill and not just intent.'

Mahendra said mockingly, 'If you know the guru's

whereabouts please divulge it to me—at this age I'm ready to go and take tuitions from him. Then we shall see about skill.'

Binodini said, 'If you fail to locate your friend's address, do not utter words of love to me. After the way you have treated Behari-thakurpo, who can trust you?'

Mahendra said, 'If you didn't trust me totally, you would not have humiliated me thus. If only you hadn't been supremely confident of my love, I would have suffered less today. Behari knows the art of not-being-tamed and if he had taught me that art, he'd have been a true friend indeed.'

'Behari-thakurpo is human and hence he cannot be tamed,' Binodini said as she stood by the window as before, her black tresses snaking down her back. Suddenly, Mahendra stood up, bunched up his fists and shouted in fury, 'How do you have the nerve to humiliate me like this time and again? Is it your belief in my goodness or your superiority that makes you so sure I won't retaliate? If you truly believe I am sub-human, know me to be a brute indeed. I am not so unmanly as to be unable to inflict a wound when I'm hurt.' He gazed at Binodini's face for a few silent seconds. Then he said, 'Binod, let's go away from here. Let's begin our journey—be it the west or the mountains, wherever you wish to go. This is no place to live—it's killing me.'

Binodini said, 'Let's go right away then—let's go towards the west.'

Mahendra said, 'Where in the west?'

Binodini said, 'Nowhere in particular; we shan't stay in the same place for more than two days, we'll keep moving.'

Mahendra said, 'That's good; let's leave tonight.'

Binodini agreed and went away to cook Mahendra's meal.

Mahendra understood that the news item about Behari had escaped Binodini's notice. She no longer had the powers of deliberation necessary to concentrate on a newspaper. He spent the whole day on edge, lest that particular news reached Binodini somehow.

46

MAHENDRA'S LUNCH WAS PREPARED AT HOME, IN THE HOPE THAT he'd come back after looking up Behari. When he didn't return, an ailing Rajlakshmi grew anxious. Lack of sleep the night before had already weakened her and worrying over Mahendra did her no good at this stage. Asha went to check and found that Mahendra's carriage had returned. The coachman informed her that from Behari's house Mahendra had gone to the flat in Patoldanga. At this news, Rajlakshmi turned her face to the wall and lay still. Asha sat by her head, her face turned to stone, and fanned her. On other days Rajlakshmi always urged Asha to go and have her meal on time. Today she didn't say anything. If, even after seeing how ill she was the night before, Mahendra felt drawn towards Binodini today, Rajlakshmi had nothing left to live for. She was well aware that Mahendra was not taking her ailment seriously; he was secure in the knowledge that this time too, as on every other occasion, her illness was a temporary malady, curable in a few days. And this casual complacence struck Rajlakshmi as very cruel indeed. In the throes of passion, Mahendra refused to acknowledge any anxiety or any concern and hence he was making light of his mother's pain; he rushed to Binodini at every brazen opportunity lest he found himself bound to his ailing mother's bedside. Rajlakshmi lost all interest in recovery—in a fit of sorrow, she wanted to prove to Mahendra how unfounded his complacence was.

At two in the afternoon Asha said, 'Mother, it's time for your medication.' Rajlakshmi didn't respond. When Asha rose to go and fetch the medicine, she said, 'There's no need for medicines, Bou-ma. You may go.'

Asha could fathom Rajlakshmi's pain and when its ripples touched her own heart, she could hold still no longer. She tried to stifle her sobs, but they broke forth nonetheless. Rajlakshmi half-turned on her side, took Asha's hands in her own and stroked them with gentle compassion as she said, 'Bou-ma, you are very young, there's time yet for you to find happiness. But don't work so hard on my account, my dear— I have lived long enough; there's no point in going on.'

Asha's sobs only increased at these words and she pressed her anchal over her lips.

In this way, the cheerless day dragged on. In spite of their misery and hurt, both Rajlakshmi and Asha hoped in their heart of hearts that Mahendra would arrive at any moment. Both of them realized that they were sitting up at every little sound that came to their ears. Gradually, twilight cast its shadow into the inner chambers of the house—it held neither the joy of light nor the comfort of darkness. It made sorrow weigh heavier and despondency tearless; it stole away the power to work or hope and yet, didn't bring the peace of respite or liberation. In that withered, graceless dusk of the sick house Asha rose, lit a lamp and brought it into the room. Rajlakshmi said, 'Bou-ma, the light bothers me. Keep it outside.'

Asha took the lamp outside and came back to sit by Rajlakshmi's side. When the darkness grew thicker and brought the endless night from the outside into the tiny room, Asha asked in gentle tones, 'Mother, should I send word to him?'

Rajlakshmi answered firmly, 'No Bou-ma, this is my order to you—do not inform Mahendra.'

Asha stood there speechless. She didn't even have the strength to weep.

Outside, the bearer said, 'The master has sent a letter.'

In that instant Rajlakshmi thought that perhaps Mahendra was suddenly afflicted by some ailment and so he couldn't come; hence he had sent the letter. Contrite and concerned, she said, 'Go and take a look Bou-ma—see what Mahin has said.'

Asha held the letter with trembling fingers and read it in the light of the lamp outside the door. Mahendra wrote that he wasn't keeping too well lately and so he was off to the west. There was no need to worry overmuch about Rajlakshmi's health; he had instructed Nabin-doctor to check up on her regularly. He had left instructions for bouts of insomnia or headaches and along with the letter had sent two bottles of light and nutritious tonics that he'd fetched from the chemist's. In the postscript there was a request to be kept posted on his mother's health at an address in Giridih for the moment.

Asha stood there dumbfounded after she finished reading this letter. Her sorrow was overtaken by a terrible sense of guilt—how was she to convey this brutal news to Rajlakshmi?

Seeing the delay in Asha's return Rajlakshmi grew more concerned. She called out, 'Bou-ma, come here and tell me what Mahin has written.' In her eagerness she sat up on the bed.

So Asha came in and read out the letter slowly. Rajlakshmi said, 'What has he said about his health—just read that bit once again.'

Asha reiterated, 'I haven't been feeling too well lately and so I—'

Rajlakshmi said, 'That's enough, stop—how *could* he feel well! The old mother refuses to die and only bothers him with her sickness! Why did you have to tell him of my illness? At least he was at home; he sat in a corner with his books and didn't meddle in anybody's business. But you had to go and drag him into his mother's troubles and where has that got you—he has left the house! If I had died in one corner of the house, would that have been too bad? Even after all this, you haven't learnt a thing, Bou-ma.' Rajlakshmi lay back on the pillows, panting.

Outside, there was the sound of boots. The bearer said, 'The doctor is here.'

The doctor cleared his throat and stepped into the room. Asha quickly pulled her anchal over her head and moved to the side of the bed. The doctor asked Rajlakshmi, 'Could you tell me what your complaints are?'

Rajlakshmi roared angrily, 'What complaints! Won't you let a woman die in peace? If I have your medication, will I live forever?'

The doctor spoke placatingly, 'You may not live forever,

but at least I can reduce the pain—'

Rajlakshmi exclaimed, 'A true remedy for anguish was available to widows who jumped into their husband's pyres. Now, it's only a matter of prolonging the agony. Doctor, please go away—don't bother me; I want to be alone.'

Apprehensively the doctor said, 'May I check your pulse—'

Rajlakshmi spoke irately, 'I'm telling you to leave. My pulse is fine—there's no hope of it giving way in the near future.'

The doctor had no choice but to leave the room. From the door he sent for Asha. He quizzed her in detail about the symptoms of the ailment. After he had heard her out, he re-entered the room with a grave expression and said, 'Look here, Mahendra has entrusted a responsibility to me. If you refuse to let me treat you, he'd be hurt.'

Mahendra feeling hurt sounded like a joke to Rajlakshmi. She said, 'Don't worry too much about Mahin. Everyone is hurt some time in his life. This hurt will not kill Mahin. Please go now, doctor. Let me sleep a little.'

Nabin-doctor realized it was best not to disturb the patient further. He walked out slowly and gave explicit instructions to Asha about what had to be done.

When Asha came back Rajlakshmi said, 'Child, you go on and take some rest—you've been at my bedside all day long. Send the old maid here—she can sit in the next room while I rest.'

Asha knew Rajlakshmi well. This wasn't an affectionate request—it was a command that had to be obeyed. She sent Haru's mother, went into her own room and lay down upon the cool floor in the dark. The day-long fast and privation had left her feeling very weak. The wedding band was playing in some neighbour's house. Now the shehnai struck up again. The notes of the tune echoed in the dark of the night and reverberated everywhere, wounding Asha continually. Upon the dreamscape of the night unfolded every minute incident of her own wedding night: the lights, the chaos, the people, the garlands, the sandal paste, the smell of new clothes and the fumes of the holy fire, the timid, shy, joyous trembling of her new bride's heart; the more the memories took shape and embraced her, the more her sorrow took root and the more her heartache grew. Just as the hungry child, in the midst of a terrible famine, strikes out at his mother, demanding food, these animated memories of past joys looked to Asha's heart for nourishment and struck out at it vehemently when they found no response. A weary Asha could scarcely be quietly supine. She brought her palms together to pray to God; as she did so, the image of the only god she ever knew, that of her chaste and loving aunt, appeared within her tearful soul. Asha had vowed not to drag that saintly figure back into the murk and gloom of mundane lives ever again. But today she could see no way out for herself—the thick, dense anguish surrounding her did not permit even a tiny crack of hope. So Asha lit a lamp, pulled a notepad onto her lap and wrote a letter as she wiped away the tears that streamed from her eyes:

My respected Aunty,

You are all I have left in this world; please come over just this once and draw this unfortunate soul into your bosom.

Or else I'll surely die. I do not know what else to write.
I place a hundred thousand salutations at your venerable
feet.

Affectionately yours,

Chuni

47

ANNAPURNA RETURNED FROM KASHI, WALKED INTO RAJLAKSHMI'S
room slowly and touched her feet with respect. Despite the
intervening tiffs and rows, the sight of Annapurna gave
Rajlakshmi a new lease of life. Only after Annapurna's arrival
did Rajlakshmi realize that she'd been seeking her all this
while, reaching out to her, unknown even to her own self. In
an instant she recognized that much of her distress, much of
the ennui of the past few weeks were due to Annapurna's
absence. In one single moment she became her old self.
Rajlakshmi was flooded with memories of the old camaraderie
between the two sisters-in-law, which had been there even
before Mahendra's birth—from the day they had entered this
house as new brides and accepted the good and bad in it as
their own, in festivals, in death and sorrow—when they had
pulled the vehicle of this household together as one, with one
destination in mind. The dearest friend of her youth, with
whom she had once begun her journey, had come back to her
side after many interludes and interruptions. But the one for
whom Rajlakshmi had inflicted such wounds on this friend of

hers was now nowhere to be found.

Annapurna sat beside the ailing woman, took her hand in her own and said, 'Didi.'

Rajlakshmi said, 'Mejo-bou,' but she could not say anything more. The tears flowed from her eyes. Asha could no longer check herself; she went into the next room, collapsed on the floor and cried her heart out.

Annapurna did not dare to ask Rajlakshmi or Asha any questions about Mahendra. She called Sadhucharan and asked, 'Uncle, where is Mahin?'

Sadhucharan narrated the entire episode of Mahendra and Binodini. Annapurna asked, 'Where is Behari?'

Sadhucharan replied, 'He hasn't come here for many days now—I don't know his whereabouts.'

Annapurna said, 'Please go to Behari's house and get me news of him.'

Sadhucharan came back to say, 'He is not at home. He is in a farmhouse by the Ganga in Bally.'

Annapurna sent for Nabin-doctor and asked after the patient's health. He said, 'Along with her weak heart, she has now developed dropsy. Death may come suddenly, without warning.'

That evening, when Rajlakshmi's pain worsened, Annapurna asked her, 'Didi, may I send for Nabin-doctor?'

Rajlakshmi said, 'No Mejo-bou, Nabin-doctor won't be able to do anything for me.'

Annapurna said, 'Then tell me who would you like to see?'

Rajlakshmi said, 'It'll be good if you could send word to Behari.'

Annapurna was touched to the quick. One day at dusk, in a far-off land, she had slighted and sent Behari away from her doorstep, and the memory still perturbed her. Behari would never come back to her doorstep again. She had never imagined that in this lifetime she'd get another chance to set right that rebuff.

Annapurna went up to Mahendra's room on the terrace. Once this room had been the one cheerful spot in the house. Today it looked forlorn—the beds were unmade, the décor dishevelled; no one had watered the plants on the terrace and they looked withered.

Asha realized her aunt had gone up to the terrace and she followed her slowly. Annapurna pulled her into her heart and kissed her forehead. Asha went down on her knees, touched Annapurna's feet and laying her head on them said, 'Aunty, bless me, give me strength. I had never imagined that a person could bear such immense heartbreak. Oh Lord, how much longer can I bear this!'

Annapurna sat down on the floor and Asha lay down at her feet. Annapurna picked up her niece's head onto her lap and without saying a word, folded her own hands and meditated in silence.

This silent, loving benediction from Annapurna was like balm to the depths of Asha's soul; after an age she felt at peace. She felt her prayers were nearly answered—the gods may well ignore her, a silly and stupid girl, but they'd surely hear the prayers of her aunt.

With this reassurance and strength in her heart, Asha stood up with a sigh after a while. She said, 'Aunty, please write a letter to Behari-thakurpo.'

Annapurna said, 'No, a letter won't do.'

Asha said, 'But then, how will you send word to him?'

Annapurna said, 'Tomorrow I shall go and meet him in person.'

48

WHILE BEHARI WAS TRAVELLING IN THE WEST, HE HAD REALIZED THAT if he didn't bind himself to a mission, he would know no peace. He resolved to take up the onus of providing treatment to Kolkata's indigent clerks. The life of a low-income, needy clerk living in a shack in a narrow lane, burdened with a family, was like that of a fish in a pond in summer, when it thrashed about helplessly in the mud and gasped for breath as the water around it dried up. For many years Behari had nurtured sympathy for this pallid, emaciated, fretful bunch of gentlefolk. So he wanted to confer upon them the shade of the woods and the breeze of the Ganga.

He bought some land in Bally and with the help of some Chinese artisans started building tiny cottages there. But his heart knew no peace. As the day grew closer for him to inaugurate his mission, his soul rebelled against his chosen vocation. His heart echoed with one thought, 'There is no joy, no pleasure, no beauty in this work—it is nothing but a dreary burden.' Never before had Behari felt so oppressed by the prospect of work.

In the past, Behari had never needed anything. He had

always been able to apply himself with ease to the task at hand. But now he felt a strange kind of hunger without appeasing which he couldn't bring himself to feel an interest in anything. In keeping with his old habits he tried his hand at this and that; but in the very next moment he wanted to give it all up and be free of everything.

The yearning of youth which had lain dormant within him and whose existence he had been unaware of had suddenly come alive at Binodini's magic touch. It now began to prowl through the landscape, looking for objects to satisfy its hunger. Behari was unsettled by this hungry animal within himself; what would he do now with the sickly, withered community of clerks from Kolkata!

The Ganga, overflowing in the monsoon, streamed ahead. Every now and then indigo clouds inclined towards each other in intimate embrace over the thick foliage on the other bank. The river sometimes glinted like a steel sword and sometimes it glittered like a flashfire. Every time Behari's glance fell on this festive monsoon scenery, someone emerged from his heart and stood all alone beneath the serene blue glow of the sky; someone with her moist, jet-black tresses cascading in waves over her back—she collected all the scattered rays of the monsoon-laden clouds and directed upon him the unblinking, burning fire of her gaze.

Today, Behari felt that his past, which he had spent in peace and quiet, had actually been a grave loss. Many such overcast evenings and moonlit nights must have come with their untold boon of joys to Behari's empty heart, and gone back unfulfilled—so many melodies had remained unsung, and so many joyous occasions incomplete. Today, Binodini's uplifted face, with the proferred kiss hanging in the air, cast its rosy glow upon all his memories of the past and turned them into wan, insignificant shadows. He had wasted the larger part of his life as Mahendra's bosom friend! What had he gained from it? Behari had been unaware that the pathos of romance could exhume from the very heart of creation such a melodic tune on the flute. How could he now remove from his mind the memories of that woman, who had held him in her arms and elevated him all at once to this unimaginable place of beauty? Her gaze, her desires were everywhere now; her fervent, deep sighs raised waves in Behari's blood and the gentle warmth of her touch embraced Behari again and again and enlivened his heart like a blossoming flower.

And yet, why was Behari so far away from Binodini today? The reason was that he couldn't imagine a relationship that would be as beautiful as the beauty of the emotions with which she had drenched his soul. If you tried to pluck the lotus, the sludge came with it. Where could he place her in the web of relationships so that the exquisite would not be turned into the hideous? Besides, if a tug-of-war ensued with Mahendra, the whole thing would take such an ugly turn that Behari couldn't even bear to think about it. Hence, Behari had come away to this solitary bank of the Ganga, placed his idol on a pedestal and burned his heart like incense at her altar. He did not even write to Binodini or ask after her for fear that he would hear something that would destroy his house of cards.

On this cloudy morning Behari sat pensively in the southern corner of his garden beneath the berry tree. Tiny boats ferried to and fro on the river and he watched them idly. The sun rose higher in the sky. The servant came to ask him if he should get started on lunch. Behari said, 'Not now.' The chief artisan came to him for some urgent consultation and Behari said, 'Later, please.'

Suddenly, Behari was startled to find Annapurna standing before him. He sat up in a rush, held her feet in his firm grasp and bent to the ground, seeking her blessings. Annapurna stroked his head affectionately with her right hand and spoke in a voice laced with tears, 'Behari, why have you grown so thin?'

Behari said, 'So that I could get back your love, Aunty.'

Tears streamed down Annapurna's cheeks. Behari stood up attentively, 'Aunty, have you eaten yet?'

Annapurna said, 'No, it's not time yet.'

Behari said, 'Come then, let me lend you a hand. Today, after all these months I am dying to eat food cooked by you, off your plate after you are finished.'

Behari did not ask a word about Mahendra or Asha. One day, Annapurna had closed her door on Behari's face ruthlessly. With hurt pride, he obeyed her indictment to this day.

After lunch Annapurna said, 'Behari, the boat is ready at the quay—come to Kolkata right away.'

Behari said, 'But I have no work in Kolkata.'

Annapurna said, 'Didi is very ill, she has asked to see you.'

Behari looked up in startled disbelief. He asked, 'Where is Mahin da?'

Annapurna said, 'He is not in Kolkata. He is travelling in the west.'

Behari turned ashen as he heard this. He sat for a while in wordless silence.

Annapurna asked, 'Don't you know everything, Behari?'

Behari said, 'I know some of it, but not what has happened recently.'

So Annapurna narrated to him the events leading up to Mahendra's escape to the west with Binodini in tow. In a flash of a second the colour of the earth-sky and water changed before Behari's very eyes; the nectar of his imagination turned bitter all at once: 'So Binodini, the temptress, played with my emotions on that night! The surrender of her heart was a mere illusion! She left her village brazenly with Mahendra and headed westwards! Shame on her, and shame on me—I was a fool to have trusted her even for a moment.'

Alas for the overcast monsoon evening, alas for the rain-soaked full-moon night—where was their magical charm now?

49

BEHARI WONDERED HOW HE WOULD BE ABLE TO BRING HIMSELF TO look at the heartbroken Asha. When he stepped into the courtyard, the palpable pathos of the desolate house overwhelmed him. He looked at the servants and on behalf of Mahendra, culpable and absent, he hung his head in shame. He could not bring himself to ask of the familiar old retainers how they were, as he'd always done in the past. On the threshold of the inner chambers, his feet fairly dragged. Mahendra had hurled a vulnerable Asha into a naked humiliation that robbed a woman of all protective mantles and exposed her to the pitying, curious glances of the whole world. How could he bear to gaze upon Asha who would be injured and cringing?

But there was no time for these ruminations and quandaries. The moment he stepped inside, Asha walked up to him quickly and said, 'Thakurpo, please come quickly and take a look at Mother—she is really suffering.'

This was the first time Asha had addressed Behari directly. In times of trouble, masks are ripped away suddenly; people from far and wide are brought together in one lightning stroke and held close.

Asha's forthright fervour struck a chord in Behari. This tiny event told him much about the state in which Mahendra had left his family. The trauma of harsh times robs the household of charm and grace and the woman of the house has no opportunity, to shield herself. Trivial shields and barriers come crashing down—no one has time for them.

Behari stepped into Rajlakshmi's room. Rajlakshmi had lost all colour due to a sudden attack of breathlessness—but that passed and she soon composed herself.

Behari touched her feet and sought her blessings. Rajlakshmi indicated for him a seat beside her bed. She spoke slowly, 'How are you, Behari? It's been so long.'

Behari said, 'Mother, why didn't you let me know that you are unwell? I would have rushed to your side immediately.'

Rajlakshmi spoke softly, 'I know that, my child. I may not have given birth to you, but you are all I have left in this world.' Tears coursed down her cheeks as she spoke.

Behari got up hastily and pretended to examine the bottles and jars of medication on the shelf as he controlled his emotions. When he returned to check Rajlakshmi's pulse, she said, 'Leave my pulse alone—let me ask you, why have you grown so thin, Behari?' She reached out her bony fingers and stroked Behari's collarbone.

Behari replied, 'If I don't have fish curry cooked by you, my bones will wither away thus. Get well soon, Mother, and I'll keep everything ready in the kitchen.'

Rajlakshmi smiled wanly and said, 'Behari, you must bring home a bride; there's no one to look after you. O Mejo-bou, all of you must find him a bride now—just look at what he has done to himself.'

Annapurna said, 'Didi, you get well first. This is your duty and you will fulfil it. We shall all join in the fun and enjoy ourselves.'

Rajlakshmi said, 'There's no time left for me to do it, Mejo-bou; I leave Behari in your care—you must make him happy. I could not repay his debts. But God will be merciful to him.' She stroked Behari's head affectionately.

Asha couldn't stay in the room any longer—she went out to cry her heart out. Annapurna gazed lovingly at Behari through her tears.

Suddenly, Rajlakshmi seemed to remember something and she called out, 'Bou-ma, O Bou-ma!'

When Asha re-entered the room she said, 'Have you arranged for Behari's meal?'

Behari said, 'Mother, everyone knows this glutton of a son of yours. The minute I stepped into the courtyard I noticed Bami, the maid, rushing into the kitchen with a large, fresh fish. I knew then that this household still remembers my tastes.' Behari laughed and looked at Asha.

Today, Asha wasn't embarrassed. She smiled sweetly and accepted Behari's banter indulgently. In the past she hadn't known the full weight of Behari's place in this family. Often, she had taken him for an intruder and disregarded him; many a times her exasperation had shown through in her gestures. Today, she regretted it all and it lent a new edge to her respect and sympathy towards Behari.

Rajlakshmi said, 'Mejo-bou, the cook won't be any good— you'll have to take charge of the cooking today. This country lad of ours from the other side of the river needs his food very spicy or he doesn't take to it.'

Behari protested, 'Your mother came from Bikrampur, in East Bengal; and you call a gentleman from West Bengal's Nadia district a country lad from the other side of the river! This I cannot stand for.'

There was a spate of good-humoured exchanges and after many days, the pall of sorrow lifted a little from the house.

But amidst all this conversation, not one person mentioned Mahendra's name. In the past Rajlakshmi only talked of Mahendra to Behari. Mahendra had often teased his mother for this. And today, when the same Rajlakshmi never once mentioned Mahendra, Behari was silently shocked.

When Rajlakshmi seemed to drift into sleep, Behari came out of the room and said to Annapurna, 'Mother's ailment is quite grave.'

Annapurna said, 'That is very obvious.' She sat down by the window in her own room. After many minutes of silence she said, 'Don't you think you should go and fetch Mahin, Behari? We shouldn't wait any longer.'

After a long pause Behari said, 'I shall do as you say. Does anyone have his address?'

Annapurna said, 'Not exactly, you'll have to hunt for it. Behari, let me tell you one more thing. Take a look at Asha. If you cannot salvage Mahendra from Binodini's clutches, she will surely die. If you look at her face you can tell that she has no will left to live.'

Behari laughed at this irony deep in his heart and thought, 'I'm the right choice to go and salvage another—and who, pray, will be my salvation?'

Aloud he said, 'Aunty, do I possess the secret of keeping Mahin da away from Binodini forever? He may come now due to his mother's illness. But how can I promise that he won't go back later?'

At this point Asha walked in slowly with her anchal pulled slightly over her head and sat down at her aunt's feet. She knew that Annapurna was discussing Rajlakshmi's illness with Behari and she was eager to hear about it. When he saw the glow of mute anguish on the chaste Asha's face, Behari was filled with a sense of reverent admiration. This young woman had bathed in the holy waters of sorrow and acquired a divine status like the goddesses of ancient times—she was no longer an ordinary mortal; terrible grief seemed to have made her as old as the acsetic women that the Puranas described.

After Behari discussed Rajlakshmi's diet and medication with Asha and sent her on her way, he heaved a sigh and said to Annapurna, 'I must salvage Mahin da.'

Behari went to Mahendra's bank and found out that the latter had recently begun transactions with their branch in Allahabad.

50

AT THE STATION BINODINI CLAMBERED STRAIGHT INTO THE LADIES' coupe in the intermediate class. Mahendra said, 'What are you doing—I'll buy a second-class ticket for you.'

Binodini said, 'But why? I'll be fine here.'

Mahendra was a little surprised. Binodini enjoyed her luxuries. In the past all hint of paucity had been anathema to her. The inherent poverty of her own home had always mortified her. If there was one thing that Mahendra had realized, it was that once Binodini had felt drawn to the comforts of his home, and to its reputation of being richer than average. She had felt restless at the thought that she could very easily have been the mistress of these comforts and the rightful claimant to the household's dignity. But today, when she had a complete hold over Mahendra, when she could easily bring all his wealth to her service, why was she displaying such careless obstinacy and rebelliously welcoming the path of arduous, degrading hardships? The fact was that she wanted to curtail her dependence on Mahendra as far as possible. She didn't want to accept from Mahendra, the man who had dislodged her from her rightful sanctuary forever, anything that could be counted as recompense for her disgrace.

When Binodini lived in Mahendra's home, she had never followed the rigid rules of widowhood. But now she had begun to deprive herself of all pleasures. Now she had only one meal a day, wore a coarse sari and her perpetual laughter and banter were things of the past. Now she was so taciturn, masked, so distant and so forbidding that Mahendra didn't dare speak a harsh word to her. In amazement, impatience and fury, Mahendra said to himself, 'Binodini tried so hard to attain me—like the effort one makes to pluck a fruit from a lofty bough; why then did she cast the fruit away without even smelling it?'

Mahendra asked, 'For which place should I buy the tickets?'

Binodini said, 'Anywhere in the west—we can get down wherever the trains halts tomorrow morning.'

This kind of journey didn't appeal to Mahendra. He hated the disruption of his comfortable life. It would be difficult for Mahendra to survive without a proper dwelling in a big city. He wasn't the sort who could fend for himself and go where his fortunes took him. He boarded the train in a very irritable frame of mind. The fear that they were in separate compartments and that Binodini could get off the train without his knowledge made things worse.

In this manner, Binodini spun around on her orbit like a malevolent planet in the skies and she made Mahendra spin likewise—never letting him rest. Binodini had the capacity to make friends easily. Very soon she made friends with the women travelling with her. She gathered information about their desired destinations, put up in the dormitories and went about touring the sights worth seeing with her new friends.

Every time Mahendra felt he was superfluous to Binodini, it was like a fresh blow to him. His only task was to buy the tickets from here to there. The rest of the time it was a ceaseless scuffle between him and his desires. At first, he accompanied Binodini on her forays in sightseeing—but gradually he grew tired of it. So he had his meal and tried to sleep while Binodini roamed about all day. No one could have dreamt that Mahendra, the apple of his mother's eye, would one day come out into the streets thus.

One day, the two were waiting for the train at Allahabad station. For some reason the train was late. Meanwhile, Binodini was scanning the faces of the passengers alighting from and boarding other trains. Perhaps she nurtured the hope that since they were in the west, if she looked hard enough, she'd be able to find one particular person. For her, there was a kind of tranquillity in this daily search amidst the chaotic throngs of people; at least it was better than her lonely life, captive in a solitary home, dying each day under the weight of stillness.

At Allahabad station her glance fell upon a glass box on the platform and she got a shock. The postal-department box displayed the letters addressed to all those who could not be located. On one letter carefully arranged inside the box, Binodini spotted Behari's name. The name 'Beharilal' wasn't uncommon and there was no reason to imagine that the Behari whose name was on that letter was the same one that Binodini longed for; yet, his full name spelt out on the letter left her in no doubt that it must indeed be Behari. She memorized the address on the envelope. Mahendra was seated on a bench, wearing a dour expression. Binodini went up to him and said, 'Let us stay here in Allahabad for a few days.'

Mahendra's male ego had felt increasingly slighted and rebellious at the thought that Binodini drove him as per her wishes and never bothered to provide fodder for his hungry, craving heart. At this point he would have been happy to stay longer in Allahabad and get some rest—but he felt like cutting off his nose to spite his face, not wanting to fall in with Binodini's wishes. He spoke irritably, 'Since we have set off we shall continue. I can't go back.'

Binodini said, 'I shall not go.'

Mahendra said, 'You stay alone then, I am off.'

Binodini said, 'That's fine.' She gestured to a porter, picked up her luggage and headed out of the station.

Mahendra with his male ego remained seated on the bench with dark thunderclouds hovering on his face. He could hold still only as long as Binodini was still visible to the eye. When she left the station without once looking back, he quickly summoned a porter, asked him to pick up his luggage and followed her. When he came out of the station he found that Binodini had already hired a carriage. In silence, Mahendra loaded the baggage atop the carriage and jumped into the coachbox. He had no inclination of sitting inside, facing Binodini and his defeated ego.

The carriage went on and on. Nearly an hour later they'd left the city behind and the carriage now rolled over fields and farmlands. Mahendra was embarrassed to ask questions of the coachman lest he thought that the woman inside was the mistress and she hadn't even bothered to consult this man about their destination. He silently chewed on his wounded ego and sat in the coachbox wordlessly.

The carriage came to a halt in front of a solitary, well-kept farmhouse on the banks of the Yamuna. Mahendra was dumbfounded. Whose farm was this? How had Binodini come upon this address?

The house was shuttered. After much hollering an aged caretaker came out. He said that the owner was a rich man who lived nearby and if his permission was obtained they could stay in the farmhouse. Binodini glanced at Mahendra just once. He was tempted at the sight of this beautiful mansion—the prospect of a few days' relaxation thrilled him no end. He said to Binodini, 'Let us go to this rich man's house. You can stay in the carriage while I go inside and fix the rates.'

Binodini said, 'I am too tired. You go ahead. I'll stay here awhile. I think it's quite safe.'

Mahendra got into the carriage and left. Binodini called the old man to her side and asked after his children—how many there were, where they worked and where his daughters were married and so on. When she heard of his wife's demise she spoke compassionately, 'Oh, it must be hard on you. At this age you are all alone in this world. There's no one to look after you.'

In the course of conversation Binodini asked him, 'Did Beharibabu stay here once?'

He said, 'Well yes, he did for some time. Does madam know him?'

Binodini said, 'He is related to us.'

The description that the old man gave of Behari removed the last traces of doubt from Binodini's mind. She made the old man open up the house, and went into the rooms where Behari had stayed. Since they were locked up after his departure, it felt as if his spirit still lingered in the rooms, the wind had failed to sweep it away. Binodini drew in a deep breath and sucked it into her soul, let the still, silent air touch her all over; but she could not get any information about where Behari had gone. He could come back—nothing was certain. The old man assured Binodini that he'd check with his master and return with the news.

Mahendra paid the advance, meanwhile, and came back with permission for them to stay there.

51

THE WATERS THAT THE HIMALAYAS GIFTED TO THE YAMUNA FROM ITS snowy peaks were eternal, as were the torrents of poetry that generations of poets had presented to her. The rippling stream of this river contained sparkling rhythms in its currents and its waves surged with the exuberant emotions of many centuries.

When Mahendra came and sat on its banks at dusk, the sensation of romance conjured up a trance in his eyes, in his breath, in his veins and in his bones. The rays of the setting sun played a golden sitar of secret melodies and tremulous agony. The day cast speckled colours on the expansive banks, and wore to an end. Mahendra sat with half-closed eyes and heard as if from the elegiac dreamworld of Vrindavan the sounds of calves returning home at dusk.

The skies were overcast with monsoon clouds. The darkness was not a mere sheath of pitch-black but also something that echoed with curious mysteries. The bare shapes that were apparent through it in a strange glow spoke in nameless, unspoken languages. The indistinct pallor of the other bank, the inky blackness of the still waters, the huddled stillness of the massive, leafy lime tree at the riverside, the wan, dusty horizon in the distance, all merged together in the dark in various indefinite, indistinct shapes on this rainy evening and embraced Mahendra from all sides.

The rainy trysts of the Vaishnava padabalis came to his mind. The lady has set off on her tryst. She had come to the banks of the Yamuna all by herself and stood at the water's edge. How could she cross the river? 'Please ferry me across,' the cry rang in Mahendra's ears, 'oh please, ferry me to the other side.'

On the opposite bank of the river, in the dark, the lady stood far away—yet Mahendra could see her clearly. She was timeless and ageless, the eternal lover of Krishna and yet, Mahendra recognized her—she was none other than Binodini! She had begun her journey from beyond time with all her anguish, the pangs of separation and the full burden of her youth; her tryst had finally brought her to this river bank today through many melodies and many rhythms—today, the skies above the remote river reverberated with her voice, 'Oh please, ferry me across.' For how many more ages would she stand there thus, waiting for the boatman to ferry her across?

The clouds in a corner of the sky parted, revealing a

sickle moon. The elusive magic of the moonlight took the river and its banks, the sky and its horizon far beyond the limits of reality. They were free of all earthly ties. The reins of time snapped, entire histories of the past disappeared, consequences of the future vanished—just this deluge of silvery water on the Yamuna remained—and this moment held Mahendra and Binodini in it, as time and the world stood still.

Mahendra was inebriated. He felt sure that Binodini wouldn't reject him today, she wouldn't refuse to fill this solitary, moonlit paradise with her gracious beauty. He stood up instantly and went towards the house in search of Binodini.

When he reached the bedroom he was overwhelmed by the scent of flowers. Through the open doors and windows the moonlight streamed onto the shimmering bed. Binodini had picked flowers from the garden, threaded them into garlands that she wore in her hair, on her arms and neck—adorned with flowers she lay upon the bed like a creeper in spring, bent under the weight of its blossoms.

Mahendra's yearning intensified. He spoke in a choked voice, 'Binod, I waited on the banks of the Yamuna. The moon in the sky brought me news that you are waiting and here I am.' Mahendra stepped forward and made to sit on the bed.

But Binodini sat up in startled surprise, stretched out her right arm and said, 'Go, go away—you must not sit on this bed.'

The wind went out of the ship's sail and it faltered to a halt—Mahendra stood there, dumbfounded. He couldn't speak for a few minutes. Lest he refused to obey her, Binodini got off the bed and came to stand before him.

Mahendra asked, 'Then why have you dressed up—who are you waiting for?'

Binodini gripped her heart and said, 'The one I wait for is right here, in my soul.'

Mahendra said, 'Who is it? Is it Behari?'

Binodini said, 'Don't you dare utter his name.'

Mahendra said, revelation striking him, 'Is he the reason why you are roaming around in the west?'

Binodini replied, 'Yes, he is.'

Mahendra said, 'And he is the one you are waiting for now?'

Binodini said, 'Yes, he is.'

Mahendra asked, 'Have you found his address?'

Binodini said, 'No, I haven't—but I'll get it somehow.'

Mahendra said, 'I shall not let you find it.'

Binodini said, 'Even if you do that, you cannot take him out of my heart.'

Binodini closed her eyes and perceived Behari within her heart at once.

Thus intensely attracted to and violently rebuffed by this image of a beflowered yet disdainful Binodini, Mahendra suddenly grew fierce—he clenched his fists in rage and said, 'I shall take a dagger, rip your heart out and remove him from it.'

Binodini spoke with unruffled detachment, 'Your dagger will enter my heart more easily than your love.'

Mahendra said in baffled wonder, 'Why are you not afraid of me—who is there to protect you here?'

Binodini said simply, 'You are there—you will protect me even from yourself.'

Mahendra said, 'So there is still this much respect and trust left?'

Binodini said, 'Otherwise, I'd rather have killed myself than set off with you.'

Mahendra said, 'You should have. Why have you hung that slender noose of modest faith around my neck and dragged me around the country? Just think how much good will come of your death!'

Binodini said, 'I know that; but I cannot die as long as my hopes of Behari live.'

Mahendra said, 'As long as you don't die, my aspirations won't die either—I shall not be free. From this day on I shall pray to God with all my heart that you should die. Don't belong to me; don't belong to Behari. Just go. Set me free. My mother weeps, my wife weeps—their tears lacerate me from afar. Unless you die and go beyond my aspirations, I shall not get the chance to wipe away their tears.'

Mahendra rushed out of the room. He ripped away the lacy webs of illusion that Binodini had been weaving in solitude. Binodini stood in silence and gazed out of the window—the skyful of moonlight had disappeared, taking with it the magical nectar. The manicured lawn, the river bed beyond, the inky depths of the water and the obscurity of the other bank—all seemed like a pencil sketch on a large white sheet of paper—quite dreary and hollow.

Today, when she realized afresh just how intensely she'd fascinated Mahendra, how she'd uprooted him like a terrible storm and felled him to the ground, Binodini grew more agitated. She *had* all these powers. Why then did Behari not come and crash at her feet like the swollen waves on a full-moon night? Why did the powerful memory of a redundant love come sobbing into her meditation every day? An unfamiliar lament continually intruded and stopped her own inner dirge from being fulfilled. What would she do for the rest of her life with this massive upheaval that she had caused? How would she calm it and lay it to rest?

As she realized that the flowers decking her had attracted Mahendra's appreciative gaze, she tore away at them. All her powers, her efforts, her life were in vain——this garden, the moonlight, the river banks, this picturesque world were all in vain.

Such futility——and yet everything stood exactly where it had earlier. Nothing mattered in the least in this world. The sun wouldn't fail to rise tomorrow and life wouldn't forget the tiniest of details. And Behari——impassive and detached—— would stay distant as before and teach Vasant a new lesson from his textbook.

Tears welled up in Binodini's eyes. What was this unyielding stone that she was trying to move with all her strength? Her heart knew bloodshed every day, but her fate didn't move an inch from its place!

52

MAHENDRA DIDN'T SLEEP ALL NIGHT——BUT TOWARDS DAWN SLEEP overcame his tired body. He woke up at around nine and sat up hastily. The anguish from last night had threaded its way into his sleep. The moment he was awake Mahendra felt the pain afresh. Within a few moments the events of the night before came flooding back to him. In the scorching late-morning heat, the fatigue of a fitful night set in and his life appeared quite distasteful to his eyes. Why was he bearing this burden, leaving his family, feeling the guilt of going astray and enduring the discomforts of a nomadic life? In the stark morning light Mahendra suddenly felt he was not in love with Binodini. He glanced at the street and saw the whole world rushing about, people getting on with their work. The stupidity inherent in forfeiting all self-esteem and dedicating his whole, redundant life to the feet of an unwilling woman was suddenly apparent to him. On the heels of a tremendous passion comes terrible fatigue—the weary heart wants to keep away the object of its desire for some time. In these times of waning, when the tide is at an ebb, the sludge and grime of the river bed is clearly visible—the object of desire then provokes revulsion. Today, Mahendra could not understand why he had been dragging himself pointlessly through the mud all these days. He said, 'I am superior to Binodini in every way and yet I endure all kinds of insults and injury and follow her around like a hideous beggar—what kind of a devil put such strange ideas in my head!' Today, Binodini seemed like any other woman and nothing more. When the wonderful glow that had emanated from the world around her and from the poetry and tales involving her vanished suddenly like a mirage, all that was left was an ordinary woman, with nothing to set her apart from the rest.

Mahendra grew impatient, wishing to extricate himself from this insufferable web of illusion and head home at once.

The peace, love and affection he had once experienced at home, now seemed like the most sought after elixir to him. He realized that Behari's loyal friendship of many years was the most precious thing in the world. Mahendra said to himself, 'Since it is easy to drown yourself effortlessly into that which is truly profound and eternal, we take it for granted and do not realize its true worth. And since the restless illusion, which brings no pleasure even if you drain it to the dregs, leads us by the nose and makes us dance a merry dance to its tune, we take it to be the most desirable thing.'

He decided, 'I'll go home today—let Binodini stay wherever she wants to stay. I'll make the arrangements and then I'll be free.' As he uttered the words, 'I'll be free', a tremor of delight shook Mahendra's being; he felt the burden of incessant quandary that he had carried around all these days suddenly lifting. For so long, he had been forced to do in one instant what had seemed odious to him a moment ago—he didn't have the power to assert himself; every command that came from his conscience was strangled as he took the other road instead. Today, when he asserted 'I'll be free', his vacillating heart found shelter at least and applauded him.

Mahendra left the bed instantly, washed his face and went to meet Binodini. He found her door closed. He banged on it and asked, 'Are you asleep?'

Binodini said, 'No. Go away now.'

Mahendra said, 'I need to speak to you—it won't take long.'

Binodini said, 'I don't wish to speak to you or hear anything any more—go away, don't bother me now; I wish to be alone.'

At any other time, this rejection would have made Mahendra's heart grow more impassioned. But today he only felt disgust. He thought, 'I have sunk myself so low in this ordinary woman's esteem that she has acquired the right to dismiss me at any time, in any manner! This is not her rightful privilege. It is I who gave it to her and made her think too much of herself.' This rebuff made Mahendra resolute to establish his own superiority to himself. He said, 'I shall win—I'll break her hold over me and I'll go away.'

After lunch Mahendra went to the bank to pick up money. Thereafter he roamed the shops of Allahabad in search of some nice things to buy for Asha and his mother.

Once again, there were knocks on Binodini's door. At first she was irritated and didn't respond. But when the knocking went on, she lost her temper and hurled the door open as she shouted, 'Why must you disturb me again and again?' But her last words hung unspoken in the air. She had seen Behari standing outside.

Behari glanced inside just to check if Mahendra was there. The room was strewn with withered flowers and torn garlands. His heart turned sour in one instant. Away from Binodini, Behari had often been beset by doubts about her, but his imagination was powerful enough to shroud his doubts of immorality and paint a pretty picture over it all. Yet, as he entered the farmhouse, he had shuddered and cringed lest the image in his heart be shattered. Standing at Binodini's door, he received the very jolt he'd dreaded.

From afar, Behari had once imagined that with the power of his love he'd be able to wash away all the grime from Binodini's life. But now, close at hand, he realized it wouldn't be easy—his heart was scarcely filled with compassion! The sudden waves of revulsion that rose within him took him by surprise. He found Binodini looking quite listless.

Behari turned away and called, 'Mahin da, Mahin da.'

Binodini spoke in soft and gentle tones, 'Mahendra is not here, he has gone to the city.'

When Behari made as if to leave, Binodini said, 'Behari-thakurpo, I beg of you, you must sit here awhile.'

Behari had decided he wouldn't give in to any plea and he would remove himself from this hideous scene instantly. But the pathetic pleading in Binodini's tone held him rooted to the spot for a second.

Binodini said, 'If you turn away and leave today, I swear on you that I shall give up my life.'

Behari turned around and asked, 'Why do you try to entangle me in your life? What have I ever done to you? I have never stood in your way or meddled in your joys and sorrows.'

Binodini said, 'I have once told you just how much you mean to me—you did not believe me. Today, faced with your disgust, I shall say the same thing again. You have not given me the time to communicate this wordlessly, or coyly. You have pushed me away and yet, I hold your feet as I say that I—'

Behari interrupted her, 'Don't say those words ever again. There's no way I can believe them now.'

Binodini said, 'Other people may hold their presumptions true, but you too? That's why I have asked you to sit awhile.'

Behari said, 'How does it matter if I believe it or not? Your life will go on as before.'

Binodini said, 'I know it will not make a difference to you. I am so unfortunate that I shall never be able to take my place beside you with honour and esteem. I will have to stay away from you. But my soul wishes to lay just one claim on you—wherever I am, you must think well of me. I know that once you had felt a little respect for me—I shall hold that dear to my heart. That's why you have to hear me out. I beg of you Thakurpo, sit awhile.'

'All right, let's go,' Behari made as if to go someplace else.

Binodini said, 'Thakurpo, it is not what it seems. This room hasn't been touched by dishonour. You had once slept in this room—I have dedicated it to your memory; those flowers were used to worship your thoughts and they lie there now, withered and lifeless. You must sit in this very room.'

Behari felt a secret thrill course through him. He stepped into the room. Binodini silently indicated the bed to him. Behari sat on the bed—Binodini sat on the floor at his feet. At this, he tried to rise in haste and she said, 'Thakurpo, sit down. For my sake, do not get up. I am not even fit to sit at your feet—you are kind enough to give me that space; even if I am far away from you, I shall retain that privilege.'

Binodini was silent for some time. Suddenly, she remembered something and looked up. 'Thakurpo, have you eaten?'

Behari said, 'I ate at the station.'

Binodini said, 'Why did you send back the letter that I'd written to you from the village, through Mahendra?'

Behari said, 'But I did not receive any letter.'

Binodini asked, 'Didn't you and Mahendra meet in Kolkata?'

Behari said, 'I met Mahendra the day after I dropped you off at your village. Soon after that I left for the west and I have never met him since then.'

Binodini enquired again, 'Before that, did you read a letter from me and send it back without an answer once?'

Behari said, 'No, I've never done that.'

Binodini sat there, speechless. Then she heaved a sigh and said, 'Now I know what happened. And now I must tell you everything. If you believe me, I shall consider myself fortunate; if you don't I won't blame you—it is difficult to believe me.'

Behari's heart had melted. He couldn't bring himself to affront the devotion of the pious, devout Binodini. He said, 'Bouthan, you do not have to say anything—I believe you entirely. I am not capable of hating you. Please do not say another word.'

Binodini's tears flowed unchecked as she touched his feet in gratitude. She said, 'I shall die if I don't confess everything to you. You must be patient and hear me out. I surrendered myself to the sentence you meted out to me. In spite of not getting a single letter from you, I would have spent the rest of my life enduring the jibes and taunts of the villagers; I would have gladly settled for your reprimand instead of your love. But fate denied me that too. The sins that I gave birth to, didn't let me remain in exile. Mahendra came to the village, to my door and dishonoured me before everyone. I could no longer stay in the village. I hunted high and low for you, in order to seek your judgement a second time. But I couldn't find you. Mahendra brought back my letter to you, opened, and betrayed my trust. I thought you had given up on me forever. After this, I could have sunk to my doom—but you have untold powers, you can protect one even from afar. I could remain chaste only because I have placed you in my heart. The day you sent me away you revealed your true self, the harsh self, as harsh as pure gold, as harsh as the uncut diamond—it stayed lodged in my heart and made me precious too; my lord, I swear at your feet that its purity has not been defiled.'

Behari sat there in silence. Binodini did not say another word. The afternoon sun had begun to lose its glare. At this point Mahendra returned—and stood stunned seeing Behari. The indifference to Binodini that had taken over his mind was nearly driven out by a sudden force of burning envy. When the slighted Mahendra found Binodini sitting at Behari's feet, his pride was wounded. He was left in no doubt that this meeting was a consequence of prolonged correspondence between Binodini and Behari. All these days Behari had been away; now if he came to her, who could stop Binodini from rushing to him? Today, on seeing Behari, Mahendra realized that he could let go of Binodini, but he couldn't give her up to another man.

In thwarted anger, Mahendra hurled harsh sarcasm at Binodini, 'So now it is exit Mahendra and enter Behari on stage, is it? Quite a pretty scene—one feels like clapping. But I do hope this is the last act. Nothing else can follow this one.'

Binodini's face turned red. Since she had been forced to take Mahendra's help, she had no answer for this slur—she merely cast a fervent glance at Behari.

Behari got up, took a step forward and said, 'Mahin da,

you will not insult Binodini like a coward; if your civility doesn't forbid you from doing so, I have the right to forbid you.'

Mahendra laughed. 'Oh, so we have already worked out rights and all, eh? Let us give you a name from this day— Binod-Behari!'

When Behari realized that the invectives were crossing their limits, he gripped Mahendra's hands and said, 'Mahin da, let me inform you that I intend to marry Binodini; from now on do control your language.'

At these words Mahendra went speechless with surprise and Binodini looked up, startled. The blood rushed to her ears.

Behari said, 'I have something else to tell you—your mother is on her deathbed; there's no hope for her. I am leaving tonight. Binodini will come with me.'

Binodini was stunned. 'Aunty is ill?'

Behari said, 'Fatally. Anything can happen at any time.'

Mahendra left the room without saying another word.

Binodini said to Behari, 'How could the words that you just spoke come from your lips! Is it a joke?'

Bchari said, 'No, I spoke the truth. I would like to marry you.'

Binodini said, 'So that you can save this sinner?'

Behari said, 'No. It's because I love you and respect you.'

Binodini said, 'This will be my final reward. That you have accepted me is all I could ever hope for. Anything more will not last, and the heavens won't stand for it.'

Behari asked, 'But why not?'

Binodini went red. 'Oh, for shame, even the thought is

shameful. I am a widow, I am tarnished—I shall bring dishonour to your name in the eyes of society—no, no, this cannot happen. For pity's sake, never say these words again.'

Behari said, 'Then, you will leave me?'

Binodini replied, 'I do not have the right to leave you. You are involved in beneficial activities for others—give me some duties in one of your missions. I shall perform them all my life and consider myself at your service. But for pity's sake—you cannot marry a widow. Your generosity may have room for anything, but if I do this and ruin your name in society, I shall not be able to hold up my head for the rest of my life.'

Behari said again, 'But Binodini, I love you.'

Binodini said, 'I shall use that privilege today to take just one liberty.'

She knelt on the ground and kissed his feet. She sat at his feet and said, 'I shall pray that I have you in my next birth—in this lifetime I hope for no more, I deserve no more. I have inflicted much misery, received much sorrow, I have learnt a lot. If I had forgotten those lessons, I would have sunk lower by dragging you with me. But since you remain on your pedestal, I am able to hold my head high today—I shall not raze this monument to the ground.'

Behari was silent and grave.

Binodini pleaded with folded hands, 'Don't misunderstand me—you will not be happy marrying me. I, too, will lose my self-esteem. You have always been detached and contented with your lot. Stay that way—I shall serve you from afar. I hope you will be happy and fulfilled.'

53

MAHENDRA WAS ABOUT TO ENTER HIS MOTHER'S ROOM WHEN ASHA quickly stepped out and said, 'Don't go in there now.'

Mahendra asked, 'But why?'

Asha said, 'The doctor has said that if Mother gets a sudden shock, of joy or sorrow, the consequences may be grave.'

Mahendra said, 'Let me go and stand by her bedside quietly, just this once—she wouldn't know a thing.'

Asha said, 'The slightest sound is enough to startle her these days—she'll know as soon as you enter the room.'

Mahendra said, 'So what do you suggest?'

Asha said, 'Let Behari-thakurpo come and have a look first—we'll do as he says.'

As she spoke, Behari arrived. Asha had sent for him.

Behari said, 'Bouthan, did you send for me? How is Mother?'

Asha seemed relieved to see Behari. She said, 'After you left, Mother seemed to grow more restless. The first day, when she didn't see you she asked me, "Where is Behari?" I said, "He has gone on some urgent work. He'll be back by Thursday." Ever since then she starts at the slightest sound. She doesn't say anything but she seems to be waiting for someone. When I got your telegram yesterday, I knew that you'll be here today. She heard that and she's arranged a special meal for you today. She sent for all the things that you like to eat; she also arranged for the cooking to be done in the veranda upfront so that she could supervise it from her bed. She refused to obey the doctor's instructions. A little while ago she called me and said, "Bou-ma, you will cook everything with your own hands. I shall sit with him during his meal."'

Behari's eyes grew moist at these words. He asked, 'How is she feeling?'

Asha replied, 'Come and take a look yourself. I feel her condition has worsened.'

Behari stepped into the room. Mahendra stood outside in stunned silence. Asha had taken up the responsibility of the household with ease—how effortlessly she forbade Mahendra from entering the room! There was no hesitation, no hurt. Mahendra's position was so weak today. He was culpable, he stood outside the door silently—he couldn't even enter his mother's room.

It was also surprising how comfortably Asha spoke to Behari! Her entire discussion was with him alone. Behari was the sole guardian of this household today, dear to everyone. He had access everywhere and everyone took his advice. Mahendra had left the space vacant for a while and on his return he found it was no longer there for him to lay claims on.

As Behari approached her bedside, Rajlakshmi laid her grief-stricken eyes on his face and said, 'Behari, you're back!'

Behari said, 'Yes Mother, I am back.'

Rajlakshmi asked, 'Is your work done?'

She looked at him with eager anticipation. Behari smiled cheerfully and said, 'Yes Mother, my mission is accomplished and I have no more worries.' He glanced at the door as he spoke.

Rajlakshmi said, 'Today Bou-ma will cook for you and I shall supervise. The doctors forbid me, but what is the point of all this, my child! Must I leave without once watching you all eat heartily?'

Behari said, 'I don't see why the doctors should object—it won't do if you don't supervise everything. Ever since we were children, we have learnt to love food cooked only by you—Mahin da is heartily sick of the daal and roti they serve in the west—he'd be delighted to have some of your fish curry. Today, we two brothers will compete with each other and eat like old times—let's hope your Bou-ma cooks enough rice.'

Although Rajlakshmi knew that Behari had brought Mahendra along, the very mention of his name made her heart leap and she found it difficult to draw breath. When the feeling passed, Behari said, 'Mahin da's health has improved from the change of air. Today he's a little drawn due to the travails of the journey—nothing that a shower and a proper meal wouldn't put right.'

Rajlakshmi still didn't take her son's name. So Behari said, 'Mother, Mahin da is waiting outside the door. He cannot come in unless you call him in.'

Rajlakshmi glanced at the door mutely. Immediately, Behari called out, 'Mahin da, come in.'

Mahendra stepped into the room slowly. Rajlakshmi couldn't bring herself to look at his face for fear that her heart would suddenly miss a beat and stop entirely. She lowered her eyes. Mahendra looked towards the bed and got the shock of his life—he felt someone had dealt him a mortal wound. He fell at his mother's feet and placed his head on them.

Rajlakshmi shuddered as her heart raced with emotion.

A little later Annapurna spoke softly, 'Didi, please ask Mahin to get up or he'll stay there forever.'

Rajlakshmi opened her mouth with difficulty and murmured, 'Mahin, get up.'

As she said his name, after an age, the tears welled up and rolled down her cheeks. They lightened the burden on her heart. Mahendra rose, knelt on the floor and sat close to his mother. Rajlakshmi turned over with difficulty, took his head in both her hands, fondly breathed in the scent of his hair and kissed his forehead.

Mahendra choked with emotion as he said, 'Mother, I have hurt you no end—please forgive me.'

Now much calmer, Rajlakshmi said, 'Don't talk that way Mahin—how can I live without forgiving you? Bou-ma— where's Bou-ma?'

Asha was cooking Rajlakshmi's food in the next room. Annapurna went and fetched her. Rajlakshmi gestured to Mahendra to get off the floor and to sit upon the bed. When he did so, Rajlakshmi indicated the spot beside him and said, 'Bou-ma, you sit here—today I want to make you sit beside each other and take my fill of the sight—that'll ease all my misery. Bou-ma—don't be shy, and cast away your grudges against Mahin—come and sit here, just for once. Let me feast my eyes, child.'

Asha raised her anchal, veiled her head and bashfully, with a trembling heart and a gentle tread, she came and sat beside Mahendra. Rajlakshmi picked up Asha's right hand and pressed it into Mahendra's hand as she said, 'Mahin, I leave this child of mine in your care—mark my words Mahin, you won't find a finer woman anywhere. Mejo-bou, come and bless them; let your virtue prove benevolent for them.'

When Annapurna came forward, the couple was in tears as they bent low and touched her feet. She kissed their foreheads and said, 'May God bless you.'

Rajlakshmi said, 'Behari, come my son, come here and say you forgive Mahin.'

Instantly, Behari came and stood in front of Mahendra, who drew him to his bosom with a firm pull and held him in a tight embrace.

Rajlakshmi said, 'Mahin, I pray to God that Behari stays as close to you as he has been since your childhood—it would be the greatest boon for you.'

Rajlakshmi was tired by now and she fell silent. Behari held a revitalizing drug to her lips, but she pushed it away and said, 'No more medicines, my child. Now let me think of God—He would administer the final cure to release me from all wordly pains. Mahin, you go and rest for a while. Bou-ma, you get started on the cooking.'

That evening, Behari and Mahendra's place was laid in front of Rajlakshmi's bed as they sat down to eat. Rajlakshmi had given Asha the responsibility of serving food and she began to serve them.

Mahendra's heart was surging with tears and he could scarcely eat. Rajlakshmi coaxed him again and again, 'Mahin, why aren't you eating anything? Eat heartily—let me watch and be happy.'

Behari said, 'You know him, Mother, he's always been that way. He can hardly eat anything. Bouthan, you must give me some more of that curry, it's really delicious.'

Rajlakshmi was delighted and she smiled as she said, 'I know Behari loves that curry. Bou-ma, that's not enough, give him some more.'

Behari said, 'This daughter-in-law of yours is so tight-fisted—nothing slips through her fingers.'

Rajlakshmi laughed. 'Look at that Bou-ma—Behari is critiquing you even as he eats your food!'

Asha plied Behari with a ladleful of curry.

Behari said, 'Oh dear me, I suppose I'll have to make do with the curry and all the other delicacies will go to Mahin da!'

Asha chastized him in a whisper, 'The critic's lips can never be sealed.'

Behari replied softly, 'Try some rice pudding and see if it works!'

When the two friends had finished their meal, Rajlakshmi sighed with pleasure and said, 'Bou-ma, you go and have your meal quickly.'

Asha left to do her bidding and Rajlakshmi said to Mahendra, 'Mahin, you go to bed now.'

Mahendra said, 'Why should I go to bed so early?'

He had decided he'd stay up at his mother's bedside that night. But Rajlakshmi wouldn't hear of it. She said, 'Mahin, you are tired, go to bed.'

After her meal, Asha picked up a hand-fan and tried to sit by Rajlakshmi's bed. But the latter conspiratorially whispered to her, 'Bou-ma, just check if Mahin's bed has been made—he is all alone.'

Asha nearly died of shame and made her escape from the room, leaving Behari and Annapurna behind. Rajlakshmi asked Behari, 'Tell me something Behari—do you know what became of Binodini? Where is she now?'

Behari replied, 'Binodini is in Kolkata now.'

In reply to Rajlakshmi's unuttered question, Behari said, 'Mother, don't be afraid of Binodini causing you any more grief.'

'She *has* caused me a lot of grief, Behari, but deep in my heart I care about her.'

'And she cares about you, Mother.'

'I feel the same, Behari. No one is perfect, but she must have cared about me. No one can fake that kind of tender ministration.'

Behari said, 'She is eager to nurse you again.'

Rajlakshmi sighed and said, 'Mahin and Asha have gone to bed—what's the harm in sending for her in the night?'

Behari said, 'Mother, she is hiding in one of the rooms in this very house. I haven't been able to get her to take even a drop of water through the day—she has vowed that until you send for her and forgive her, she won't have anything to eat or drink.'

Rajlakshmi was concerned. 'Starving the whole day—oh dear, send for her, quick!'

The moment Binodini stepped into her room hesitantly, Rajlakshmi said, 'Shame on you, Binodini, what have you done? You have starved yourself the whole day! Go and eat first and then we'll talk.'

Binodini touched Rajlakshmi's feet and said, 'Aunty, first you must forgive this sinner and only then will I eat.'

Rajlakshmi said, 'I do forgive you, my child—I am no longer angry with anyone.'

She took Binodini's hand in hers and said, 'May you be happy and may no one be harmed by you.'

Binodini said, 'Your blessing won't go in vain, Aunty. I swear at your feet, no harm will befall this household on my account.'

Binodini bowed low and touched Annapurna's feet, too, before she left to have her dinner. When she came back Rajlakshmi looked at her and said, 'Are you leaving now?'

Binodini said, 'Aunty, I will attend to you. As God is my witness, you have nothing to fear from me.'

Rajlakshmi glanced at Behari. He gave it some thought and said, 'Let Bouthan stay, it won't do any harm.'

That night Binodini, Behari and Annapurna nursed Rajlakshmi together.

Meanwhile, Asha woke up very early the next morning, abashed at not having gone into Rajlakshmi's room even once through the night. She left Mahendra still asleep in bed, washed and changed before she came downstairs. The dark of the night still lingered. When she came and stood at Rajlakshmi's door, the sight that greeted her eyes made her wonder if she was dreaming.

Binodini was heating some water over a spirit lamp; it was to make some tea for Behari who hadn't slept all night long. When she saw Asha, Binodini stood up and said, 'Today, with my burden of crimes, I seek refuge from you. No one else can evict me, but if you say "go", I will leave this very minute.'

Asha couldn't say a word—she couldn't even fathom what her heart was saying. She just stood there, overwhelmed.

Binodini said, 'You'll never be able to forgive me—don't

even try it. But please, do not fear me any more. Please let
me stay here and serve Aunty as long as she is in need of it.
Afterwards, I shall leave.'

The day before, when Rajlakshmi had placed Asha's hand
in Mahendra's, Asha had wiped away all traces of hurt and
rejection and surrendered herself to Mahendra all over again.
But today as Binodini stood before her, the pangs of her
rejected love refused to be calmed. The thought that swelled
in her bosom was that Mahendra had once loved this woman,
and perhaps he still loved her deep in his heart. In a short
while Mahendra would wake up, he'd see Binodini—how
would he feel? The night before Asha had perceived her
whole life to be free of thorns henceforth. But this morning
she found the thorny bush planted right at her doorstep. Joy
was the most delicate of objects—there was scarcely a place
to keep it safe.

With a heavy heart Asha stepped into Rajlakshmi's room
and with great mortification she said, 'Aunty, you have stayed
up all night—go to sleep now.' Annapurna looked at Asha's
face searchingly. Then, instead of going to bed, she took Asha
to her room and said, 'Chuni, if you want to be happy, try
and forget what happened. The misery of remembering the
crimes of others is greater than the pleasure in laying the
blame at their door.'

Asha said, 'Aunty, I do not want to remember—I want
to forget—but I *can't.*'

Annapurna said, 'Child, you are right. It's easier said than
done. Let me tell you a way of doing it—you must keep the
pretense alive that you have forgotten everything. If you
succeed outwardly, it'll also take root in your heart. Keep

this in mind, Chuni—if you do not forget, you'll keep it alive in others' minds too. If you cannot do it on your own, I command you hereby—behave with Binodini as if she has never done you any harm and neither is she capable of it.'

Asha humbly asked, 'Please tell me what I must do.'

Annapurna said, 'Binodini is making tea for Behari right now. You take the cups, saucers, milk and sugar—work together, the two of you.'

Asha rose to obey her command. Annapurna said, 'This was easy, but I will tell you something much more difficult, which you *must* do. There will be times when Mahendra will run into Binodini and I know what will pass through your mind—at those times, you must not try to see Mahendra's or Binodini's reaction, even with a covert peep. Even if your heart breaks, you must stay unruffled. Mahendra must come to think that you do not suspect him, you do not grieve, you nurse no fears or worries—things are exactly the same as they were once, before the rift; even the traces of the fissure have vanished. Mahendra, or anyone else for that matter, should not look at you and feel weighed down by guilt. Chuni, this is not a request or advice; this is your aunt's command. When I go back to Kashi you must not forget this for even an instant.'

Asha fetched the teacups and saucers and approached Binodini, 'Is the water ready? I've brought milk for the tea.'

Binodini looked at Asha in amazement and said, 'Beharithakurpo is sitting on the veranda—you have the tea sent to him while I go and arrange for Aunty to wash her face; she should be waking up any minute.'

Binodini did not take the tea to Behari. She felt embarrassed to claim the rights that he had granted her by admitting her love for him. In order to retain the due respect for privileges, one must use them judiciously. Only the beggar would pull and stretch at his whole booty at once. The true worth of wealth lay in savouring it prudently. Now Binodini couldn't bring herself to go in front of Behari under some pretext, unless he sent for her specifically.

As she finished speaking, Mahendra arrived on the scene. Although Asha's heart missed a beat, she composed herself quickly and addressed him calmly, 'Haven't you woken up early today? I shut the doors and windows lest the sunlight wakes you.'

When Mahendra found Asha speaking to him so normally in Binodini's presence, a burden seemed to lift off his heart. He replied cheerfully, 'I've come to check on Mother—is she still asleep?'

Asha said, 'Yes, she's sleeping—don't go in there now. Behari-thakurpo has said she is much better today. After many days, she slept through the night last night.'

Mahendra was relieved. 'Where is Aunty?'

Asha showed him to Annapurna's room.

Binodini, too, was taken aback to see this calm and controlled Asha.

Mahendra called, 'Aunty!'

Annapurna had finished her bath at the crack of dawn and was about to sit down to her puja, but she called out, 'Come, Mahin, come.'

Mahendra touched her feet and said, 'Aunty, I have sinned and I hate to stand before you thus.'

Annapurna said, 'Oh no, don't talk that way Mahin—the

little boy comes to his mother's lap even when he's covered in mud.'

Mahendra said, 'But this mud cannot be washed off.'

Annapurna said, 'A few flicks, a good dusting down and it'll be gone. Mahin, it's all for the best—you were very proud of your ideals, you were too confident in your beliefs— the squall of sins has shattered your arrogance but left you unharmed.'

Mahendra said, 'Aunty, this time we won't let you go— your absence brought all this upon us.'

Annapurna said, 'If the mishap was held at bay by my presence alone, it is better that it has taken its toll. Now you will not need me any more.'

There was another voice at the door, 'Aunty, are you doing your puja?'

Annapurna said, 'No, you may come in.'

Behari stepped into the room. When he found Mahendra awake at this early hour, he said, 'Mahin da, this is perhaps the first time that you are seeing the rising sun!'

Mahendra said, 'Yes Behari, it's my first sunrise. Perhaps you need to discuss something with Aunty—I'll be off then.'

Behari laughed. 'You can be included in the cabinet of ministers. I have never concealed anything from you and if you have no objections, I won't start doing so now.'

Mahendra laughed. 'Objections and me! But of course, I can no longer demand it. If you do not conceal anything from me, I shall be able to respect myself again.'

These days it *was* rather difficult to say everything in Mahendra's presence. Behari nearly stumbled, but he went on resolutely, 'My marriage to Binodini was a subject broached earlier and I have come to conclude the discussion with Aunty.'

Mahendra shrank away and Annapurna looked up in surprise. 'What's all this, Behari!'

Mahendra made a great effort and shrugged away his qualms. 'Behari, there is no need for this marriage.'

Annapurna asked, 'Is Binodini with you on this talk of marriage?'

Behari said, 'Not one bit.'

Annapurna said, 'Will she agree to this?'

Mahendra spoke up, 'Why wouldn't she agree to it, Aunty? I know that she is devoted to Behari—why would she throw away this chance of a safe haven?'

Behari said, 'Mahin da, I proposed marriage to Binodini— she has turned it down.'

At this Mahendra fell silent.

54

FOR RAJLAKSHMI, THE NEXT TWO OR THREE DAYS PASSED SOMEHOW, with some good moments and some bad. One morning her face grew contented and all signs of pain vanished. She sent for Mahendra and said, 'I don't have much time—but I die in peace, Mahin, I have no regrets. Today my heart wells with the same kind of joy that I once felt, when you were a child. You are the apple of my eye, my own little boy—I am taking with me all your troubles and that fills me with joy.' Rajlakshmi stroked his face and arms. Mahendra couldn't check his tears as the sobs rose to his throat.

Rajlakshmi said, 'Don't weep, Mahin; the queen of grace is still in your home. Give the household keys to Bou-ma. I have kept everything in order—you two wouldn't lack for anything in the house. One other thing, Mahin, don't tell anyone before I die—there are two thousand rupees in my box that I bequeath to Binodini. She is a widow, all alone in this world—the interest from this money would suffice for her. But Mahin, my request to you is don't keep her within the walls of your own home.'

Rajlakshmi sent for Behari and said, 'Behari my son, Mahin was telling me that you have bought a property where you want to treat impoverished gentlemen. May God grant you a long life to do the poor a good turn. At the time of my marriage my father-in-law had gifted me a village, I bequeath that to you. Use it to serve the poor; it'll bring peace to my father-in-law's soul.'

55

WHEN THE LAST RITES FOR RAJLAKSHMI WERE CONCLUDED, MAHENDRA said, 'Dear Behari, I have studied medicine—please make me a part of your mission. With the way Chuni has gained control over the household chores, she'd be able to lend you a hand too. We shall all live there.'

Behari said, 'Mahin da, please think this through—would

this work satisfy you at all times? Don't take on permanent duties in the throes of a sudden surge of altruism.'

Mahendra said, 'Behari, you think about it too—the life that I have made for myself, can no longer be savoured at leisure. If I do not occupy myself with a worthwhile cause, my restless soul can haul me into the nadir of despair one day. You must make room for me in your mission.'

So it was decided.

When it was time for them to say goodbye, Annapurna and Behari sat immersed in restful sorrow, discussing the days past. Binodini came and stood at the door. 'Aunty, may I sit here for a while?'

Annapurna said, 'Come, come, my child—sit.'

Binodini came in and sat down. Annapurna spoke a few words with her and then under the pretext of making her bed, she went into the veranda.

Binodini asked Behari, 'Tell me what I should do now— what is your command?'

Behari said, 'Bouthan, why don't you tell me what you want to do?'

Binodini said, 'I've heard that you have taken a house by the Ganga to treat poor patients. I'd like to be of some use to you there. If nothing else, I could cook there.'

Behari said, 'Bouthan, I have given this a lot of thought. Through circumstances the webs of our lives are now utterly tangled. The time has come for us to sit in solitude and undo the knots one by one. First, we must clear everything. Now I no longer have the courage to indulge in all that the heart desires. Without laying to rest every upheaval, every tumult that has resulted from the events till now, from all that we have borne, we cannot settle down and anticipate the end of our lives. If our pasts had been different, you are the only one who could have given my life completion—but now I must part from you. Now, it would be a vain effort to strive for happiness. Now we can only repair the damages slowly and surely.'

At this point Annapurna stepped into the room and Binodini said, 'Mother, you must give me shelter at your feet. Please don't push me away as a fallen woman.'

Annapurna said, 'Child, come then, come with me.'

On the day that Annapurna and Binodini were to go to Kashi, Behari sought out Binodini at some point and said, 'Bouthan, I want something from you—a mark—to keep with me always.'

Binodini said, 'What do I have to give, that you can keep as a mark, by your side forever?'

Abashed and diffident, Behari said, 'The English have a custom—they keep a few locks of the dear one's hair as a memento—if you—'

Binodini recoiled, 'Oh no—how shameful! What would you do with my hair? That tainted, dead item means nothing to me, that I would gift it to you. Hapless that I am, I could not be of any use to you—I'd like to gift you something that can help you in my stead. Will you accept it?'

Behari said, 'I will.'

Binodini untied the knot at the end of her anchal, took out two notes of a thousand rupees each and handed them to Behari.

Behari gazed at her steadily, his eyes alight with intense

fervour. A little later he said, 'Is there nothing that *I* can give you?'

Binodini said, 'I have a mark ftom you, it graces my body—no one can take it away from me. I do not need anything more.' She showed him the scar on her elbow.

Behari was astounded. Binodini said, 'You may not be aware but this was given by you and it is worthy of you. Even you cannot take this back now.'

Despite her aunt's counsel, Asha had not been able to free her mind entirely of vitriol towards Binodini. They had nursed Rajlakshmi together, but every time Asha's eyes had fallen on Binodini, her heart had smarted, the words had dissolved on her tongue and the effort to smile had been painful. She had resented it if she had to accept even the slightest help from Binodini. She had accepted the paan made by Binodini out of courtesy, but later thrown it away in distaste. But today, when it was time to take leave, when her aunt was departing from the household a second time, Asha's heart swelled with tears, and she found herself pitying Binodini too. There are few hearts hard enough to be incapable of forgiving the one who is taking leave forever. Asha was sure Binodini loved Mahendra—and why wouldn't she? Asha knew from her own heart just how inevitable it was to feel love for Mahendra. It was the anguish of this love that made her feel compassion for Binodini now. Asha could not wish upon her worst enemy the agony that Binodini was bound to feel as she left Mahendra forever; the very thought brought tears to Asha's eyes. In the past, she had loved Binodini and that love touched her heart again. Slowly she walked up to Binodini and with great compassion, affection and sadness, she said,

'Didi, so you are leaving?'

Binodini held up Asha's chin and said, 'Yes, my sister, it's time for me to leave. Once, in the past, you had loved me—now, in times of joy, set aside a bit of that love for me, my friend—and forget everything else.'

Mahendra came and touched Binodini's feet as he said, 'Bouthan, forgive me.' Two teardrops brimmed over the corners of his eyes and rolled down his cheeks.

Binodini said, 'You forgive me too, Thakurpo. May God grant you two eternal happiness.'